BARBARIAN'S MATE

BARBARIAN'S MATE

RUBY DIXON

BERKLEY ROMANCE
New York

BERKLEY ROMANCE
Published by Berkley
An imprint of Penguin Random House LLC
penguinrandomhouse.com

Library of Congress Cataloging-in-Publication Data

Names: Dixon, Ruby, 1976– author. |
Dixon, Ruby, 1976– Ice planet honeymoon.
Title: Barbarian's mate / Ruby Dixon.
Description: First Berkley Romance edition. |
New York: Berkley Romance, 2023. | Series: Ice planet barbarians |
Originally self-published in 2016.
Identifiers: LCCN 2023000963 | ISBN 9780593639467 (trade paperback)
Subjects: LCGFT: Science fiction. | Romance fiction. | Novels.
Classification: LCC PS3604.I965 B3766 2023 |
DDC 813/.6—dc23/eng/20230113
LC record available at https://lccn.loc.gov/2023000963

Barbarian's Mate was originally self-published in 2016.

First Berkley Romance Edition: July 2023

Printed in the United States of America
3rd Printing

Book design by Kristin del Rosario

*For all those completely invested
in their own happy ever afters*

BARBARIAN'S MATE

What Has Gone Before

Aliens are real, and they're aware of Earth. Fifteen human women have been abducted by aliens referred to as "Little Green Men." Some are kept in stasis tubes, and some are kept in a pen inside a spaceship, all waiting for sale on an extraterrestrial black market. While the captive humans staged a breakout, the aliens had ship trouble and dumped their living cargo on the nearest inhabitable planet. It is a wintry, desolate place, dubbed Not-Hoth by the survivors.

On Not-Hoth, the human women discover that they are not the only species to be abandoned. The sa-khui, a tribe of massive, horned blue aliens, live in the icy caves. They hunt and forage and live as barbarians, descendants of a long-ago people who have learned to adapt to the harsh world. The most crucial of adaptations? That of the *khui*, a symbiotic life-form that lives inside the host and ensures its well-being. Every creature of Not-Hoth has a khui, and those without will die within a week, sickened by the air itself. Rescued by the sa-khui, the surviving human women take on a khui symbiont, forever leaving behind any hopes of returning to Earth.

The khui has an unusual side effect on its host: if a compatible pairing is found, the khui will begin to vibrate a song in each host's chest. This is called resonance and is greatly prized by the sa-khui. Only with resonance are the sa-khui able to propagate their species. The sa-khui, whose numbers are dwindling due to a lack of females in their tribe, are overjoyed when several males begin to resonate to human females, thus ensuring the bonding of both peoples and the life of the newly integrated tribe. A male sa-khui is fiercely devoted to his mate, and most humans are now claimed by the males, and pregnant.

The humans have now been on the ice planet for over a year and a half, and most have adapted to tribal life. Almost all have taken mates; new babies are being born of human and sa-khui pairings, and the tribe stirs with life once more. Only two human women remain single . . . and then Tiffany resonates.

This is where our story picks up.

CHAPTER ONE
Josie

I'm the last single woman on the entire ice planet. I watch Tiffany and her new mate, Salukh, head off to their cave as everyone celebrates, but I'm not really in a celebratory mood. I'm worrying. I'm not a big fan of stressing about things I can't change, but this is something that concerns me. Being the singlest single woman that ever singled? It's distressing. Am I going to have a cave by myself? Am I going to be stuck in someone else's cave like a reject? Am I going to have to listen to everyone else make out and know that I'm never going to have a mate because Harlow can't fix the stupid surgery machine?

I stare glumly at the fire, thinking about my stupid, stupid IUD that won't come out, even though it's been over a year and a half since we landed and my cootie's supposed to fix that sort of thing. Around me, everyone's happy and celebrating, but I don't feel like sharing in their enjoyment. It wasn't so bad when I wasn't the last human alone. I didn't feel like a total reject then.

Now? The cheese stands alone and I *do* feel like a total reject.

It's a feeling I'm kind of used to, after being dumped from a half-dozen foster homes growing up. I've never had family to call my own, and the people that wandered into my life wandered right back out again just as quickly. But I don't dwell on the past. Shit happens to everyone.

Here on the ice planet, though, I felt like I was part of a family, at least for a while. There were twelve human women, and the sa-khui only had four women to their thirty-something men. To them, we were special, a gift from the stars to be cosseted and taken care of. I was part of a group for once, a family. Then one by one, the girls started to pair off with mates. First Georgie, then Liz, then the others—Stacy, Nora, Ariana, Harlow, and all the rest. One by one, they paired up with big, hunky, utterly devoted blue guys who think that their fated mates can do no wrong and dote on them at every turn. And now they're all popping out babies and having the bestest time ever on the ice planet.

It's kinda hard not to be jealous. And it wasn't so bad when it was me, Claire, and Tiffany left after the initial rush of matings. That was all right, because it wasn't just me being rejected by my cootie—the symbiont that keeps me alive and plays matchmaker.

But then Claire got a mate.

And then Tiffany got a mate, too.

I'm the only one whose cootie has gone out to lunch. The cootie's supposed to be looking out for me. It's supposed to keep me healthy at all costs, fixes up my body so I can withstand the harsh environment on the new planet, and it's supposed to find me the perfect mate. Once it does, I'll resonate—my cootie will vibrate once it gets near the perfect male so I can know that it's chosen, and then we can have really intense, repeated sex until we make a cute, fuzzy blue baby. But I don't resonate, and I know it's because of the stupid IUD stuck up in my you-know-what.

You can't get pregnant if you're on birth control, and you can't resonate if you can't get pregnant.

It sucks to know the exact reason why you're warming the bench and not being able to change it.

I stare into the central firepit. So much for not being a gloomy Gus. It's hard when you see everyone getting everything you've ever wanted—a mate, family, babies—and you keep getting passed up.

A small movement catches my eye and I look up from the flickering fire to see a familiar face scowling in my direction. Haeden. Ugh. My least favorite person in both of the sa-khui caves. He looks pissier than usual, which is kind of a feat for him. If he wasn't such a dick, maybe he'd be handsome. Maybe. He's big, of course, and heavily muscled like all sa-khui men. He's got the big, arching, curling horns jutting from his forehead like a ram on crack. He's got pale blue skin and his forehead is covered with thick, platy ridges that should make him look like a mutant but only emphasize how strong the rest of his features are. And he's got the long, black hair of the sa-khui, but he wears his shaved on the sides and in one extra-long braid over the top of his head and down his back. He might be someone's type, but he's not mine. His tail flicks angrily at the sight of me, as if just looking in my direction pisses him off.

Our eyes lock and he crosses his arms over his chest, as if daring me to get up and confront him.

Whatever. I make a face at him. I don't know why he's got a hate-boner for me but I'm tired of it. I'm a little pleased—and weirdly disappointed—when he stalks away. I'd almost welcome a fight with him, except he doesn't really fight. He mostly spits out a few choice words, glares a lot, and then storms away when I irritate him enough.

I nudge Farli, who's settling in next to me with her paint pots. She's doodling a festive red line down her arm. "So what's with Haeden lately?"

"Hmm?" She dabs a brush in red and then paints a dot on my arm.

"He looks more angry than usual," I tell her, and obediently turn my arm toward her so she can paint an accompanying blue dot next to the red one.

"Oh. He was very . . . sour . . . when he found out you went to the main tribal cave alone. He yelled at Taushen for many hours."

My eyebrows go up. "Why? He hates me." He should have been glad that I'd taken the scary, dangerous journey so recently. He'd probably been hoping that I'd fall into a snowdrift and never come out again.

She shrugs and holds my arm, painting a tickling circle on it. "He is protective of females. He thinks it is foolish to risk them."

Oh barf. So he's a chauvinist. "I was perfectly fine." Sure, it was a little scary, but I handled it. I went because we didn't have a choice. Tiff, Taushen, Salukh, and I were visiting the elders' cave—a crashed sa-khui spaceship from several hundred years ago—when Tiff noticed a big storm coming in. We'd decided to send out runners to warn both the South Cave (my home) and the main cave. Tiff had hurt her ankle, so Salukh stayed behind with her. Taushen took the longer walk back to the South Cave, and I headed to the main cave to warn them, despite the oncoming blizzard and despite the fact that I'd never traveled by myself before.

I'd been pretty proud of the fact that I made it and saved the day, darn it. Sure, I could have died in a snowdrift, but I didn't. I found the cave all on my own and showed that I'm not useless. I'm glad I made the journey and I'd do it again.

Farli draws a bigger blue circle on my arm with her paint-brush. The sa-khui like to paint their bodies with bright swirls when they celebrate, and I love it. It makes me happy just to look at it, and Farli knows she has a willing canvas with me. She doodles on my arm a bit more, then holds on to my wrist to keep me still. "Yes, but humans are weak. He says that risking your life means risking more than just one life. It is potentially robbing another male of his mate and kits."

I gape at her, then realize she's parroting Haeden's words. "Good thing I'm only worth my vagina to him." Joke's on him, my girl parts have a permanent no-vacancy sign on them, alas.

"What is *va-shy-nuh*?" Farli asks. "I do not know this word."

"Never mind." I probably shouldn't be teaching Farli inappropriate human words. She can't be more than fourteen years old. "He's just a jerk. Always has been and always will be."

"What is *yerk*?" She draws another circle on my arm, this time a sickly green. "You're fun to paint on, Jo-see. You are pale like Chahm-pee's belly. The colors show up nicely."

Greeeaaaat. I'm being compared to her pet dvisti. "A *jerk* is a man who thinks with his male parts." It totally applies for scowly Haeden, I don't care what the others say.

She giggles at my words. At least someone finds me amusing.

Nope. I can't go down that path, mentally. I need to think about happier things. Things like the baby Tiffany and her mate are rather noisily making back in our cave. I do love babies, and Tiffany's my best friend here on the ice planet, so I'm totally go-ing to volunteer to godparent the crap out of that poor kid. I stare at the fire, contemplating living circumstances. If Salukh and Tiffany are getting it on twenty-four seven, they'll need a cave of their own.

Farli finishes decorating my bared arms and picks up her paint pots, heading toward someone else. I remain where I am, the paint drying. No one comes over to talk to me. It's not like there's a lot of us left in the South Cave. Half of the cave has already moved back to the main caverns. The ones left are probably not feeling that celebratory, if Taushen's sad mood is any indicator. I don't blame him. He lost out on the girl, and the only one left is me.

Or Farli, but she's a kid still. So he's either got to put the moves on me, or wait for Farli to grow up. No wonder he's depressed. I'm kinda bummed myself. I don't want to go back to the cave, because I'm afraid I'm going to see a lot of Salukh and Tiffany . . . which would be awkward. Maybe I'll go borrow a blanket from Kira and hide in one of the now-empty caves.

I get to my feet. Something soft taps against my leather boot.

I look down, and there's an object gleaming in the firelight on the tip of my shoe. I pick it up, frowning. It fell out of my leggings. What on earth? It looks like a plastic little Y of sorts, which is weird. There shouldn't be any plastic here in the sa-khui caves. Did it get stuck in my boot from when we were at the elders' spaceship? But if so, how . . .

I gasp as I realize what I'm looking at. It's not from the elders' ship.

It's my IUD.

Somehow, my body has forced it out. My khui must have been silently working on pushing it out of my system. I clutch it in my hand, my heart hammering with excitement.

This changes *everything*!

Now, I can get pregnant. Now, I can resonate. I can have a mate!

I can have a family, a happy ever after. I can have everything I always dreamed of. I don't have to wait for Harlow to fix the surgery machine back at the elders' ship, because my cootie decided to be awesome after all. *Thank you, khui! Thank you! You're the best! I take back all the awful things I said about you.*

I look around eagerly at the people in the main cave. Who's going to be my mate? There are several males in the tribe that are attractive and all of them are nice . . . except Haeden.

I'm not picky. I'll let my cootie choose someone for me. It knows best, after all. It's going to pick the perfect male for me so we can make sweet little babies together and I can live a life of joy and happiness. My mood has totally changed and I'm so happy I could shout with pure joy.

Nearby, Vaza catches my eye and gives me a speculative look. To my relief, my khui remains silent. Good. It's not desperate. Vaza's older and he's tried hitting on everything with tits. He's seated next to Bek, and I'm glad that my khui isn't making a sound for him, either. *Cootie, you are one smart cookie.*

Hassen is probably my number one draft pick at the moment, because he's sexy and all alpha, and I'd be down with that. At the moment, he's nowhere to be found. Taushen, either. Both of them are probably still moping after losing Tiffany. Well, hello, I'm perfectly willing to be a consolation prize. Time to find my guy and make his day.

There are two elders talking off to one side but I'm pretty sure one had a mate back in the day and the other could be my grandpa. Just to make sure, though, I stroll past them. Nothing happens. Whew. *No problem, cootie. We still have lots of man-meat in this cavern before we run out.* "Anyone seen Hassen?" I ask.

"He's in his cave, packing," Vaza says.

"Super." I jump to my feet and head in that direction before Vaza can decide if he wants to hit on me or not. *Come on, Hassen. Be my mate!* Of course, even if I don't resonate to Hassen, there's always the guys back in the other cave. I immediately think of Rokan. He's hot, and he's nice. I'd be down with that.

I head for the cave that many of the single hunters live in, and the privacy screen isn't up. "Yoo-hoo," I call out, my voice sweet. I'm excited, and I push away thoughts of Rokan. The other cave seems so far away right now. It's going to happen tonight, I can feel it. Rokan's going to lose out, because he's not here. I feel like my mate is here. My chance.

I'm going to get my happy ever after. Tonight, my life starts. Tonight, I get my family. Tonight, I'm no longer a reject.

Hassen pops out of his cave, a confused look on his face. His gaze settles on me. "Yes? What is it?"

I smile at him, but . . . nothing happens. Rats. Hassen was hottie number one on my list. "Just . . . thought I'd say hi? Have you seen Taushen?"

He narrows his eyes at me, as if trying to figure me out. "He is here."

"Can I say hi to him, too?" Might as well kill two birds with one stone.

"Is this a human custom?"

I keep smiling, because even his puzzled look is not going to get me down. Not tonight. "Yes, yes it is."

He grunts and heads back into the cave. I admire his ass for a moment, because, darn, it *is* a rather nice ass. Not *my* ass, though. Oh well. I'm sure mine will be awesome. Taushen's got a tight little bod himself, and—

—and he pops out of the cave a moment later, giving me an eager look. "Ho, Jo-see. What is it you need?"

My chest is just as quiet as before. No resonance, no nothing. Dammit.

I make my excuses to him, citing a sudden need to find a potty, and hurry away. Who's left? There's Vadren talking to Harrec, and while both are older than me, I could learn to love me some May-December relationship action. I sidle up to them, pretending to listen to their conversation. Nothing.

Is . . . my cootie on vacation? Is it tired because it worked so hard to get rid of the IUD? I put a hand to my heart, worried. I've approached every guy in the cave that's single. Maybe my mate's back at the other tribal cave? That's disappointing, but I guess I can wait another day or so. Rokan might be the one for me after all. I picture him and start to imagine what our kids would look like.

As I walk toward the fire, my chest feels funny.

I look down and my small boobs are vibrating. My entire chest is, actually.

Holy crap. *Resonance.*

Yes. I knew it would be tonight! I gasp, clutching my leather tunic tighter to my body so no one sees my boobs jiggling except my mate. My chest continues to vibrate, and as it does, the noise grows louder. I'm resonating.

I'm motherfucking *resonating*!

I want to scream with joy. I look around with excitement, trying to see who it is that set my cootie off. Who did I forget? Who did I walk past that made my cootie pay attention? Did someone trigger me on a second chance? Or—

I turn around and Haeden's standing right behind me, frozen in place.

My eyes widen and I clutch my vibrating boobs.

No.

Hell to the no.

"It's not you," I whisper.

He looks down at his chest, and then at me.

Then, I hear it. A matching thrum, a low purr.

He's resonating. I'm resonating.

For a moment, I hope that he's somehow decided to resonate to someone else. That there's another woman somewhere nearby and she's going to spring from the shadows and yell "Surprise!" That this is all just a bad joke.

But then Haeden takes a step toward me.

My cootie gets even louder. My chest is vibrating so hard with the force of the resonance that it's making my nipples ache. I hold my breasts down and look up to see Haeden's reaction.

He's staring at me. There's a look of such anger and agony on his face. He doesn't want this.

I don't, either. I'm devastated. This is my worst nightmare. All I've ever wanted is a family. Someone that loves me. A happy ever after.

Resonating to Haeden?

My dream is completely destroyed.

CHAPTER TWO
Josie

It's happening.

Oh God.

I never thought it would be like this. This intense. This immediate.

And I never thought it would be to *him*.

I . . . don't know what to do. I stare blankly at him, holding my boobs like if I can get them to stop, I'll somehow stop resonating to him.

I wanted resonance. I wanted it so badly. I want a mate and babies. I should have been more specific. *Anyone but him, cootie. Let's take it back. I'll go with anyone else but him. Please.*

But the stupid cootie in my chest only purrs even louder.

Haeden's eyes narrow at me and he takes another step forward. His fist presses to his chest as if he's trying the same bargaining tactic with his own.

"This isn't happening," I blurt out. "This isn't us."

He scowls and grabs my hand. "We need to talk." He drags me toward his cave, the one he shares with Salukh and Taushen.

I try to pull my hand out of his grip, mostly because his touch is . . . okay, it's making my hormones go wild. I'm freaking out. Touching Haeden's hand—no matter how warm or strong or callused it is—should not make my nonexistent leather panties go damp, but that's exactly what's happening. "I'm not going anywhere with you!" I hiss at him.

He stops and turns to look back at me like I'm the crazy one. "You want to do this out here?"

"I don't want to do anything with you!"

"You don't have a choice. This," he says, and thumps his chest hard with his free hand, "has made our choices for us."

He's not wrong about that.

Haeden moves in closer to me. "So unless you want to resonate in public and all the things that entails, come with me so we can talk."

He's so close to me that I can feel the heat of his big body. How did I never notice that Haeden's enormous? That he towers over me, all brawny blue muscle and smoky-scented skin? Dammit, cootie, your timing is shit. Your taste is shit, too. "Fine," I say faintly. "I'm coming."

Because if I don't go with him, I worry that I'm going to, you know, come if he steps any closer. And the thought makes me blush.

To my relief, he doesn't grab my hand again, but puts his on my back, guiding me toward his cave. If anyone notices us departing together, no one says anything or stops us. I'm guessing everyone's either drunk or not paying attention. It's a small cave and sometimes there's nothing to do but gossip. If someone sees me going to Haeden's bunk with him? It'll be all over the caves in the morning.

Then again, so will our resonance.

Shit. Shit shit. I don't know what to do. I'm in a haze of worry and hormones and doubt as he leads me into his cave. Salukh isn't there—he's busy nailing Tiffany in *my* cave—but Taushen is. He's seated on his furs, sharpening his blade.

He looks up at the sight of us entering together. My cootie's purring a mile a minute at Haeden's closeness, and I'm sure I have a deer-in-headlights look on my face. "What's going on?" Taushen asks, getting to his feet.

"Get out," Haeden tells him bluntly. "Jo-see and I need to talk."

"But—"

"Out," Haeden snarls, moving forward and looming over the smaller male.

I clutch at the neck of my tunic. I should be appalled at how ferocious Haeden's being, but I'm kind of . . . aroused by it. He's so decisive. *Oh, you jerk of a cootie. How could you do this to me? I thought we were friends!*

So far? Not loving this whole resonance thing. I give Taushen a mute look of apology as he frowns at both of us and scurries out of the cave. Then it's just me and Haeden.

My new mate, if my cootie has anything to do with it.

He turns slowly, rubbing a big hand over his face. And then he looks at me. "This . . . is not what I wanted."

I'm a little stung by his words. Hearing that you're someone's last choice on earth—or Not-Hoth—stings, no matter who's saying it. "Like I wanted this? I *hate* you."

"That does not matter any longer," he says bluntly, beginning to pace. It's like he's twitchy and can't stay still. I know how that feels—I'm ready to crawl out of my own skin. "Our khuis have chosen. We are mates."

I shake my head. It's like my entire world is crashing down

around me. This is a nightmare I can't wake up from. "I don't want to be your mate."

He turns on me, and his face is filled with anger. "We do not choose, Jo-see. The khui chooses!"

"Yeah? Well, our cooties are assholes! I don't want this! I don't want you!"

He just rubs a hand down his face again.

"I don't even get how this is possible," I say brokenly. "I thought you had a mate."

His eyes narrow at me. He stalks away a few feet, and then his hands go to his hips. His tail is lashing wildly, and I watch it with a kind of horrified fascination. It's clear Haeden doesn't have a mate, or else I wouldn't be stuck with him. You can only resonate to one person, ever. Once a cootie makes its mind up, there's no changing it.

I sink to my knees. I feel utterly helpless and alone. I don't know what to do. All I know is that my symbiont has arranged a marriage with the person I hate most in this world, and I'm completely at its mercy. Hot tears spill down my cheeks and I swipe at them.

I'll allow myself to cry over this for one night, and then I need a plan.

Haeden

I thought you had a mate.

Jo-see's simple, brutal words cut to my heart, dredging up terrible memories. I've never had a mate, but I did resonate to another female. But she died, along with my khui and along with any hope I had. I never imagined in all the long, lonely years since that the new khui in my chest would also select a mate for me. I have never hoped to have a mate or a family, or a warm body curled against mine in the furs.

And yet, I look at Jo-see's round human face and realize I still will never have those things. It is a cruel, cruel khui that has chosen her as my mate, and me as hers. I watch as she sinks to the floor in the cave and tears spill from her eyes down her cheeks.

She is weeping at the thought of being mated to me. She hates the idea so much that she cries. The thought fills me with helpless frustration and self-loathing. I watch her, unable to offer comforting words. I have nothing to say to her that will ease her pain and misery. Already my body reacts to her nearness, stiffening with excitement at the thought of a mate. My cock aches under my loincloth. This gnawing need to claim a female to the point of mindlessness? I've felt this before, with Zalah, and hated every moment of it.

I gaze down at her misery. I have seen that before, too. Zalah had been devastated at the thought of resonating to me. Jo-see is no happier.

And me?

I am filled with utter terror. Humans are fragile creatures, ill-suited to live here amidst the snows. They must be carefully watched, guarded at all times, and kept warm with fire. They shiver at a stiff breeze and must have their food burned over a fire. Some are a bit more hardy, like Raahosh's Leezh, but Jo-see? She is smaller than the others, and when I look at her, I see the tiny size of her wrists, her small hands, her delicate shoulders.

I . . . do not know what I will do if I resonate to another female only to have her die. It will destroy me.

I turn toward the wall of the cave and clench my hand against a rocky outcrop. It is taking all of my willpower not to grab

Jo-see and pull her to my furs, where I can protect her from anything and everything. To drag her under me and claim her. I reach out to touch a lock of Jo-see's brownish-yellow hair, and she flinches away.

I am the only male to have two mates and yet have never touched a woman.

"This is awful," she sobs, struggling to her feet. "You hate me and I hate you."

She hates me. The words cause an ache in my chest that outweighs the ache in my groin. She thinks I hate her. I deserve that. I have pushed her away with every opportunity.

The truth is that I do not hate her. I could not. She is sunlight and warm smiles. She is laughter and happiness, and those things are lost to me. I have not been happy since Zalah died cursing my name.

And every time I look at Jo-see's face . . . I have known this day would happen. I have known there was a connection between us from the day I picked up the small, broken human female out of the strange cave they arrived in and carried her back to the tribal caves. I knew then there was something between us, and I have fought it ever since.

Not because she is not worthy, but because humans are fragile and I am terrified at the thought of losing a mate . . . again. I frown at the thought, and that is when Jo-see looks up. Her jaw stiffens at the sight of my frustration and she glares at me. "Don't look at me like that. I would have picked anyone but you. I can't believe I've wanted this for so long and now this . . ." Her lip wobbles and the tears start to fall again.

Each teardrop is like a knife in my chest. "Stop crying," I tell her, and it comes out more harshly than it should.

She dashes a hand over her cheeks and finds the strength to

glare at me again. I will take her glares. I will take anything but her tears.

"We must be sensible about this," I tell her and step closer. My entire being reacts to her nearness. The khui in my chest hums its song so loudly I think the entire cave can hear it.

Jo-see gives me another irritated look and sniffs. "Of course we're going to be sensible."

Good. Then we are thinking along the same path. My cock surges against my leathers, desperate to be buried inside her and fulfill the bond that resonance has brought between us. My entire being aches with the need to possess her, and the resonance is quickly taking over my thoughts. I can see nothing but Jo-see, smell nothing but her delicate scent, imagine nothing but running my fingers through her soft mane and pressing it to my lips. I cannot help myself—I reach out and touch her soft mane. "I will be gentle, Jo-see."

She skitters away from me as if burned, her eyes going wide. "W-what?"

Does she not grasp how a kit is created? "We will go slow if this is your first time." I do not tell her it is mine as well.

The look on her face changes to one of disbelief. Her jaw drops and she clenches her fists at her sides. "Are you *men-tahl*?" She hisses the words at me and then looks around as if to make sure no one else has seen. "I'm not sleeping with you!"

Sleeping? She truly does not know how a kit is made. "We will not be sleeping. When a male takes a female—"

She presses her small fists to her forehead. "*Ohmigahd.* I know how babies are made, you *twit*!"

I frown at her anger. There is no point in getting frustrated. "This is not my choice, either, Jo-see, but resonance cannot be denied—"

"I. Don't. *Care*!" She slices a hand through the air, as if cutting something. "We are *not* mates. I am *not* sleeping with you."

Irritation is flooding through me, a potent mixture with the ache of desire and the onset of resonance. I am a mix of emotions, all of them strong, and my patience is nearly gone. I cross my arms over my chest. "Then what would you have us do?"

"We're not going to do anything!"

I give her a skeptical look. I have seen too many resonances to think that this plan will work. There are some pairings that fight the inevitable, but they always give in. Then there is my unfulfilled resonance with Zalah, which haunts me to this day. But if Jo-see thinks we can just ignore the call of our khuis, she is mad. "That will not work."

She presses a hand to her forehead again, and strangely enough, I want to pull her against my chest and comfort her. Jo-see's frustration and unhappiness are distressing to me, even more so because I am causing them. "I need time," she says after a moment. "I can't handle this tonight. I can't."

Her words chill me. They remind me of Zalah, and Zalah's refusal to answer the call of resonance. But that was many, many turns of the seasons ago, and Zalah is long dead. Jo-see is here, and Jo-see is now my mate. It will not turn out the same.

It cannot.

I will not survive it.

But Jo-see's pain eats at me. Even though my every instinct is demanding that I pull her into my furs and touch her until her "no" becomes "yes," then she would hate me.

And I could not bear to have my mate's hatred. Already the desire to please her floods through my body and my mind, the need to care for her and make her happy foremost in my thoughts.

I nod slowly. "It will be as you say. I will not touch you until you ask me."

She bares her teeth at me, furious. "You think I'm going to come to you begging for you to touch me? You have another think coming to you, buddy."

I tilt my head. Why does everything I say enrage her? "You say you want to wait. I will leave it in your hands."

"Don't throw this all on me! You mean to tell me that if I said 'go ahead,' you'd toss me down on your furs right this moment? Me?"

"Of course." I am puzzled by the question. Why does she think there is a choice? "The khui has decided. It does not matter what I want." Nor does it matter that the thought of touching her makes my cock ache, or even the sight of her makes my blood pound in my veins. Already I cannot separate my need for Jo-see from the resonance. She is my mate; therefore she is mine.

Nothing else matters.

She throws her hands in the air. "I'm done here." She turns to walk away.

"Where are you going?" Her soft mane brushes over her shoulders and my fingers itch to grab a handful of it, to pull her back against my body and bury my face against her soft skin. Everything I am rebels against the thought of her walking away without fulfilling resonance. I clutch at the wall again for support.

"Away," she says, and there's desperation in her voice. She hugs her small body and doesn't turn to look at me. "Say nothing of this, all right? I'm sure it'll come out eventually but . . . I just need time."

And because she is already my mate, I can refuse her nothing. "Very well."

Jo-see leaves my den and it feels as if a fire has gone out the moment she disappears from sight. I am filled with a keen sense of loss so great that it staggers me. The ache in my body has not decreased, and my khui's song seems to have a lonely sound to it before it stills in my chest. It is as if it misses its mate as well. I stagger to my furs and drop to my knees, tearing at the ties to my loincloth and leggings.

If she will not let me touch her, my hand will have to do for now. Yet even as I pull my cock free and take it in my grip, I know it will not be enough.

It is never enough.

CHAPTER THREE
Josie

I sleep in Chompy's cave that night. It's not that I wouldn't be welcome back in my own cave, but Tiff and Salukh are probably having a throw-down to end all throw-downs and I don't want to listen to it. Not tonight, not when my body's freshly aching and full of need from my own resonance. I could stay at someone else's cave, too, but that would involve questions I don't want to answer. I hug the furry dvisti close and let it lick the salty tears off my cheeks.

Tonight, I'll let myself cry. Tomorrow is a new day.

When I wake up the next morning, I'm a little disoriented. The smell of fresh dvisti poop far too close nearby reminds me of where I spent the night, and I crawl out from under the borrowed fur blanket and stretch. My entire body feels feverish, and when I press my thighs together, my pussy feels wet. Well, isn't that just ducky. I suck it up, because I'm done crying over my lot. I'll figure something out. Somehow.

The rest of the cave is busy, and I can hear the sounds of people rushing around. I fold up the blanket and open the pen so I can get out. Chompy pushes his way past my legs and bounce-trots away, likely to find his favorite person, Farli. The thing's more loyal—and more smelly—than a dog. Cute, though. It's hard to be sad watching his fuzzy butt bound away, and my mood lightens a little.

"Where's Josie?" I hear Tiffany ask. "Is she packing?"

I emerge into the main cave and there's a flurry of people cramming stuff into baskets, packing sleds, and adjusting backpacks. Looks like I slept late. Today, we're taking the hike back to the main cave and reuniting with the rest of the tribe. I should be excited. I can't wait to hold all the babies and talk with all my friends again, but my mind is on other things.

Against my better judgment, I glance around the cave, looking for a familiar pair of horns, dark blue skin, and a surly attitude. I don't see him anywhere, though, and I feel a pang of disappointment, but I'm pretty sure that's just my cootie reminding me of what it wants.

"There you are," Tiffany says, and hurries over to me with a backpack and my fur wraps. Hers is already strapped to her back and she's wearing her traveling furs. "Come on. We're not dragging sleds, so we need to hurry up and move ahead with the hunters. They're waiting on us."

"Aren't you bright-eyed and bushy-tailed," I tease her as she hands me my fur wraps and helps me into them. "Here I thought you'd be yawning this morning."

Tiffany giggles. *Giggles.* Oh my God. Practical, can-do Tiffany is giggling like a schoolgirl at my teasing. "Where did you sleep?" she asks.

"Oh, I just found a quiet spot in the back and curled up," I tell her. "Didn't want to bother anyone."

"Silly. You know you could have come back to the cave."

And listened to sex noises all night as they tried (and failed) at being quiet? Gosh, no thanks. Especially not with my own cootie being all hormonal. "Didn't seem like a good idea."

She helps me tie the strap of my backpack under my breasts and then pauses. "You're . . . okay with this, aren't you, Jo?" Her cootie-blue eyes, so brilliant in her pretty brown face, look at me imploringly. "I don't want anything to come between us as friends."

My poor heart nearly breaks all over again. "Don't be silly, Tiff. I love you, and I'm happy for you and Salukh. You're going to have a family and you have a mate that loves you. How can I not be beside myself with joy?"

"Because it's been just us for a while, and now I feel like I'm leaving you behind." She gives me a crooked little smile. "You know you can live with us in the new cave, right? I'm sure Salukh won't mind."

"Don't worry about me," I tell her brightly. "Something will shake itself out." And again, I resist the urge to look around for Haeden. Living with him would be a nightmare, I tell myself, even as I squeeze my stupid thighs tightly together. He's grumpiness personified.

Tiffany casts me another worried look, so I hug her. She doesn't need to worry about me. She's got enough on her plate. I squeeze her hand and then pull her toward the front of the cave. "Let's find our snowshoes and get going. I can't wait to see everyone at the other cave again."

She laughs but allows me to tug her along. "You just saw them a few days ago, silly."

"Yes, but they've got babies, and babies seem to grow up overnight." Plus, I've totally got babies on the brain. Always have. I love their sweet scent, the way they clutch at you like you're the most important thing in the world, the trust in their eyes. I've wanted a baby of my own so badly, because I want to do right by my child. I want it to grow up in a world of love where parents never disappear, people only touch you with kindness, and there's nothing but joy and welcome and love at home.

I want my child to have what I never had.

And I don't know if my child will get that if Haeden is the father. I don't know if I can be mated to him without losing it. He's everything I've never wanted. I thought my cootie would pick a mate that would be kind, and gentle, and caring. Instead, I get the sa-khui Oscar the Grouch, minus the garbage can.

As if my thoughts have summoned him, we head to the front of the cave and Haeden is there, waiting next to Salukh. His gaze immediately goes to me and he drops the snowshoes he was holding and storms away into the snow.

For some reason, I feel a pang of regret. I mean, I also feel a pang of lust deep between my thighs (thanks, cootie) and my chest starts to thrum quietly with resonance, but I also feel . . . sad.

Tiffany brightens at the sight of Salukh and practically skips over to him, despite the heavy pack on her back. I follow after her, picking up the discarded snowshoes that Haeden has abandoned. They're mine.

He was waiting for me.

I don't know how that makes me feel.

I move next to Tiffany and sit down on a rock beside her so we can put on our snowshoes. There are several others waiting at the front of the cave, and behind us I can hear Kira talking with Aehako, the baby crying. Farli's back there, too, chattering up a storm, and ahead are Taushen, Hassen, and if I peer out hard into the gray day, I can barely make out Haeden's retreating back.

"Is Haeden leaving?" I ask.

"Mmm," Salukh says, nodding. He kneels down and begins to strap Tiffany's snowshoes to her boots for her, like the sweetheart that he is. "He says he is not in the mood for company and will scout ahead."

"Oh." My cootie doesn't like this and gives a disappointed little purr, just as Salukh breaks one of Tiffany's leather shoe straps. He gets up and walks away to get a new one, and as he does, thankfully, my cootie gets over the fact that Haeden's not here and shuts up.

Tiffany peers around. "What was that noise?"

Uh-oh. "What was what?" I rub my stomach. I'm going to have to pretend indigestion unless I want to be found out. I'm not ready to see Tiffany's sympathetic expression when she realizes I've resonated to *Haeden* of all people.

"I thought I heard . . . resonance." Her brows draw together and she glances around the cave entrance and then looks at me. "Was it you?"

"Girl, please." I force out a laugh. "You sure it wasn't your man nearby?" I gesture at Salukh, who has his back turned to us. His tail is flicking and I see her gaze go to his butt. I can't blame her. He's got a fine butt. "His cootie might not be satisfied after last night."

Tiffany ducks her head and gives another girlish giggle, and I can hear her own resonance begin in her chest. Jealousy gnaws through me. I'm happy for her. I really am. I'm just sad that I'm so miserable. I rub my own chest thoughtfully.

Salukh returns a moment later, and immediately Tiffany starts humming like a cat in heat. She giggles again, and Salukh's chest takes up the song.

And me? Me, I want to barf. They're so giggly-giddy with

happiness that it's driving me crazy. I hate that. I want to be happy for her. I really do. But I'm lost in my own thoughts and none of them involve being excited about the prospect of waking up next to Haeden for the rest of my life.

I . . . just don't know what to do.

Our secret resonance? The dirty secret I don't want to tell anyone about?

It lasts until all of midday.

The walk to the main tribal caves is a half a day by most hunters' standards. But humans have to walk with snowshoes, which makes us slow. Add in backpacks and the sleds full of goods behind us that are being dragged along by the men while the women and elderly walk beside?

We are a slow-moving, wide-spread group. Tiff and I hang out somewhere toward the front, walking next to Salukh and Taushen. Taushen, bless his heart, is chatting up a storm as we walk, and doesn't even seem to mind that Tiffany's holding hands with Salukh. He seems to be in a good mood and I hope it's because he's just naturally a cheery person and he's not pinning his hopes on me . . . because that would be awkward.

Haeden remains far ahead, a blue and leather blur on the horizon. I'm glad he's staying away so my cootie remains silent.

After a few hours of walking, the twin suns are high in the sky, casting their weak light over the snowy ground, and the chilly air becomes a little too warm. We take a break in the shade of an icy cliff, and Kira comes to sit next to me and Tiffany. I take her fat baby from her arms to give her a break, and spend the next while cuddling and kissing her sweet, round face. Kira looks more tired than Tiffany and me, and I'm sure it's because of the baby. Kae's a pudgy little thing, fat and healthy at two months old, and wriggles constantly. Kira has no backpack but she looks wiped.

"You want me to carry this little inchworm for the next bit?" I ask Kira, pressing a kiss to Kae's cheek. The baby's a pale, pale blue but has almost completely human features except for the soft, downy covering on her skin that the sa-khui have. She grabs my nose and gives a delighted baby giggle, as if it's the most fascinating thing ever.

"Would you mind?" Kira sounds exhausted. "She gets heavy, and the snowshoes aren't helping."

"Of course I don't mind. I'll hand her back if she gets to be too much," I promise, knowing I'll do no such thing. This baby is all joy and bright smiles and I want to hold her forever. I kiss her tiny little nose, not even caring a bit that she grabs my face again and digs little nails into my lip. Everything she does is cute.

"Don't look now, but here comes Grumpy," Tiffany murmurs. "I'm sure he's coming back to yell at us."

I hold Kae a little tighter and avoid looking up, even as I hear snow crunching with approaching feet.

"Why are we stopping?" Haeden asks, his tone surly. "The sooner we get to the cave, the sooner the females can rest. It is not safe out in the open."

"They are tired now," Salukh says, his voice reasonable. He doesn't get up from his spot next to Tiffany. "Let them rest for a few moments. There is plenty of day left to walk."

Haeden snorts with derision.

My stupid cootie chooses that moment to start purring. Loud. Like, super loud. Like it's turned on by Haeden's grumpiness.

Aw, crap.

I hunch over the baby for a moment, hoping no one will notice.

"Josie?" Tiffany whispers.

I guess it's too late to fake indigestion again. I sit up and look over at Haeden. He doesn't look a bit tired, all big, muscular arms and irritation. I scowl at him. "Really? You couldn't wait, like, ten minutes for us to keep on going? You had to come back and set me off?"

"Me? You are blaming me for this?" The look on his face is both irritated and incredulous.

"Josie?" Kira asks. "Don't . . . Wait. You guys resonated?"

"Not by choice," I say, angry. Haeden came back on purpose to force my hand, didn't he? "And we're not doing a damn thing about it. I'm not his mate and he's not mine."

"Oh my God," Tiffany breathes. "What are you going to do?"

Pray for a miracle? Hope a rock falls on him? Something? I look up and his gaze is burning into me. My nipples prick and I feel my thighs quiver, and I bite back a groan. I'd say I'm not going to do anything . . . but I don't think my cootie is going to allow it.

"I don't know," I say honestly, and hold the baby closer.

Haeden

The group is somber as we trudge through the snow. No one seems to know what to say to me, and Jo-see is pretending I do not exist. The mood changes as we crest one of the last hills between the tribal cave and our location, and Rokan jogs forward. "Ho!"

I nod at him and give him a half-armed embrace of greeting. "My friend. It is good to see you."

He nods and scans the line of people straggling distantly behind me. "I am glad you have returned. All of you. Especially the females." He gives me a wicked grin. "It is lonely in a cave full of mates and babies, and you at the South Cave keeping all the young females to yourselves."

It takes all of my power not to shove him down into the snow. I am shocked at the surge of jealousy that powers through me. He does not know of what he speaks. "They are no longer unmated," I growl at him, and then I storm past. I ignore the confused question he sends my way and head on to the caves. Let the others answer him. I am in no mood.

I continue on until I am in the caves. There are no family members to greet me. There are many friends, but my mother and my father and my brothers died in the khui-sickness of many years ago. I am alone.

Vektal approaches me, smile wide. "I am glad to have all of my tribe home," he says, glancing behind me. "Are the others close behind?"

"Close," I agree, terse. "Which cave is to be mine?"

"The hunters—"

"I will not be staying with the hunters," I tell him, and I feel a surge of bittersweet pride at being able to say the words. "My khui has chosen a mate. I will need a cave for my family."

The look of surprise on his face is gratifying. "Who—"

"Jo-see."

His eyes narrow, but that is the only reaction he gives. He is my chief and he is wise and knows when to be silent. After a moment, he nods. "Come, then. I will show you. We have several caves that have opened up, thanks to Har-loh and her *ma-sheen*."

I pick out one of the larger caves for my new home. It's toward the very back of the cave system, tucked away in the new section that has been cut from the smooth walls. Here, the rock is rougher and small rock icicles hang from the ceiling, but the cave I select is roomy and private and will hold a large bed of furs as well as plenty of room for hunting equipment and supplies. It is a good cave. Jo-see cannot help but be pleased, even if she must share it with me.

Vektal leaves when it is clear I am not in a mood to talk, and I set down my pack and unroll my bed furs. My cock stirs at the thought of Jo-see lying in them, and I resist the urge to take myself in hand again. I did three times last night and it did not ease the ache. Only claiming my mate and planting my kit inside her will make the need go away.

Or the death of my khui.

I rub a hand over my chest, my mind full of bad memories from many, many seasons ago, back when I was newly made a hunter. Of Zalah and her pleasure mate, Derlen, laughing by the fire, feeding each other. Of the look of dread on her face when she realized her chest was resonating to me and not to her pleasure mate. She was many years my elder and much in love with Derlen, but my khui did not care. It wanted her. It hit me, hard and fast, and I was young and foolish enough to assume that she would comply with the demand of the khui.

But Zalah was always complicated. She pushed me away, said she needed time to think. And because I had been a foolish boy, I gave her time. I watched from afar as she went to her pleasure mate's furs every night. I watched with longing as she ignored me, trying to avoid the demands of her khui. I remember approaching her, determined to mate and slake the burning need in my body, only to find her in the arms of her lover. And because I had been young, I turned away. I waited for her to come to me.

But then the khui-sickness came.

Here, my memory is full of clouds. I remember nothing of this except returning home from a hunt, aching and miserable with unresolved resonance, my breast humming with an angry song. Zalah was not there to greet me. She was sick in her furs, and I assumed it was from khui-sickness. I went to join her, but I never made it. I collapsed in the main cave, burning with fever.

Vektal has told me that I was one of the first sick, but one of the last to have the light go out in my khui. It must have struggled mightily. Others died within a day or two of the sickness— like Zalah. Like Derlen. Like my mother and my father.

There was nothing worse than waking up and hearing only silence in my chest.

I shake off the memory with a shudder. I lived. I survived. I was given a new khui and I lived through it. I am whole and healthy now, and my new khui has given me a mate—Jo-see.

And this time, there is no khui-sickness to keep her from me.

I unpack my things and then go to the storage cave to gather more furs for bedding. The humans are small creatures who need much warmth, and not very strong. Jo-see is tiny and I frown, thinking of how she carried Kira and Aehako's kit all the way to the cave, along with the pack strapped to her back. She will be exhausted. She will need food and hot tea and a warm bed to sleep in, even if she does not want me in it. She is my mate, and the urge to take care of her is overwhelming. I grab additional things from storage—leather, pouches of dried tea, salted dvisti. I will replace them at a later date, but for now, my mate needs food.

When I return to my new cave with supplies, the main cavern hums with happy voices. The others have arrived, and the sound of happy chatter is a constant hum in the air. I think Rukh and his mate Har-loh—who live at the elders' cave more often than not—have the right of it. With everyone returning, there will be faces everywhere and no privacy. This thing between Jo-see and me will play out before all.

At the thought, another surge of fierce possessiveness rises in me. Whatever she may think, she is *mine*.

Jo-see is standing in the cave when I return, her pack at her feet. My khui immediately begins a pounding beat in my chest at the sight of her, and my blood pulses hard with the need to claim her. But her face is drawn and tired, her small shoulders hunched with exhaustion. Her khui starts to sing to mine and she looks down at her chest, confused, then jumps with surprise when I set my bundle down. "What are you doing here?" Her small human brows draw together. "They said this is my cave."

"The cave you will share with me," I agree, keeping my tone even, though it is a struggle. "We are mated."

Her small, pink mouth pinches into an angry line. She rubs her forehead and there is exhaustion on her face. "Do not do this, Haeden. Please. I'm too tired."

"I did not say I would climb into your furs. I know you are tired." Her refusal of me rankles, but I expect it. I must learn patience. My khui sings on, unaware of the tension between us. I must remember that this is different. Jo-see is not Zalah, to parade her pleasure mate in front of me. She is small and human and fatigued. "Sit and take off your boots. I will build a fire and make some hot tea."

There's a look of surprise on her small face, as if she didn't expect me to be courteous to her. Have I truly been so terrible to be around? If I snap at her, it is because she pulls me to her and it worries me. Now, it seems my fears were not unfounded.

She hesitates for a moment, and then gracefully collapses in the furs with a little sound of pleasure. My cock tightens in response, but I ignore it, digging out the firepit in the center of the cave. Someone has already lined it with round, smooth rocks, and so I set up a pyramid of dung and tinder, and then go to retrieve a burning coal from another's fire. When I return, her boots are off and she's curled up under the blankets, her delicate, pale face the only thing showing under the furs. Her eyes are closed and she doesn't stir when I move to the firepit and blow on the coal, feeding it tinder until it becomes a flickering flame. I set up a tripod and a bladder to create the tea, but I suspect Jo-see will be asleep before it is ready.

I glance over at her, and the urge to stroke her smooth cheek with my finger is overwhelming. What will she feel like in my arms? Zalah was tall and wiry, as muscular as me. Jo-see is nothing like her. She is small and soft and full of smiles that have genuine joy.

Someday, I would like for those smiles to be aimed at me.

"You won't try anything, will you?" Her words are a soft husky murmur. "Just because I'm sleeping?"

I am offended at her words. Does she think I would crawl over her while she sleeps and shove my cock between her legs? My khui thrums harder at the thought, and I scowl to myself. "I would never do such a thing."

"Just checking," she says softly. A moment later, I hear the gentle sound of her snore. I adjust my aching cock in my breech-cloth and drop tea leaves into the bladder of water.

I am disturbed by her ideas of what I would do to claim her. Does she truly think I would force her? Is that why she is so miserable at the thought of mating to me? Are human men like this? If so, she should be glad that she resonated to a sa-khui hunter. We do not mount females without their welcome.

I rub my chest thoughtfully. The purr there is both comfort and torture, but I am glad it is there.

CHAPTER FOUR
Josie

I wake up from an exhausted slumber feeling rather refreshed . . . and horny. God, so horny. My hand is between my legs and I absently cup my sex. The heat of my body seems to be greater there, and I'm a little shocked to realize that I'm so wet that my leather leggings are damp against my pussy. I push against the folds of the fabric and let them rub against my aching flesh, and a tiny moan escapes me.

A breath sucks in nearby.

I freeze. Shit. I'm not alone. What the fuck am I thinking?

My eyes fly open and I gaze around the cave. It's dark, a small fire flickering in the firepit. There are stalactites overhead, and the cave itself is much bigger than the one I shared back with Tiffany, the ceiling higher.

Crap. This is my new home I'm sharing with Haeden. And judging by the breath sucking in? He's somewhere nearby and heard my little moan. Crap crap crap.

I slide my hand out from between my legs and rub it on the blankets to get rid of the, well, pussy smell. I sit up with a yawn and decide to pretend like nothing is wrong. "Thanks for letting me sleep."

Glowing blue eyes watch me from across the cave. Haeden is there, his big, muscular body squatting near the fire. I watch the tip of his tail flick near the stones and I hope against hope he can't smell just how aroused I am . . . because that would be awkward. "How do you feel?" he asks.

I watch as his shadow moves and he pours some hot tea into one of the shallow bone cups favored by the sa-khui. He hands it to me. I take it, and to my relief, he moves back to the other side of the cave, even though he returns to watching me with that frank, possessive gaze.

I cross my legs, careful to keep the blankets over my lap, and cup the tea in my hands. I sip it—still warm and spicy with flavor. "I'm better, thank you."

He grunts but doesn't move.

Nor does he say anything else. All right, I guess it's up to me to break the silence. "I feel like we should talk."

"Why?" His voice is wary.

Not a great start. "Well, everyone seems to think we're mated."

He makes a sound like a huff of frustration. "We are."

Oh fun, now I get to argue with him over this. I slurp my tea, wondering the best way to tell a guy that I'm not married to him just because my chest decides to play the drums every time he's around . . . like right now. My chest is jiggling with the force of my khui's song, and it's downright uncomfortable, especially with him sitting nearby. "I'm not going to argue about this tonight, okay? I just want to talk about our situation."

"You do not want to talk?" Again he makes the huffing sound. "This is new to me."

All right, we're resorting to being bitchy, are we? "Are you trying to pick a fight?"

Again, he falls silent.

Good. At least I'm getting through to him. "I think we need to come to an understanding, since we're going to be together in this." I stress the last word, deliberately choosing to refer to our mating-not-mating in vague terms.

"What is there to understand?" His voice is defensive. "There is no bargaining with a khui. It chooses."

I sip my tea, giving myself a few moments to choose my words. "I guess I just don't understand this. I mean, I do. The khui is pretty specific. And I get that people think we're automatically mated because of the resonance. I guess I understand it even if I don't think it's right." I take another sip of my tea, waiting for him to argue. When he's silent, I go on to the part that's bothering me. "But . . . I thought you were a widower?"

He's silent for so long that I wonder for a moment if he even hears me. "It . . . is complicated."

"What about this isn't?"

"Mmm."

I wait patiently. When it seems like nothing else is forthcoming, I prompt him again. "Well?"

I can practically hear his scowl. "It is not something I like to talk about."

"But as your"—I look for a word other than *mate*— "resonance partner, don't I deserve to know the whole story?"

"Drink your tea," he says in a sour voice. He gets up and moves to the fire, stirring the coals with a long, smooth bone.

I toy with the idea of tossing my tea in his face, but I end up drinking it because it's tasty and that would be a waste of perfectly good tea. Jerk. Why did I think he'd be any different if we were mated? He's as prickly and unlikable as ever.

Even as I think vindictive things about him, he sighs heavily and his shoulders seem to slump. "It is . . . hard for me to speak of it."

I feel a twinge of pity. "I'm sorry."

"You have a right to know," he says, and his voice is gruff. "And it will get no easier, no matter my reluctance." He pokes at the fire again, staring down into the red coals. "Her name was Zalah."

Oh. So . . . it's true? I feel a gnawing sense of jealousy, which surprises me. Why do I care that he was mated to someone else before me? "I thought you couldn't have more than one mate?" My tone is snippy and I feel a little ashamed, but I also want to know the truth. "Is that a lie?"

"Not a lie." He pokes at the fire again. "As I have said, it is complicated. I think I am the only male in such an unlucky situation."

"Wow, thanks for that slap."

He grunted. "It was not meant as a slap at you. I would . . . I would have preferred not to resonate to her. But I did. She was only a few seasons younger than my mother and had long been with her pleasure mate. I was younger than Taushen, barely out of my kit seasons, and had just been made a hunter. I resonated to her and she took one look at me and laughed."

I cringe. I try to imagine Haeden—proud, scowling Haeden—as a teen boy, barely older than Farli. I picture him excited over the prospect of resonance, because every male sa-khui wants nothing more than a rare, prized mate. And then I imagine her being old enough to be his mom and laughing in his face. It's not a pretty scenario. I clutch my teacup harder. "What did you do?"

Haeden gives a grim little laugh. "What could I do? I was young, untried, and uncertain of myself. All I knew was that my khui said she was mine, and she said she was not. So I thought I would be patient and wait for her."

I'm surprised. Patience is not one of his virtues. And something tells me that it didn't turn out well. "What happened?"

He stares into the fire. "I never claimed her. She refused to yield to her khui's demands and days turned into a moon. I was sick with need and so was she, but she did not care. I think she wanted to hold out for as long as she could to punish me for disrupting her life."

That hits a little close to home. "Maybe she liked the way things were."

"It does not matter. The khui chooses, always." He shakes his head at the fire and won't look over at me. "Around this time, the khui-sickness struck. My mother and father were hit by it, and so were Zalah and her mate. I was, too. There were very few in the tribe that were not affected, and Maylak had not developed her healer's powers yet."

The spicy tea I've been enjoying sours in my stomach. "Oh."

"When I returned to consciousness, my body was weak and near death. My khui was gone, burned up in my chest from its efforts to save me." He rubs his breast thoughtfully. "I am the only one struck by the sickness to survive." He looks over at me, and his eyes are glowing blue. "Zalah and her pleasure mate did not live. Those of the tribe that remained hunted a sa-kohtsk and placed a new khui in my breast in the hopes it would take. It did, and I grew better."

I'm silent. What can I possibly say? It's a horrible story, from start to finish. My khui continues to hum, ever vocal about its choice.

"So you ask how I can have a mate and yet resonate to you? That is how. And that is why I consider myself unlucky." There is a harsh tone to his voice, and I don't blame him for being angry at the telling. It's clear they're bad memories.

"I see." So basically no one can get around resonance unless a horrible tragedy happens and the khui dies.

Or is removed . . .

My hands tremble and tea sloshes on my fingers. The surgery machine back at the elders' ship—it would work. I was going to use it to have my IUD removed, like Kira had her translator removed. Harlow said it was broken . . .

But Harlow can fix a lot of things.

I feel a surge of hope for the first time in days. "Haeden," I breathe, looking over at him. "What if we had our khuis removed to get out of the resonance?"

"What?" He turns to look at me, his voice an angry growl. His khui hums loudly, as if protesting my idea.

"There's a machine back at the elders' cave," I say, breathless. "It can fix physical ailments—mend wounds, things like that. We could have it remove our khuis! Then we aren't stuck resonating to each other!"

He gets to his feet. "Madness—"

"No!" I say quickly. "It'll work! And we'll just do another sa-kohtsk hunt and get fresh khuis! Khuis that won't resonate to each other. We'll be free." I mean, surely a khui wouldn't resonate to the same person a second time, would it?

"You would ask me to give up my chance at a mate?" Haeden's voice is incredulous. Angry, too. He starts to walk over to my bed, crossing the cave.

I shrink back. Okay, it is a little selfish, but I'm thinking of myself and the fact that I don't want to be tied to him. I'm thinking of the child we would inevitably have that would grow up in a home where the parents hated each other. "Then I'll be the one to get it done."

"It does not matter," he bellows, leaning over me. "Vektal burned with resonance for Georgie before she ever had a khui! Do you think this ache for you would go away if your khui was gone?" He slams a hand over his vibrating chest. "Do you think it cares?"

He's roaring with anger now, so loud that I'm sure people several caves over can hear him. I wince. "Not so loud—"

"Why?" He gets even louder, shouting the words. "Do you think anyone in this cave does not know we are resonating, Josee? Do you think no one knows of your dislike for me? You have made that quite clear." His eyes are blazing. "I should not be surprised that you would be so selfish."

"Selfish?" I gasp, angry at his words. "I'm selfish because I want to be happy? Because I don't want to be tied down to a miserable bastard?" I get to my feet and shove the near-empty cup of tea into his hands. "So it's either my happiness or yours, is that it? Am I wrong for wanting to pick mine?"

"You are! The khui has chosen. You cannot unchoose!" He moves closer, leaning over me. He's enormous, over seven feet tall and all muscle. Oddly, though, I'm not scared. I know he would never hurt me. I'm just pissed. I'm pissed that I find him sexy when he's angry, and I'm pissed that I keep noticing how good he smells. "You think you can unchoose resonance?"

"I'm willing to give it a shot," I retort.

"You may say what you want, but you are wrong. You think there is nothing worse than resonating to me? I know what is worse. The silence in your chest when your mate is gone." His words are rough with anger. "And you would do that to me a *second* time?"

I glare at him mutely.

"You think I cannot smell the juices in your cunt, Jo-see? You think I do not hear your little moans as you sleep? Your body wants mine." He leans in closer, and his face is so close to mine I'd swear he's going to kiss me. "Your body has accepted that I am your mate. Give in."

I'm scandalized, a bit aroused, and utterly appalled all at once. I slap a hand on his chest. "Back off."

He takes a step backward, but I sense smugness in those narrow, glowing eyes. "I will not touch you unless you request it, Jo-see. In that, I have not changed. You will need relief soon, and I will be here waiting."

He's right. Unless I figure out a way to remove our khuis and make us both happy, I'm going to have to crawl to him at some point. Already my pulse is pounding and my pussy throbbing at the thought. It's just going to get worse, too. It's like an itch or a sunburn that's escalating in its discomfort. At some point, I'm not going to be able to stand any more of it.

And then I'll be trapped.

But today's not that day. "You know what? I'm done here." I push my way past him and head for the mouth of the cave. "You can go fuck yourself. I'm going to go stay with Tiffany."

"You will return," he says darkly.

I hate that he's not wrong. I storm away to find where my bestie is moving in, unnerved and aroused.

I sleep like shit that night.

It's not that Tiffany and Salukh are super noisy in their bed-play. I mean, they are, but I'm used to that. It's like the entire tribal cave is awash with horny, humping couples and their babies. And the blankets I'm nestled in are comfy enough. The cave is roomy and I don't have to rub elbows with anyone else as I sleep. I've even got a nice fluffy pillow, courtesy of Megan.

But I still can't sleep.

I think about Haeden and his terrible story. He wants me to be his mate, his second chance at a family. If it were anyone else, I'd feel sorry for the tragedy they'd endured . . . but it's Haeden. I can either make him happy and be miserable, or I can look out for myself.

But if I get my own khui removed, he's going to relive his nightmare of losing another mate.

I toss and turn, unable to find an answer. My body isn't helpful, either. Every time I hear a moan carried on the air or the soft slap of bodies coming together, my hand steals between my legs and I press, hard. It's not helping. I'm achy and throbbing with resonance, and it sucks. I've never been one to crave sex—all of my experiences with it haven't been fun in the slightest—but right now? I'd give anything for a guy to throw me down and make sweet love to me for hours.

Well, any guy but Haeden, that is.

I wake up early and tiptoe past where a sleeping Tiff and Salukh are twined together in their furs. I can hear people in the main cave and I head in that direction, looking for food and company and, above all, a distraction. Maybe someone will have their baby with them and I can get in a little cuddle time.

I move down the twisting passage of the cave addition. The old part of the tribal cave was smooth and built like a doughnut, complete with the hole in the ceiling for ventilation and a hot spring pool at the center. The caves were spaced along the walls and Harlow had theorized that the elders had used rock cutters of some kind to set up their home. The new passage that had been opened up was a lot rougher, with a narrow path leading to the main portion of the cave. Everyone's thrilled that we can all be together again and no one minds if their new cave has a stalactite or two and a rough wall instead of a smooth one, because the addition of more caves opened up means that each family gets their own place instead of doubling up.

I arrive in the main cave and see a male crouching by the big central firepit, stoking the flames. Farli's by the cave entrance with Chompy to take him for his morning walk, and she's chatting with one of the hunters. Stacy's leaning over the fire, her baby on her back, papoose-style. Over at the pool of water in the center of the cave, one of the hunters is bathing, his back to me. Nearby, Megan relaxes in the water, her big belly sticking out. Behind her, her mate has a comb and is brushing her hair for her. She looks as if she's ready to pop, and I head over to say hello.

As I do, the bathing hunter turns and pushes his big body out of the water, and I see that it's Haeden.

Eeep.

I watch, transfixed, as he braces strong arms on the lip of the pool and hauls himself out of the water. There's nothing but acres and acres of taut blue buns and a lashing tail before my eyes, and I'm half-worried and half-hoping he'll turn around and I'll get some full-frontal action. The sa-khui live in close quarters and they're not shy about their bodies. The bathing pool is in the center of the main portion of the cave and everyone uses it without a qualm as to what they're showing. When the humans first arrived, they were a bit more modest about things until we adjusted, but now, a year and a half in, well, let's just say I've seen more sausage than I would at a meat market. Not that I normally have a problem with this.

But today? Today it's a problem . . . because when Haeden turns around and starts to dry his hair with a soft hide, I can't stop staring at him like I've never seen dick before.

This is the first time I've ever seen Haeden naked and, well, he's packing some serious heat. All of the sa-khui are equipped in a rather impressive way, but I think Haeden has the thickest dick I've ever seen. It's rather magnificently broad, his balls heavy underneath the length of him that rests against his thigh. The sight of his substantial dick makes me ache deep in my belly, and my khui starts its needy thrumming. Haeden's must be starting to thrum, too, because he looks up and our gazes meet.

And I feel oddly vulnerable, standing there, gawking at his naked bod. My mind wars with my body's need to touch him. My hands itch with the need to brush over his skin and feel the velvet texture against the pads of my fingertips. Images of touching him all over move through my mind, and I have to fight the urge to rush over to him and tackle him to the cave floor.

This isn't what I want.

I want a mate that loves me, not someone that can barely tolerate me. I can't bring a baby into this world in any other way, no matter how badly I want to be a mother.

Legs stiff, I force myself to walk over to the pool and sit down. I smile, even though my mind is raging with thoughts of Haeden and not the couple in front of me. "Hi, Megan, Cashol."

CHAPTER FIVE
Haeden

Jo-see's stubbornness is infuriating. I watch as she settles in next to Cashol and his mate, ignoring the fact that I am present. I know she saw me—I watched her gaze move over my body with a hungry look. I know she's as affected by the resonance as I am.

Stubborn female. Why does she insist on trying to fix things that cannot be changed? I would not have chosen Jo-see for my mate, and yet now it is clear to me that there is no one for me but her. The khui has decided; there is no more arguing to be done.

My chest sings an angry song of need, and I rub a hand over my breast, willing it to calm. My cock aches at her nearness, but I won't approach her. She will have to come to me and tell me she is ready, and I must be patient, no matter how long it takes. Eventually, the resonance will become so strong she will be unable to resist its call. I must simply wait the endless nights and days until then.

And until then, I cannot linger in the cave.

I return to my cave—empty and lonely without her annoying

presence—and dress quickly, then tie my wet mane back in a knot to keep it out of my face. I grab my spears and my sling. If I cannot slake the thirst of my body with my mate, I will put my energy toward hunting and feeding the tribe. The brutal season will be here in a few turns of the moon, and my mate's belly will be full with my child and will need taking care of.

The image of Jo-see's slight body, full with my child, fills me with a fierce pleasure and craving . . . and utter terror. She is fragile. What if she cannot carry my kit? What if the reason she has not resonated until now was that her khui was not strong enough? I grip my spear tightly and resist the urge to rush back to Jo-see's side and push food into her small hand. She does not like my attention.

But I picture her as my mate again, curled in my furs, her belly round. My cock nearly spills in my loincloth and I lean heavily on my spear.

Never have I wanted anything as badly as this.

I must be patient. I must wait for her to acknowledge me as her mate.

Until then, I must remain busy.

I hunt with a ferocity that surprises all of the tribe.

Grim with the need to exhaust my body, I leave at dawn every morning and bring a sled, and when I return each night, it is full of fresh meat for the growing tribe. There are young, tender dvisti fawns, the hardier mothers with the thick hides that are so useful. There are delicate scythe-beaks with the feathers that the humans prize for their pillows. There are quill-beasts and two-fangs and snow-cats, fish of all kinds, hoppers, and I even grab the sweet, reedy *hraku* plants that the human women are so fond of. All creatures land in my traps or fall prey to my spears. The other hunters marvel at my dedication.

I say nothing. The only reason I work myself as brutally as I do is because of the small human who holds my future in her hands.

Every night, I return to the cave exhausted in body. I return to my empty furs and feel the echo of my empty, empty cave around me. It fills me with a hollow ache to know that my mate would rather sleep in another's cave than be in my presence.

She is not like Zalah, I tell myself. *Be patient. Give her time.*

So I do. I stroke my cock until I come, and it fills me with less satisfaction each and every time. My khui's song is an angry protest at my self-pleasure, but Jo-see is nowhere to be found and my body craves release. When I fall to sleep, I dream of her and our kit. On good nights, the dreams are happy. On bad nights, I dream that they die and are lost to me.

As time goes on, there are more bad nights than good.

So I hunt even more. I stay out of the caves later every day, until the twin moons are high in the night sky. I would leave for several days if it would help, but I must be near her. My khui will not accept any less. I must see her, even if only to watch her turn away from me.

I cannot eat. I cannot sleep. And as the days crawl past, I hope that something will change soon.

WEEKS LATER

"You look like a sick hopper on its last legs," Aehako teases me one morning as I sharpen my spear.

I glare at him, not welcoming the company. "You should find your mate and chatter in her ear, not mine."

He just grins, sharpening his own spear point as if I did not just snarl at him. Aehako is a male who is bothered by very little, and sometimes I envy him. It seems as if everything bothers me lately.

"You should eat something," Aehako says easily. "You are nothing but a tail and skinny legs. That's not the way to please your mate."

I snort and concentrate on my spear. There is very little that pleases my mate. Just thinking about her fills me with a gnawing need, and I have to fight the urge to press my head into my hands.

I am tired. Tired, and ill, and full of unfulfilled need. It has been nearly a full turn of the big moon since my breast resonated to Jo-see, and still she denies our bond. My body feels sick and achy and there are times that I must lie flat simply to catch my breath. My khui is making me ill because I am denying its wants.

But I have no choice. Jo-see has not relented. When I am in the cave, she ignores me or leaves the room. My attempts to talk to her are shut down with a few bitter words. For the most part, I try to ignore her, because being around her and not touching her makes things worse.

Something will have to change soon. If I am struggling, how must Jo-see feel?

Patience, I tell myself again. *She will come to you soon. You must wait it out.* But I think of the haunting dreams of last night, of Jo-see dying to khui-sickness, her belly flat, her eyes dull. A shudder racks me.

Aehako's hand falls on my shoulder.

I jerk away, surprised.

He looks equally surprised at my reaction. "Haeden, my friend . . . I worry about you." His normally laughing face is solemn. "You cannot keep hunting like this. Something will happen and you will fall, or trip on your spear. I worry you're going to get hurt. You need to talk to the stubborn female and make her realize that you cannot win against a khui."

I start to sharpen my spear again, though my hands are shaking. "The decision is in her hands."

He snorts. "There is no decision. The khui has made its choice."

Ah, but it is so simple for him. His mate adores him and they have a fat, healthy kit. My mate? She loathes the sight of me. She would walk away and never look at my face again and be glad of it. And the realization of this fills me with such gnawing sadness that I put my blade down and hang my head.

Was there ever a male discarded by two mates? I am the most unlucky of them all. I sigh, thinking of Jo-see's smiles . . . the ones she never has for me. A wistful ache blooms in my chest. "I want her. I want her to want me. Is that so unreasonable?"

Aehako squeezes my shoulder again. "Talk to her again. Make her see reason."

I nod and put my spear down. My hands are still trembling as if I am ancient and weak. There will be no hunt for me today; Aehako is right. I would fall into my own pit trap or trip over my own spear. "She does not want to talk to me," I tell him. "She loathes me."

"Talk to her anyhow," Aehako says bluntly. "Both of you are sick with resonance. It will not end until you give in. Surely she has enough sense to realize that."

I want to snarl at him. Jo-see is smart. Of course she's smart.

She just . . . hates me. I am the part she cannot come to terms with. But I nod. His words have decided me. *Both of you are sick with resonance.*

I will gladly suffer on my own, but the thought of my mate in pain? Suffering as I do? It fills me with misery. I do not want that for her. So I heave myself to my feet and go to find her.

The privacy screen is up on Salukh's cave, so I do not head there. I can hear the soft noises of mating and cannot imagine they would be so loud with Jo-see asleep in her furs a few paces away. She must be sleeping elsewhere. The thought fills me with vague unease and I check in several occupied caves with their screens down, earning me a few confused and sleepy looks from tribemates. No Jo-see.

There's a storage cave near the hunter caves, small and cluttered with food and goods. Surely she did not squeeze into the storage cave rather than sleep in the same cave as me? But when I enter it and see a small bundle of furs wrapped around a small human form in the corner, I feel my chest squeeze with misery. She does not look comfortable. Is this all that she can claim as a home now? All because she has been placed with me?

It . . . does not feel right.

I rub my chest as my khui begins to hum in her presence. "Jo-see," I call out.

The furs shift but she doesn't wake up.

Irritation flashes through me and I move to her side. She cannot ignore me forever. I kneel next to the furs and rip them back. "Wake. We must talk."

Her eyelashes flutter and she lifts one weak arm to reach for the blankets. "Stop it."

My heart clenches with fear at the sight of her. This isn't Jo-see. This isn't the bright-eyed female with the tart tongue. This female has sunken eyes and is thinner than she should be. She looks tired, and when she tries to reach for the blankets, her movements are sluggish.

I have done this to her.

My heart sinks. "Jo-see?"

"Go away," she breathes, averting her face from mine. "I don't want to see you."

I touch her cheek before she can push my hand away. I am filled with longing, an aching need that will never be fulfilled. She will never be my mate. She will never let me claim her. She will never accept me into her arms and let me fill her belly with our child.

Those things will not be mine.

I realize this now and I am filled with a sense of loss greater than when I awoke and my khui was silent. My breast hums now with resonance, but the song is desperate and sad, and Jo-see's answering song does not make me feel better.

She would rather live in misery than take me as her mate. We cannot continue on like this. I will endure whatever I must, but the sight of her in so much pain fills me with agony.

She is my mate; it is my job to take care of her and to keep her safe, even if it is from me. I touch her cheek again and ignore how she tries to bat my hand away. Her skin is soft, and my entire body aches with the need to claim her.

But I will not. She does not wish to be mine. "You are making yourself sick, Jo-see. If you will not take me as your mate . . . I will take you to the elders' cave."

Her eyes flutter open and she looks at me in tired surprise. "You will? To get our khuis removed?"

I nod. I will not get mine removed. To do so seems wrong. But if she gets hers removed, she will no longer suffer, and that is what I want. "We will do as you ask. I cannot bear to see you suffer any more."

A small smile touches her mouth and she clasps my arm. "Thank you, Haeden. Thank you so much."

I nod. What else can I do? I can refuse her nothing, it seems.

My khui sings a sad, sad song in response.

CHAPTER SIX
Haeden

TWO DAYS LATER

"Ho," I call out as we approach the entrance of the elders' cave. I feel a mixture of emotions at the oval, snow-covered dome of the cave. I am pleased that soon Jo-see will be out of her pain, but mine will just be beginning.

I am about to lose my mate once more.

"Do you think they're here?" Jo-see asks at my side. Her hand rests on my arm. She is tired, but her eyes are bright once more, and she is not as thin as she was two days ago. Jo-see has not been eating much with the resonance attacking her body, and I have been forcing regular meals into her as part of our deal. I will take her to the elders' cave to see the *sur-jree ma-sheen* and she will eat. She no longer looks as if she is withering away, but I still worry over her.

I will always worry over her. No matter what she thinks, she is mine. I rub my chest. "They will be here. Rukh does not like to live with the tribe. They are too noisy." Vektal said that during the brutal season, they moved back with everyone else, but when the weather cleared for the bitter season, they left immediately. I understand Rukh's reluctance to be around others. Sometimes I wish they would all go away, as well.

"I hope the *ma-sheen* is fixed," she tells me. "I don't think I can stand it if it's still broken. If we're stuck."

Her hope makes my heart ache even more. I pat her hand. "There will be an answer for us inside, one way or another."

We enter the cave and Jo-see holds on to my arm as we move up the sloping ramp. My khui rumbles a pleased response, and I only rub my chest harder. She bends over to undo her snowshoes and I take over the task—she is tired. "Rest. I have this."

"Thanks," she murmurs, and stands still as I remove them from her boots. "I appreciate this, you know."

I grunt. The only reason I do this is because I cannot bear to see her grow sicker. There is no other reason. If it were up to me, I would have her on the floor with her legs spread . . . and the thought alone makes my cock ache unbearably. I ignore it as best I can and straighten.

Feet stomp down one of the hallways of the elders' cave and then Rukh appears. He puts a finger to his lips, indicating silence, and in his arms is a blanket-covered bundle, fast asleep.

Jo-see's eyes light up at the sight and she clasps her hands. "Is Rukhar asleep? Can I hold him?"

Rukh nods and offers her the kit, looking at us curiously. He's a big, burly male with sharp features and looks very much like Raahosh, if Raahosh were not scarred and ugly from an old hunt gone wrong. He studies us. "Why you here, friends? Is bad news?" His speech is rough, but has come a long way in the moons since he returned to the tribe.

"No bad news." I look over at Jo-see. She's gazing down at

the kit with an adoring look and it makes me ache even more to think she will never hold our kit like this. My khui rumbles loudly in my chest, and hers answers.

Rukh immediately tenses, alert. "Is—"

"Resonance," I say abruptly. "She wants the *sur-jree ma-sheen* to fix it."

Rukh scowls. "Nothing change resonance. It final."

I agree, but I will let Jo-see speak.

"We're going to get our khuis removed," she says, happiness in her voice. "If it's not there any longer, then we can't resonate to each other. We'll get them removed and put in new ones."

Rukh looks at me as if to say, *Why do you agree to this?*

I scowl at him. Jo-see is not stupid. I do not agree with what she wants, but I will not let him stop her. I feel the overwhelming urge to step in front of her, to protect her from Rukh's disapproval. "Just show us the *ma-sheen*."

The kit in Jo-see's arms hiccups and makes a fussy noise, and she makes a soothing sound and begins to rock it. "Not so loud, both of you."

Rukh throws his hands up, as if giving up. "Follow."

I put a hand on Jo-see's back protectively, and because I'm shaking with the need to touch her. She allows it, and my khui sings loudly in my chest at this touch. It wants more. I want more . . . but it cannot be.

Rukh leads us deeper into the elders' cave, and I realize that every time I come here, it looks less like a cave and more like the strange square made of rock that the humans arrived in. They said it was a ship, and as lights blink in the walls and strange squares and ovals dot the walls and flash, I feel uneasy. How Rukh can live here amongst this strangeness, I do not understand. His mate would follow him anywhere. Why they choose to stay here I do not grasp.

The kit makes another unhappy noise and then begins to cry. A moment later, a human female appears, extending her arms. "Feeding time. Hi, Jo. Hi, Haeden." Har-loh is a strange-looking human, with hair the color of flame and specks all over her belly-pale skin, but she smiles at the sight of us as she takes her kit from Jo-see's arms. "What are you two doing here?"

"They resonate," Rukh says.

Her eyes go wide and she looks at us. Her gaze moves quickly over me and then lingers on Jo-see. "Oh no. Jo!" Her voice is full of sympathy.

I scowl darkly. Does everyone think I am cruel to her? "Tell them your plan, Jo-see." I rub my chest again, trying to silence my humming khui.

Jo-see follows Har-loh into the next room, chattering in that bright, lively voice of hers about her plan. Har-loh puts her kit under her tunic and feeds it as they talk, and I lean against one of the long tables set out in the room and watch my mate. I pay no attention to what they say, because I do not like the plan.

But I cannot stop watching her. It fills me with pleasure to see her smile, to see her eyes light up with enthusiasm. She tucks a strand of her soft hair behind a tiny ear and my fingers twitch with the need to touch her mane. Her hands move as she talks to Har-loh and her gestures are fluid and graceful. She would be a wonderful mate.

I rub my chest again, frowning in the direction of the women.

Jo-see looks over and sees my scowl and flinches.

Her reaction only makes me scowl harder.

"So that's why we're here," Jo-see says. "If we can remove

our khuis, then we can get rid of the resonance. That's why Haeden was able to resonate to me—his old one that chose his last mate is gone."

"It is wrong," Rukh says, looking over at me as if daring me to disagree.

"I will do what Jo-see wants," I say flatly and am rewarded with a brilliant smile from my mate. My khui hums louder with pleasure, unaware of what we discuss.

"It's not our decision to make, Rukh," Har-loh says in a sweet voice. Her wide-eyed gaze flicks between me and Jo-see. "I wish I could help, but the *ma-sheen* is still broken."

Jo-see's face falls with disappointment. "W-what?"

I stagger with relief. My hands clench into fists at my side. Jo-see's sadness is terrible to see, but my own joy is nearly overwhelming me. She cannot unchoose me.

She will remain *mine*.

Josie

"Look," Harlow says, pulling out a panel in the medical bay. "I can fix a lot of stuff, but I've been working on this particular beast for a long time and I'm not getting anywhere." She holds a square out to me and then pulls out a second. "These are supposed to be identical."

I compare the one in my hands to the one in her hand. It's charred in a few spots and the middle looks a bit like melted frosting. All the tiny, glittering components have liquefied and smooshed into a silvery mess. Disappointment flares inside me. "This isn't an easy fix, is it?"

"Nope. I don't even know how they made these particular

parts, so replacing them—if we can even replace them—is going to be a real bitch." She slides her square back into the wall and then carefully takes the panel from me and replaces it. "I'm not giving up, but it's going to take time."

Time's something I feel like I don't have. I fight back tears of frustration. "How long? Weeks? Months?" Just the thought of holding out for a few more months makes me want to crawl out of my own skin.

The look Harlow gives me is sympathetic. "Maybe longer, girl. I don't know. I try to do what I can but this is alien technology. If I can't plug part A into slot B, I might not be able to do anything. What I can do is pretty basic. And my time to work on things is limited, between Rukh and Rukhar and day-to-day chores. There's not a ton of time to fiddle with machines, no matter how much I want to."

She's right. Of course she's right. There are so many additional chores to daily living that they eat up a lot of the day. You can't just buy a new shirt from a store—you have to hunt the animal, cure the leather, cut it, and sew it before you can wear it. Everything on Not-Hoth takes six steps instead of one, and it all takes time. I know Harlow's trying, but the thought of waiting months or longer? I can't. I don't have that time.

I put a hand on my forehead, trying to think. I can hear Rukh and Haeden talking quietly in the next room—I know they're close because my cootie is purring madly. It won't stop.

There's only one way to make things stop if I can't get my cootie out of me. Unease clenches my stomach. Sex with Haeden.

Sex with someone that hates me. Ugh.

I've had bad sex in the past. I've been abused by foster parents, raped by aliens, and gone on terrible dates where things got out of hand. I've made bad choices and I've had others' bad choices thrust on me. I've survived it all. I can live if I have awful, unpleasant, unwanted sex again.

But the thought of bringing a child into this? It feels so wrong.

I'm trapped. I don't know what to do.

"I'm sorry," Harlow says. Her hand touches mine. "I really do wish I could help."

"It's okay. I'll think of something." I don't know what, but there's got to be a way out of this.

I retreat to one of the old rooms of the ship, just to get away from the others. Harlow's busy with the baby and a jigsaw of components, and Rukh and Haeden are preparing food near the fire. I don't feel like talking or holding the baby—for once—so I hide away where I can have some time to myself to think.

The back of the ship isn't in use. Harlow and Rukh stay to the front, and the sa-khui never go exploring deep into the bowels. They don't trust the ship, especially since the "walls" (doors) started opening and revealing new passages. I head down one of these now, climbing up a pair of metal stairs that have withstood the test of time and moving down a narrow hall. The floor is pitted with holes and weak in some spots, wires and cables hanging from the ceiling. There's a chilly breeze moving through the air that tells me the hull has been breached somewhere close by. But it's quiet, and it's private.

It's also eerie.

There are traces that people used to live here: A forgotten scrap of clothing that's nearly rotted away. An old circular canister whose meaning I can't decipher. Something that looks like it was once a child's toy. I touch nothing, feeling the need to exist here without disturbing things. I don't want to dig up the past; I just want to make sense of the chaos in my head.

I sit on the edge of a hard cot that juts from one of the metal walls. If there was ever a mattress here, it's long rotted away. There is debris and a bit of dirt in the corners of the oversized square, and I run my gloved hand over it before lying down and staring up at the ceiling. There are cracks that let the light in, and a large chunk of black metal looks as if it's about to fall inward, but I don't move.

If fate's going to dick me over, well, it can't be any worse than it is right now.

Haeden's my mate. I taste the words on my tongue and find I still can't reconcile myself to them. I've been sick for nearly a month now due to fighting my cootie, and I'm so tired. So exhausted in both mind and body. The cootie won't let me rest. I'm constantly twitching and aware—even in my sleep—and I can't relax. My pussy aches, something I've never really experienced before. Not the ache of abuse but a deep down, empty, gnawing ache as if I need to be filled.

According to the cootie, I guess I do. I need to be filled first by Haeden, and then by the baby he's going to leave inside me. Wordless frustration spirals through me, but I force it back.

I've already had my night of tears. I won't let myself have more. I need a solution. So I lie back and think of options.

I . . . really don't have any.

I've tried denying my cootie. I've been doing that for the last month, and it's gotten me nowhere but exhausted and wrung-out. On some days, I don't feel strong enough to get out of bed. I can't go on like this forever. So that's a big X.

I can't get my cootie out of my chest safely. Not without the surgery machine, which is currently busted. So that's not an option.

I could . . . kill Haeden.

I giggle a little wickedly at the thought. Okay, I totally couldn't kill Haeden. Not only is he stronger than me, but I would never be able to live with myself if I harmed another person. I'm not like that. And I don't hate him. I just hate being attached to him.

What option does that leave?

Just one, I'm afraid.

I swallow hard, thinking about being mated to Haeden. One night of unpleasant sex with a man that scorns me and makes me feel like less? I could live through it. I don't want it, of course, but I've had worse and I've lived through it. It's what comes next that scares me.

There's a big plus to giving in. A baby. I hug my arms to my chest and imagine my belly filled with a new life. I imagine a baby of my own to cuddle and love. My heart aches with want. I'd love a child. I'd love one so badly. All my life, there's never been anyone or anything that's loved me unconditionally. I was tossed from foster home to foster home for as long as I could remember, and I've never had a pet. A child as sweet as Liz's chubby Raashel would be amazing. I'd even take a little crank-monster like Harlow's Rukhar, because when he gives that droopy baby smile, you feel like your entire world brightens.

A baby. My cootie wants me to have a baby. Tears threaten to come to my eyes, and I feel a surge of want and love so strong that my cootie immediately starts purring, no doubt thinking Haeden is in the room.

And that brings me back down to earth.

Haeden.

If I give in to the resonance—and everything in my body is just about to give out, so it's not looking like I have a choice—I'm going to be considered his mate. His wifey. I'll be tied to him forever and ever. I'll be stuck with him looking at me with scorn every day for the rest of my life. His irritated snort of derision every time I speak up. He'll break me down until I'm nothing.

And that's the life I'll bring my baby into.

A yearning ache fills my breast. I was never loved by my parents, given up for adoption at the age of two. I've always dreamed of the fantasy of a real family and a happy ever after. That one day, all the bad shit I've gone through will be behind me, and it'll be worth it because I'll have nothing but happiness for the rest of my life.

It's hard to come to terms with the fact that it's just a dream. That I'm giving up on everything I've ever hoped for.

My back aches from the hard bed and I shift, trying to get comfortable. As I do, a bit of dust falls onto my face and I cough, sitting up. Not the most comfortable place to relax. I gaze around the room, vaguely irritated that I've come to no decision.

As I do, I start to feel guilty. There's a seat built into one of the walls across from me, and it's large and obviously sa-khui sized and not human sized. There's a door off to the side, and while it's mostly collapsed, I imagine it to lead to a private bathroom, again sa-khui sized. What was it the computer called their people?

Sakh. Right.

They didn't want to come here. From what I remember of the stories Georgie told me, they were going on a nature retreat to another planet—or something along those lines—when they crashed here and couldn't leave.

They didn't have a choice in how their lives went from there.

They just sucked it up and carried on. They made do. They had children, and they lived their lives, and they did the best they could with what they'd been given.

I smooth one glove over my furry leggings, thinking.

Maybe I need to suck it up, too. Maybe I need to accept that, like the alien ancestors that crashed here, we don't always get a choice in our future, and we need to make the best of things.

That means taking Haeden to my bed and getting rid of the resonance problem. It means hitching my wagon to his for the rest of my life, and while that doesn't sound fun . . . right now I'm not exactly having fun, either.

And there will be a baby. I want that baby. If nothing else, I'll have a child to love and cuddle, a child of my own.

Hello, silver lining.

I get to my feet, and nearly collapse again. My legs are weak and trembling, another side effect of the stupid resonance. I just want to feel strong again. I want to *not* want Haeden anymore. All the lust I feel for him? It's artificial. It's meaningless, and I hate that it controls me.

But . . . maybe it won't be so bad if he is a good kisser. No one ever seems to kiss me, and I'd love for just one really wonderful kiss. I don't think I'll get it from Haeden, but I can't help but hope a little.

Time to get this show on the road, I guess. I suck in a deep breath, hold on to the wall for support, and choose my path.

CHAPTER SEVEN
Haeden

Jo-see is gone for much of the afternoon, and her absence gnaws at me. I know she is in the bowels of the elders' cave, and she is safe, but I want to see her. I *need* to. Rukh, luckily, is not talkative, and we enjoy a companionable, if surly, silence between us as we sharpen weapons and tend to the fire. I feel as if I should be doing something—hunting, watching over Jo-see, providing for her, taking care of her needs—but I remain by the fire and tend to my things instead, waiting for her. A hunter's life is such that he must always be repairing his gear. There are always fishhooks to be made out of bone, a spearhead gone blunt with use that must be sharpened, knives that must have their edges honed, nets to be repaired, straps that have grown weak with use, and shoes to be mended. Normally I find comfort in the endless chores, but today they make me impatient.

I snap a delicate fishhook with my fingers and snarl, casting the shards into the coals of the fire. "Ridiculous."

Rukh looks over at me with a narrow-eyed gaze.

I glare at him. He says nothing, but I can imagine what he is thinking. That is the third fishhook I have carved—and broken—in a row. My focus is on anything but the tasks before me. Instead, I worry about Jo-see. She has been gone for a long time. Did she hurt herself? Fall? Is she bleeding and in trouble even now? I surge to my feet. "I need to go."

"Go where?" Rukh pokes at the fire and turns the spit, roasting a quill-beast. His mate likes her meat charred and most of the supplies here are cooked beyond inedible to a sa-khui tongue, but Rukh does not seem to mind. His Har-loh is happy and that is all that matters to him.

I toss aside my carving knife. "Anywhere. I—"

I stop. Jo-see is in the doorway, her arms crossed over her chest. She's watching me, her gaze on my face. As our eyes meet, she gives me a tentative smile.

My khui flares to life, thrumming hard in my chest. Its song is wildly desperate, and my blood pounds in my ears, my weakened body unable to cope with my khui's excitement. My cock stiffens in my breechcloth and I adjust myself with one quick hand, my tail flicking.

"Can we . . . Can we talk?" Jo-see takes a step forward, her hair spilling over her shoulder. She looks vulnerable and beautiful all at once and my body hungers with the need to touch her. She's looking at me as she speaks, and it feels as if for the first time in almost a moon, she is seeing me.

I feel a surge of triumph deep in my bones.

She has come to accept the resonance.

Rukh grunts and gets to his feet, though I am barely aware of his presence. "I go check on my mate." He tosses aside the fire stick, glances at us, and then leaves the room, hitting a panel on the wall. The wall seems to close together and slides shut behind him.

We are alone, and I inhale deeply, filling my nostrils with her sweet scent.

My mate is coming to me.

My mate.

My khui hums even louder as she takes a few tiny steps in my direction. She looks fragile and hesitant, yet she is moving toward me. This is good. I force myself to remain still as she approaches. If I grab at her, I will lose her. I clench my fists at my side, determined to remain motionless, even though my khui is all but frantic in my breast. It senses her nearness and grows wild.

She moves forward and then stops, brushing a lock of her long hair back behind an ear. "I . . ." She pauses and licks her lips. I stare at the pink flash of tongue, my cock aching unbearably at the sight. Humans have smooth tongues, I have been told. At first I was repulsed by the thought, but now I imagine Jo-see's small tongue on my skin and nearly spend in my loincloth.

"Yes?" I growl the word.

Jo-see blinks, a little startled, and then rubs her arms. "So . . . remember when we talked? And I said I would never give in?" Her gaze drops and she lets out a small little sigh. "I can't hold out any longer. This is me . . . giving in. You win."

I frown at her words, not entirely certain I understand. She is speaking the human tongue, and there are some words I do not grasp. "Win?" The image that comes to mind is of conquest, not of mating. "How do I win?"

"I'm crawling to you." She spreads her hands. "I give up. I can't fight this thing any longer." Her eyes are curiously shiny, but she puts a tight smile on her face.

This . . . is not how I imagined her coming to me. In my

dreams—and there have been many—her eyes are heavy-lidded with lust and she runs her hands on my chest, as if unable to stop from touching me. In my dreams, she is eager to give in to the khui's song. The woman before me seems . . . defeated.

But my khui is singing a powerful song, and my body is excited. I reach out, hesitant at first, to see if she will shy away. When she does not, I touch a lock of her long, smooth mane and let it move through my fingers, soft like water. "You wish to be my mate, Jo-see?" My voice is husky with need, and my cock strains against my loincloth. If she moves any closer, she will feel it for herself. The thought makes me absurdly aroused.

"Honestly? No. I don't want it. I don't want you." She gives a small shake of her head. "But . . ." Her hands go over her chest, where her own khui is humming frantically. "I can't . . . I can't do this anymore. I feel like we're stuck treading water and just getting weaker and weaker. The *sur-jree ma-sheen* is no longer an option, so . . . this will have to do."

She speaks a lot of human words, and I vaguely hear them, but I'm focused on her soft hair instead, dragging my fingers through it again and watching it ripple.

Finally, she will let me touch her.

"So, um, should we find someplace private to do this?" Her voice sounds choked.

I nod. I would take her on the floor, right here, right now—but I understand that humans value quiet places where they can be alone to mate. I try to think of all the things the other human-mated males have said around the fire—how they like to be held, what pleases them—but all I can think of is the steady throbbing hum of my khui in my breast, Jo-see's nearness, and the ache in my body that is about to be slaked at last.

She moves away, and I walk behind her. She could lead me

off a cliff, and in this moment? I would follow gladly. Jo-see heads into the depths of the cave, turning down a passage I have never been in, and then stops in front of the wall. She pushes a button and the wall slides back, revealing a chamber. I twitch, uneasy at the sight of the moving wall, but when she moves in, I follow anyhow. If it is not safe, better that I am with her.

The chamber is small and square, and there is a shelf along the wall. She sits on the edge of it and looks over at me with nervous eyes.

"You want to mate here?"

Her cheeks flare with color and she nods. "Seems as good a place as anywhere else."

I nod and move closer to her. Her scent beckons, and I hear the endless hum of her khui. It calls to me, and I can't resist the chance to reach out and touch her mane again. My fingers drag through it and she shudders, her eyes closing.

She doesn't touch me, and I fight back a pang of disappointment. Maybe it is human custom for the male to take charge of the mating. I sit next to her on the hard bench, and brush a finger over her smooth, rounded cheek. My cock aches, my sac tightening against my shaft as if ready to release my seed. I cannot yet, though. I have barely touched her, and I want more.

Her scent is enticing, and I lean in to sniff her. I . . . never touched Zalah. She pushed me away and mocked me for the stripling I was. Then when I recovered from the khui-sickness, she was gone, and touching anyone else—had they even offered— seemed wrong. Now, I have my mate and no idea of how to please her. Instinct will have to guide me.

I lean in and nuzzle at her neck, licking at her soft, smooth skin. She shivers and makes a soft, whimpery noise that makes my cock jolt in response. She is not moving away from my touch, and her khui is singing loudly in her breast. Her scent is so . . . overwhelming. I want more of it, and I cup a hand to the other side of her neck and bury my face against her shoulder. She is fragile and small, my mate, and I worry I will hurt her somehow. "I . . ."

"It's okay," she breathes and puts a small hand on my arm. "Let's not talk, all right? Let's just . . . do this."

She does not want to speak? I do not know if this is another human custom. It feels strange to me, but I give in to her wishes. I pull at the collar of her tunic, loosening the laces. She remains utterly still, that tight look on her face. I wish she acted as if she were more . . . aroused by my touch. My cock jerks in my breech-cloth, unaware of her tension. All my body cares about is that I am finally touching my mate.

The khui hums in my chest, and I pull her closer against me. I want to touch her everywhere. I want that tight look on her face to change to one of pleasure. It is important to me that she like my touch . . . I want her to realize that I can be a good mate to her. That I need her. That she is beautiful to me with her silky hair and her pink, smooth face and her smiles.

Ah, her smiles. I feel pre-cum slicking the head of my cock at the thought. I am close to spending and I have barely touched her. I release her, clenching a hand into a fist, trying to keep control.

But then she leans against me. I forget all about control. My hand slides down her front and I am eager to touch her every-where. Her teat is small in my hand, but she makes a little noise of pleasure when I touch it, and it makes me want to do more. I caress her over the leather of her tunic and feel the hard little nub of her nipple. She sucks in a breath as I stroke her body, and I can smell the scent of her arousal through her clothing. My mouth floods with water, and I imagine how good she will taste on my tongue. I cannot wait to bury my face between her legs and lap at her sweet juices. I squeeze her teat, and she leans against my chest, her hand going to my face to caress it.

And I erupt in my pants.

The breath hisses from my body as the force of the orgasm overtakes me. I stiffen, stars dancing before my eyes.

"Haeden?" There's a question in her voice. Confusion. "What's wrong?"

I mentally curse. My breechcloth is hot and sticky with my spend. All she had to do was touch me and I lost control. I am . . . humiliated. Any other male would know how to please his female, but I do not. I have never touched one. I feel awkward and foolish, and my mind conjures up Zalah's mocking grin as she denies me.

I feel as if I am back to that same unwanted, untried kit I was.

"Haeden?" She reaches for me.

I jerk to my feet and turn away from her so she won't see the mess I've made of myself.

"What is it?" Jo-see asks.

"Nothing." My voice is harsh. I will never admit what just happened. "Stop pressing me with your questions."

She sucks in a breath. "God, you're still a dick. Even after I come crawling to you?"

My back goes up. I do not look at her. "You did not crawl. The khui chose. You have accepted it." And me? I cannot control myself. My shame is immense. Oblivious, my khui hums and hums in my breast, eager to take my mate.

"Bullshit," she says softly. "Bullshit that I've accepted it. You know what? I can't do this." I hear her hop down off the ledge.

"I thought I could move past this, but I can't. I can't fling myself into the arms of another person that's just going to use me. And I'm not going to bring a baby into this kind of relationship. Fuck you, and fuck your cootie."

"Do not leave," I growl as I hear the door open. I press a hand to my cock, but the front of my breeches is still wet with spend. If I turn around, she will see my shame, and I cannot bear to see the scorn in her eyes like the scorn Zalah always had for me.

But the door closes again a moment later, and the room is silent.

She has gone anyhow, and I am left with wet breeches and stinging pride.

Josie

I can't do it. I thought I could, but I can't.

He didn't even kiss me. A kiss shouldn't have mattered so much, but it feels like everything. It feels as if Haeden didn't want me there. Like I was just a body for him to jerk off on. I've been that body before, and it sucks.

All I wanted was a kiss. To feel cherished for once. I sigh and wipe the frustrated tears from my eyes. I can't cry over this. I've already had my one night of tears. No more.

I retie the laces of my tunic at my neck and head for the main computer room. For some reason, I keep expecting Haeden to come after me. To come coax me back into his arms. To shower me with kisses and show me that I was wrong, that he didn't mean to make me feel bad. But . . . no one comes.

And I can't believe I'm disappointed over that.

I feel like such an idiot. I've made things worse. Not only do I still have unfinished resonance, but now I've fought with Haeden. Again.

I just wish there was a way out of this. Somehow.

I plop down in one of the uncomfortable, slick chairs that have managed to last the hundreds of years from the crash. The one I'm sitting in is oversized, perfect for someone as big as Haeden but not so great for someone my size. My feet dangle, and I kick them, then lean forward and pick up an errant object on the counter. "Hey, computer? Where's Harlow?"

"My readouts show that Harlow is in her private quarters with her companion and her child. Do you wish to locate them? I can provide directions."

"No thanks." I toss the chip aside and pick through the items on the countertop, miserable. "What about Haeden?"

"The modified sakh male that you arrived with is still in room 3-A."

Still there? He's probably expecting me to come back. He can just keep waiting. I find a rounded circle of what looks like glass and take it in hand. It's smooth to the touch and about the size of my palm. "Computer, what's this for?"

The computer rattles off an explanation that I don't grasp in the slightest. I make a few noises of acknowledgment just to be polite and sit back in the chair, swinging my legs like a little kid and playing with my new toy. The glass is slightly thicker in the center, and I lift it to my eye and peer, because it reminds me of a kaleidoscope. When I bring it to my eye, though, everything rushes forward. Ooo, a magnifier of sorts. I bet you could make a kickass Not-Hoth telescope with this. Of course, it'd be useless on me because I never get to travel anywhere. Everyone thinks I'm too fragile.

I flip it in my fingers again . . . and an idea hits me.

What if I leave? Just leave and don't come back? Will my khui give up if I'm separated from Haeden by a hundred miles?

I keep flipping the circle of glass in my fingers. I'm not hating this idea. It'll mean leaving everyone behind . . . but I already feel left out. They've all happily mated and are expecting me to just roll over and let Haeden run roughshod over me and give me a baby. For the last month, I've been the recipient of tons of sympathy glances, or looks of pity. I hate both.

I remember Tiffany telling me a few weeks ago that she wanted to leave. Just start walking and never come back. But now I get it. I don't want to wait around for everyone to expect me to leap into Haeden's furs. I don't want them all watching my every move to see when I give in. I don't want the smug looks of pity when they find out that "silly Josie's still holding out."

I can just leave.

After all, what's tying me here? Friends? They've all been mated and are building families. They're happy and in love. Even Tiffany, who wanted to leave a short time ago. I'd thought she was crazy . . . but back then I hadn't walked from the elders' cave to the tribal cave on my own, with nothing but a crude homemade compass. I can do it.

I think of the little cave Harlow lived in with Rukh, the one by the ocean.

I've . . . always wanted to see the ocean.

CHAPTER EIGHT
Haeden

I cannot figure out how Jo-see made the wall open. I slap at it, over and over again, trying to find the way out. I want to go after my mate, to drag her back into the room—wet pants or not—and find out why she has changed her mind.

Her words echo in my head. *I can't fling myself into the arms of another person that's just going to use me.* I want to find out what she means by that. Who has used her? I will rip their heads from their bodies and stomp on their innards.

More than anything, I want more of her soft touches, the little sounds she makes when I touch her. I play them over and over in my mind until my cock is hard once more, and there is no way to ease the ache.

There is also no way out of the room. I pound against the wall over and over again, but as time passes, it becomes more and more obvious to me that she is not coming back.

So, seething, I wait. I lie down on the hard stone-like shelf, stretch out my legs, and wait for Jo-see to come back. My mind wanders to thoughts of her returning, begging my forgiveness.

She's decided she wants my touch after all. She crawls over me, all silky brown hair and eager mouth. And when I touch her? She makes more of those soft, whimpery noises that send a pulse of need right through me.

I wake up sometime later, khui humming, my cock still hard, and my breechcloth wet again from my dream.

And still no Jo-see.

Cursing, I rip one of the decorative panels from my leathers and scrub at my wet belly and groin. Twice now, I have come in my pants. I snarl as I toss the wet leather aside and then push at the wall again, trying to get it to move. When it doesn't budge, I slam my shoulder into it, over and over again. This room will not keep me from my mate.

Nothing will.

"Haeden?" I hear a confused voice in the distance, from the far side of the wall. It is Har-loh. "Is that you?"

"Let me out," I bellow. "The wall will not open."

As if determined to prove me wrong, the wall opens easily a moment later—several paces down from where I am slamming my body against it. Har-loh gives me a confused look, hefting her kit onto her shoulder. Her mate is two paces behind her. "What's going on? I didn't realize you were still here."

Still . . . here? "Of course I am here." I slap a hand at the frustrating wall and shove past. "Where is Jo-see?"

"See, that's the thing," Har-loh calls after me. "I thought she was with you."

Her words make no sense. I storm into the main area of the elders' cave. The firepit is nothing but coals. Her pack, originally next to mine by the cave entrance, is gone. Her snowshoes and her heavy outer furs are nowhere.

My khui is silent.

I rub my breast, determined not to panic. She has moved to another one of the rooms, then. She has retreated from the main cave because she needs space from me. She would not just leave. Not with resonance still singing an unfulfilled song between us.

I head back into the winding caves, toward Har-loh. "Where is Jo-see?"

"I think she left." Her eyes are wide, upset. "Did you guys have an argument?"

I snarl at the thought and race back to the front of the cave. I take a few steps outside and there, in the falling snow, is the slushy, dragging trail that snowshoes leave behind. I bend down to touch one track. It is heading away from the elders' cave, but she is not heading to the South Cave, nor to the tribal cave. Instead, she is veering in a completely different direction.

Where is Jo-see going? Alone?

Is it because of me? I rub my breast again, hating the guilt that swoops through me. Was I that cruel? I am not the most patient of males but . . . I would never harm her.

Yet she has left, and left without saying a word to me or to Har-loh. She has crept away. I imagine her sad face, the tears falling from her eyes, the cold biting at her small human form.

I grit my teeth and return to the elders' cave, determined.

Har-loh is there, holding her kit to her shoulder, worried. "Is it true? Is she gone?"

"I will go after her," I tell Har-loh. "She will be safe under my watch."

She bites her lip and looks at her mate. He puts a hand on her shoulder to comfort her. "Take food," Rukh instructs in his broken language. "For you and Jo-see."

I grunt in acknowledgment of his wise words. I can hunt for myself and will never starve, but it is always wise to have dried food on hand for the days when the weather is too bad to leave shelter. I heft my pack . . . and it's lighter than normal. Frowning, I open it to realize that my neat, orderly things are out of place. My rations are gone, along with my extra waterskin.

A reluctant smile of admiration curves my mouth. My mate has raided my pack and taken supplies. Instead of infuriating me, it makes me feel good. She is clever and smart, my Jo-see. She will not run off into the wild unprepared. I look over at Rukh. "I will need an extra spear and knife, and some rations for myself."

Rukh nods.

"You'll bring her back?" Har-loh asks.

"If that is her wish." I want to see where she is going first, and why she left without me.

Har-loh nods and looks up at Rukh, still worried. He presses his mouth to her forehead. A kiss, the humans call it.

A kiss.

I did not kiss Jo-see. I did not hold her in the tender, easy way that Rukh holds his mate. And I am ashamed. There are many things that I have done wrong this day.

I will right them, or die trying.

I set out a short time later, easily picking up Jo-see's trail. There is a light, powdery snow on the air, but not enough to cover her tracks. She has made no attempt to hide her trail, and for a time, I entertain the thought that she wishes to be found. That she will see me tracking her and rush into my arms and shower my face with the little presses of her mouth that humans call kisses. But as her trail stretches on and the weather grows steadily worse, I realize this is a fantasy.

She has no intention of returning.

My chest aches with the realization that my mate has abandoned me. I have not pleased her. I did not caress her properly, and when she touched me, I spent my seed in my loincloth like an untried kit. I thought to hide my shame from her but it seems that she has been hurt by my actions. When I find her, I will explain myself and seek her forgiveness. I will ask her how she wishes to be pleasured. This time, I will do it right.

Even though I make good time, I am many hours behind her. The twin suns set behind the distant mountains and the air grows cold. I pull on a fur wrap to block the worst of the wind, but I think of Jo-see and her fragile human body. She will be shivering with cold, unable to last a night out in the open. I must find her and build her a fire. I must shelter her with my own body so she does not freeze.

No sooner do I think it than a tiny light appears on the horizon. It flickers and then flares brighter, yellow in the dark night. I catch the faint scent of smoke.

A fire.

Pride bursts in my chest. My Jo-see is not so helpless after all. I approach, quieting my footsteps. I see the outline of the tiny cave—one of the hunter caves scattered like wind-blown seeds across the landscape—and she is at the mouth of it, feeding bits of fuel to her fire. I devour the sight of her small form. She looks healthy, wrapped in her furs, and when she stands, she seems tired but not shivering with cold.

After a moment, she pulls the privacy screen over the cave entrance, blotting out some of the light given off by the fire.

I am left out in the snow, pondering. With a fire, she is safe. Even the most aggressive of metlaks will not approach a flame, and this particular region has very few large predators. I am impressed that she was able to find one of the hunter caves, build a fire, and take care of herself.

My fragile Jo-see is stronger than I have imagined. And instead of storming into her cave and demanding that she return, I hunch in the snow and settle in for the night. I will put up a watch to ensure she is undisturbed. But if my Jo-see wants to go somewhere? I will follow until it is no longer safe for her, and then I will step in.

Josie

So far? I've got the hang of this survival-on-my-own thing. Yesterday, I hiked until I found a cave, made myself a fire (thanks to the firestarter necklaces that one of the girls insisted we all have), and spent the evening cozy and warm.

And okay, it was a little terrifying to be out on my own.

A lot, actually.

Despite being tired from a day of walking, I'd had a heck of a time falling asleep. The knowledge that I was the only one around for miles and no one knew where I was? It did a bit of a number on my head, and I clutched at my furs, terrified. Every noise made me jerk awake. Add in the fact that I'm feeling restless and out of sorts thanks to resonance? It wasn't a fun night.

At some point, I went to sleep, and when I woke up, my fire was dead, there was frost on my furs, and my breath was puffing in the air like a cloud once more. I was also aching from resonance, my nipples hard and my pussy wet. Gah. Time to get up. I stretched and shook out my furs, doing a little jog to try and make my body focus on the day instead of sex. The furs were a little damp from yesterday's travel, so I rebuilt my fire and spread them out to dry before heading on. If I started walking around lunchtime, it wouldn't be so bad.

I feed more dried dung to my fire and wash my hands with a bit of snow, then take out a pack of rations. I help myself to a handful of the granola-like stuff, wrinkling my nose as I eat. The cootie has dampened a lot of my senses—smells are not as keen, and neither are tastes—but this particular sa-khui dish is still spicier than I like. I wash it down with the last of my water and realize I have no more. Time to melt some snow.

It's a little intimidating to realize that I can't depend on anyone else to help me. If I need water, I have to get it myself. Fire? I need to pick up supplies as I walk. I put the last few bites of my trail rations back into the pouch. Who knows how long they'll have to last me? I've never hunted before, and the enormity of the task looms before me.

Well, I'll just have to figure it out somehow, because I'm not going back.

When my furs are dry enough and snow is melted for my waterskins, I put out my fire and dress in my heavy furs again, then put on my snowshoes. I leave the cave and start heading toward the west. Harlow and Rukh came from the west, and that's where the ocean is, so that is where I'm heading. She said the temperatures are milder there. I tug one of my gloves higher and figure mild is just darn fine with me.

The snow is thicker this morning, which means more must have fallen overnight. I trudge through the powder with my backpack over my shoulder. After an hour, I'm already exhausted and sweaty, but I keep going. This is what I want, so I'm going to have to suck it up. I need to enjoy the scenery—this is my chance to really see more of Not-Hoth than just the caves.

And Not-Hoth? For all that it's cold and blustery, it's also really beautiful. Hill after endless hill of white snow undulates before me. The landscape is dotted with the occasional feathery pink tree, and more of the shorter, frothier bushes, thick with piney needles. In the distance, there's a herd of dvisti, their shaggy grayish-white coats making them look a lot like overgrown sheep with spindly legs. I suppose I should think of them as food, but right now I'm enjoying the scenery. The sky is overcast as usual, but that just means there's no glare on the snow. In the distance, the purplish, spiky peaks of ice dance along the skyline, and I wonder if I'm going to have to cross them to get to the ocean. Gosh, I hope not. I'm not a mountain climber.

I head into a valley, following the easiest path to walk, and then over the next hill. Something shakes the ground and I freeze, looking around. There, in the distance, is a sa-kohtsk and its baby. It lumbers over the snow with slow, almost lazy motions of its long, skinny legs, and I find myself drawn toward it despite the danger it presents. It's hideous. The hide is shaggy like the dvisti, but the legs are a tough, sinewy hide that leads down to flat, wide hooves. The head itself is the size of a car, and dotted with glowing blue eyes like a spider. Gross. As I watch, it moves its big head back and forth, as if tasting the air.

I wonder what something so big eats. Hopefully not "people."

I follow it for a time, fascinated. I've never gone to the zoo and this is a lot like a big, icy, open zoo. I wonder if I could get close enough to touch one? The baby sa-kohtsk is bigger than I am, but still seems more approachable. I'm tempted to chase after it—

—until the mama sa-kohtsk lets loose an epic stream of piss. Squealing, I trundle away from their trail as fast as I can in my snowshoes. Gross gross gross!

After that, I decide following animals is probably not the

smartest thing. I also realize I don't have a spear. I do have a small knife that I keep with me at all times, but it's not exactly built for hunting, and I don't really want to have to kill something with a blade the size of a pocketknife. How the heck did I forget to bring a spear? I'm kicking myself for that, and in addition to scanning the ground for dung chips for the evening's fire, I look for something that will make a decent spear.

There's nothing, of course. In the icy, windy landscape, the trees are whippy and frail, and the bushes aren't big enough to provide much wood. This is why all the weapons back at the cave are bone, I remind myself. Of course, you have to be able to bring down a kill—a really honking big one—to find a bone big enough to make a spear out of.

Maybe there will be spears at Harlow and Rukh's old cave. I'll just have to make my rations last that long, and then I'll be set. Encouraged, I pick up the pace a little and head over the next rise.

It'll all work itself out. And for the first time in what feels like forever? My cootie is silent in my chest. I may be exhausted from traveling, I may be needy and sick with thwarted sexual desire, but my chest is all quiet.

I'll take the small victories.

CHAPTER NINE
Haeden

Jo-see is much stronger than I have given her credit for. She is tired, but she walks a good distance every day, even when her snowshoes drag on the ground. She has been lucky in finding shelter—the first two nights, she found hunter caves, and the third, she made herself a nest in the rocky shelter of a ledge out of the wind at the base of a cliff. She is smart. She is resourceful, too. I watch from a distance as she picks up dung as she walks, or scoops up snow and pulls her pouch under her furs to melt it.

She does not, however, look behind her.

This does not surprise me. Jo-see is the type to plunge forward in life. I am the sour one that looks behind. But if she looked just once, she would see me on the horizon, trailing behind her, watching to make sure she does not wander into a nest of metlaks, or that she is not hunted by a hungry snow-cat.

But no, Jo-see is smart and she is cautious, and I am proud of how well she is doing, even if she does not seem to want to go back.

She continues to head toward the mountains every day, always in the same direction. It is intriguing to me. Where is she going? What does she think she will find? She treads over hunting trails and goes over hills, and crosses over rocky outcroppings that make my body tense with the need to rescue her. But she is not being foolhardy. She is cautious. She pauses at every stream and checks for nelukh—the fish that humans call "face eaters"—and sprinkles crushed berries upstream to get them to leave before she crosses. If she sees tracks of other animals, she changes her route.

I rub my chest as I watch her peek her head into another hunter cave. Last night she slept in the open, and while she kept her fire going, it took everything I had not to step in and lead her toward shelter. I know these lands like I know my own tail, and I do not want to see her suffer.

But this is important to her, so I will follow her for however long it is necessary . . . or until my khui becomes unbearable. Even now, just thinking about her causes my cock to rise. When I know she is safe for the evening, I will rub myself until I come, but it does no more than whet the itch.

Just once, I wish she would look back. I wish she would see me, waiting on the horizon for her. Waiting to take care of her. To comfort her. To be her man and her mate and whatever else she needs.

But she never turns.

I hope wherever Jo-see is going, she gets there soon.

Josie

The ocean is beautiful.

After days of walking, my supplies are getting low, my feet

feel battered, and I'm utterly exhausted. But when I hike up a rocky ridge and see the distant rolling, jade-green waves of the water? It's something else. The outcropping I'm on ends abruptly, and far below, I see gritty sand a darker shade of green than the water itself, and frosty, light green icebergs floating in the distant water. This is so cool.

I remove my snowshoes and take a seat on the ledge so I can relax and gaze out at the ocean. From my vantage point, I can see for miles. It's really something. The waves are tranquil and the water looks so soothing. I pull out my trail mix pouch and eat a few crumbs as I enjoy the view. I don't have much left, but I'm at my destination. Well, sort of. I don't see anything that looks like the caves Harlow described, so maybe I'm in the wrong spot. I lick the last few crumbs from my fingers and ignore the grumbling of my stomach. It'll have to last.

On a whim, I dig out the disc of glass from my bag. I'm a little ashamed to say I stole it from Harlow, but if the surgery machine is broken, does it even matter? Nothing else is half as useful, and I plan on using the heck out of this thing. I cup my fingers around the edges and hold it to my eye like I would a telescope. At first it makes my gaze blurry, so I try focusing with one eye closed, and things zoom into place.

Now I can see much farther away. Excited, I use it to gaze down at the ocean. The water doesn't look as green—or as soothing—a little closer. In fact, the waves look downright nasty, and I can see dark blobs scuttling on the shore.

A shadow flies overhead, and I put my "telescope" down, glancing up. There's a gigantic bird overhead, rushing past at a speed I've never seen before. Holy crap, it's fast. I lift my spyglass again, but it moves so quick I can't catch a view of it. Darn.

I turn back to the ocean, and peer out at the icebergs. There are dark shapes on them that I can't make out. Maybe the Not-Hoth version of seals? Ice otters? Something? A moment later, the waves undulate and a thin, yellowish snakelike thing erupts from the depths and snatches one of the dark shapes off of the iceberg and disappears under the water with it. I shudder.

Mental note: no swimming.

I move the telescope over the water, scanning. Mostly there's nothing to see but more waves, but as I sweep over the distant horizon, a faint smear of lighter green against the water catches my eye. I try to focus in, but no matter how much I squint, I can't see what it is. At first I think it's another sea serpent, but when it doesn't move, I realize it's something else. Land, maybe? But it's . . . green. Maybe I should check it out.

I turn my telescope back to the icebergs and see another dark shape flutter under the water.

Maaaaybe I won't check out the green if it means going through Jurassic Park: Aqua Edition. Haeden would know what those things are. For a moment, I feel an unhappy pang of longing that has nothing to do with my cootie.

I put down my spyglass and rub my forehead, where a headache is starting.

It's weird, but I miss Haeden. With all this travel, my cootie's gone mostly silent, though I dream of Haeden at night, and when I wake up, my chest is vibrating with resonance. That isn't what makes me miss him, though. I miss his presence, knowing that he's *there* for me. It's strange, but no one's ever really been there for me in my life. When the shit hit the fan, everyone else ran away. Not Haeden. He might glare and put up a fuss, but he's always been there. Funny how I didn't realize it until I left.

He's still insufferable and a prick, but . . . he's growing on me. Or was. I imagine what he'd say if he knew I went all the way out to the ocean on my own. He'd scowl, his tail flicking, and cross his big arms. *You're weak, Jo-see. Females must be protected. Humans cannot travel like the sa-khui.*

I'm gleeful, imagining the smug look on his face changing to one of wonder as he realizes just what I've done. That I'm a tough cookie. And some of my enjoyment fades when I realize he'll never realize what I've accomplished, because I'll never see him again.

I hate the wistful ache in my breast. I've made my choice and I won't cry over it. Another bird flies overhead and I squint at it. Eagles? This area reminds me of a (much, much colder) Pacific Northwest and there are eagles in that area. Probably not too safe to be up on the ridge, then. I'll leave just as soon as I figure out where Harlow's cave is.

I raise the glass again, and this time, I scan the rocks. The cliff below shows nothing interesting, and I sweep up, up, up into the distance until I realize I'm staring at the base of the purple mountains, the ones that look like glass or rock candy. Pretty, but not what I want. Still, I can't help but study them for a bit, because I've seen nothing like them before.

That's when I notice the wreckage.

My spyglass sweeps over one mountain, and at the base there's a dark shape half-covered in snow. There are hard edges to it and a blinking red light, and the pit of my stomach curdles, sick.

It's a ship.

It can't be . . . can it?

CHAPTER TEN
Josie

When I decided to set off and become Ice Explorer Josie, I'd expected one of two things: sucking miserably at it and returning home, or finding Harlow's cave and hiding out there until my cootie gave up.

I didn't expect to find another spaceship.

I stare at the square. It's not our ship. It's not the one we came from. That one was near the peak of a granite-like mountain and this one is surrounded by purple rock-candy peaks. Ours had a breach in the hull on the top and the rest of the compartment we'd landed in was relatively secure. It was the only way we'd managed to survive the elements for a week despite no cold weather gear and no supplies. The snow had insulated us and our body heat kept us warm.

This wreckage is different. Even though it's a square, it looks like one end is mangled, like a cereal box torn open at the bottom. There's snow, but I see a blinking red light. Maybe it's a distress beacon of some kind.

Oh, crap. What if there's someone that needs a rescue and all they've got is *me*?

I put down my spyglass, thinking. Okay, panicking. A little panic's totally justified, though. I don't know what I'm going to do. We haven't seen any ships fly overhead in the year and a half that we've been on Not-Hoth. No one's tried to re-kidnap us.

It's a trap, Admiral Ackbar's voice says in my ears.

Yeah, it feels a bit like a trap. Of course, the more I think logically about it, the more I wonder.

A ship returned a few months after we'd arrived. They stole Kira again, shot Aehako and Haeden—oh crap, Haeden!—and left them for dead. Kira had saved the day when she crashed the ship and took an escape pod back to Aehako's side. It's a story that's been told around the campfire over and over again. I've heard it a dozen times, mostly because I gleefully enjoyed the part where Haeden got his guts shot up.

Man, I've been a jerk to the guy. I feel a twinge of guilt and then shove it away. *Focus, Jo.*

Okay. Okay. I close my eyes, picturing Kira telling the story in her solemn voice. She'd set the spaceship on autopilot and pointed it at the distant mountains, where it had crashed. Both Aehako and Kira had seen the crash.

Distant mountains.

These mountains.

I exhale a breath of relief. That has to be it. This is the ship Kira crashed, and when she'd crashed it, there were no survivors. They were all already dead. It was a little . . . well, bloodthirsty, but it's hard to feel sorry for someone that stole you from Earth and wanted to re-enslave you. I'm not sorry they're dead.

But I still don't know what to do.

Do I check out the wreckage and hope there's something useful? Or do I go hunt down Harlow's cave with its supplies?

Or do I somehow make a boat and check out the green smear in the distant waves that might be an island?

This feels like an ice-age version of *House Hunters*.

Does Josie want adventure and an island cabana despite the dangerous location? Or will she choose a beachfront property . . . provided she can ever find Harlow's cave? Or will she choose the house in the mountains, even though it might already be occupied?

I look around me. The cliff has greenery, but it's scrubby and twisted, designed to cling to the rock through the snow and the high wind. There's nothing around here that would make a canoe even if I knew how to make one, or a raft. And the thought of getting into that sea-monster-infested water scares me.

"Island, you're going to have to wait for another day," I tell it. House one eliminated. Now, in true *House Hunters* fashion, I need to narrow it down to two choices.

I ponder this even as another dark shape moves through the sky, the shadow rippling over me. Whatever I decide, it's not smart to stay here. I give another quick glance through the spyglass at the cliffs below, but I don't see a cave. Shit. I turn my glass back to the wreckage, in the opposite direction.

The red light winks at me.

If that's the wreckage I'm thinking of, there's no survivors.

But what if I'm wrong?

But . . . what if they have food? And guns? And things I can use to survive? Right now I've got a pocketknife and maybe a handful of trail mix left.

I chew on my lip, thinking, and toy with the spyglass, flipping it through my fingers. It's been surprisingly handy, and it wasn't even meant for this. Who knows what kinds of goodies the other alien ship will have? I put the spyglass in my pack. I sling it over my shoulder, put my snowshoes back on, and head down the cliffs, toward the wreckage.

If I'm here, I might as well see what I can salvage.

The wreckage is a bit farther away than it appeared in my stupid spyglass. Okay, a lot farther away. I hike for the rest of the day and don't make it there before the suns start to set. There's not much shelter around, so I find a few scrubby bushes to act as a windbreak and spend the last hour before sunset pushing the snow higher into the bushes so they form a wall. I have a bit of a dugout and I build my fire there, spending the entire night shivering and feeding more fuel to it so I don't freeze.

By the time morning comes, I'm exhausted. I let the fire die and take a quick nap in the sunlight until the bleating of a nearby dvisti herd wakes me up. I head off toward the crashed ship again, and when the suns are high in the sky, I arrive at the ship.

Haeden

It takes everything I have not to go to Jo-see's side during the night and offer to assist. She would not appreciate it, and when I see her creating the windbreak with the snow, I know she is smart. She will be fine, if not comfortable. Still, I stay closer than I normally do, my spear at the ready, and watch over her. She is in the open, and if anything tries to approach her, I will gut it for daring to get near my mate.

After her morning nap, she takes off again and I follow behind her, far enough so she will not notice me. As I do, I notice that her path crosses other tracks in the snow. I slow, letting her get ahead so I can study them. I crouch low and touch one. The snow has not crusted, which means it is fresh.

And the clawed toes? Metlak. Many of them.

Jo-see's in danger.

Josie

The flashing light I'd seen in my spyglass is a lot brighter the closer I get. It's an exterior light of some kind, and blindingly bright, making me see spots every time it goes off. I shrug off a fur wrap and throw it over the light, only to hear my fur sizzling and the smell of burning leather. I quickly yank it off again. The light's so hot the snow melts when it touches it. Well, that's not a good sign.

I circle around the wreckage to give it a once-over. There's snow piled up around it and so I can't make out the shape, but the boxy end that's torn open and sticking out of the snow? Yeah, that looks familiar. The mountains that looked like purple glass from a distance are clearly ice, and I'm amazed at the massiveness of them. This ice must be hundreds—or thousands—of years old to have formed mountains, and at the base, I see a tinge of green. Okay then, how did the ocean become green if these mountains are purple? I wish I knew. Maybe it's algae or something. I'm not a scientist, so I can only guess. But the snow that falls is white, as are the drifts covering the craft, which tells me that this is definitely a recent addition to the landscape. I circle around it one more time, trying to determine how big it is.

It's not like the ancestor ship, which is a long, rounded oval as big as a shopping mall. This one's more like a wedge, I think, and as long as a city block. Most of it is buried in snow except for the cargo end. If there was debris—or bodies—they were covered by the snow a long time ago.

I'm kind of glad for that. I don't want to see a bunch of corpses sticking out of the snow. I shudder at the thought.

I approach the busted end of the spaceship that protrudes from the drifts. It's tilted to the side and one end sticks out high from the snow, but the other end is climbable with a little effort, I think. "Hello?" I call out. "Anyone home?"

No answer. Not surprising, given the remoteness of the location and the fact that the ship's crashed. If this was Kira's ship, everyone was dead before the thing ever landed. I swallow hard at the thought, squeamish. I've seen TV shows with car accidents . . . I hope I'm not going to see corpse splatters all over the inside of the ship. Or worse, corpse-splatter Popsicles. I press a mitten to my mouth and hurk a little.

But I've come this far. I need to keep going.

After the overheated flashing light, I worry that parts of the ship will be too hot to touch. I throw my fur wrap over the part I've designated as my point of entrance, and when it doesn't sizzle, I climb into the dark, hollow pit. "Hello?"

No answer. No light, either. Crap. I retreat back out and attack one of the scrubby bushes nearby, taking twiggy limbs and ripping them off, then twisting them into a bundle. I hold my bundle against the flicking emergency light until it smokes and then lights up. It's a crappy torch and drips embers everywhere, but it'll do. I don't plan on staying down there long. It gives me the creeps.

I crawl back into the busted hull carefully, torch in hand, and start to explore. I thought this was the cargo area, but apparently not. It's a different part of the ship, and it looks like the entire thing is turned sideways. I'm in a narrow hall and standing on what was probably a space window or something. There are furniture and other small objects peppered on the floor, mixed in with debris, and I kick through the mess, looking for guns. The aliens that kidnapped us originally had guns that looked a lot like clubs the size of a rifle, and I could use one of those.

There's a door half-open ahead of me, and I hold my torch aloft, peering in.

Bodies. Lots of bodies, frozen in their seats. I stagger backward and retch, then get angry at myself for doing so. Of course there are bodies. *Quit being so girly, Josie.* I picture Haeden chastising me, but instead of irritating me, it fills me with wistful sadness. I wish he was here. He'd hold the torch and put an arm around me, and it wouldn't matter that I'm a little girly and scared, because he'd be by my side. And he only needles me because he's scared of how fragile I am.

The realization strikes me like a brick.

That's why he's so protective. That's why he's such a dick when I try to be independent and is constantly talking about how women should be protected. He's scared someone's going to die and then the remaining mate will have to suffer like he has.

Maybe I've been too mean to him.

I pick a different passageway and head through it, determined to be strong. It's a dead end, though, blocked by debris and slag and hanging cables. I can't go farther, so I turn around and look for the next passage.

A short time later, my torch is burning down to cinders in my hand and I haven't found anything useful. Well, scratch that. I found a room that was private quarters, and the only things not rotted away were a small blanket made of a weird, plastic-feeling material and a cushion-like pillow made out of the same. I stuff them both into my bag even though I don't know what I'm going to do with them. I decide to check one last hallway before heading out, because I'm determined to find something I can *use*.

But the moment I step through the next doorway, I'm hit by old memories.

This is the cargo bay. Or was. There's a hole in the ceiling that is letting light in, and there's a light dusting of snow in the middle of the floor. The cargo bay's contents are scattered everywhere, crates smashed and their contents destroyed. I swallow hard at the sight of this place. If I close my eyes, I can hear the crying, smell the unwashed bodies, see the faces of the guards as they leered at us . . . and more.

I bite the inside of my cheek until I no longer feel like screaming, or weeping. I've already cried over that, and I won't give it more time in my head. I shake the bad memories away and focus on the good things. If this is the cargo bay, maybe there's food. Maybe there's supplies.

When I turn to the left, though, I see them.

Tubes.

Oh God.

I head toward the wall, trembling. There's a thin coat of ice on it, and half of it is collapsed. I can barely make out three tubes. I brush a hand over the snow and ice and immediately amend my count. Two tubes. There's nothing but scorched remains of the third, the wall crumpled away. *I hope you didn't have an occupant.*

When I smooth away the ice and snow over the next one, though, the green light flashes. I remember that light.

It means there's someone inside.

"Shit. Fuck. Damn." Saying the words aloud doesn't make it any better, but it feels necessary. I run a hand over the next pod's panel. Yellow lights flicking to green. I don't know what that means, but I'm betting this pod also has an occupant. "Fuck! Fuck fuck fuck!"

This? This I'm going to cry over. I allow myself to burst into tears and sob.

Because now I have to go *back*.

CHAPTER ELEVEN
Josie

When I emerge from the ship, I don't expect to see another person in the distance. But up on a distant hill, I see blue skin and horns and the graceful movements of a male sa-khui locked in combat. It's obviously Haeden. I recognize his motions even as my khui starts a low hum in my chest. My anger and frustration at being followed disappear when I realize why he's turning on one leg and flinging a spear. He's fighting something that looks . . . well, a bit like a skinny gray yeti. A metlak, my brain tells me, though I've never seen one. I've heard the stories. They're tall, monkey-like creatures that are almost as intelligent as they are vicious. Liz has told me hair-raising tales of running across them in the wild, and I'm alarmed to see one here.

As another pounces on Haeden's back, only to be brushed off, I notice that there's not just one or two but a dozen of the creatures.

Oh shit. Were they following me? Is this my fault? Guilt and alarm surge through me, and as another slams into him, I rush forward to offer my assistance, only to realize that I have nothing but a tiny knife.

Fuck! What do I do?

I look over at the flashing emergency light and am nearly blinded by it as it blinks again. I need something else to burn. They're afraid of fire. But the only thing I have is my bag.

I hesitate a moment, and then dump everything, including my food and water pouch, out on the ground and gather up a few handfuls of the debris at the edge of the ship, then stuff one of my furs into the bag. Back in goes my new pillow. In goes the small blanket of the strange, shiny material. Then, I rush forward and hold my bag against the light, squeezing my eyes shut against the flare of red light as the leather sizzles angrily. There's no time to gather more wood for a torch and I pray that the leather will catch on fire.

The bag hisses angrily and smoke starts to pour forth. "Come on," I whisper, glancing up the hill where Haeden was fighting just a moment ago. He's still there, flinging another metlak aside, and my heart hammers with a mix of relief and worry. "Come on," I tell my bag again. "Hurry!"

The damn thing doesn't want to catch, though. I give a low growl of frustration and then toss my bag down. The shiny blanket catches my eye and I grab it out of the bag and hold it against the light, hoping that it's not flame retardant, or I'm really screwed. If this doesn't work, I'll have to go help Haeden with my bare hands. Leaving him is not an option.

The blanket begins to hiss against the super-heated light, and my fingertips blister as I hold it there. I squeal and jerk my hands away, but the blanket is smoking. It's working. Before I can think about it too much, I shove the blanket against the light again and hold it there, trying to ignore the pain in my hands. Hot tears pour from my eyes and I moan as my fingers continue to blister. Just when I can take it no more, the blanket catches.

Yellow flames lick at the edges and then the entire thing starts to crawl with fire. I pull it away and dash toward Haeden with my flaming bundle, yelling at the top of my lungs.

I don't know who's more surprised to see me running at them, full throttle with a flaming blanket—Haeden or the metlaks. The big blue male pauses only for a brief second, and then he slams his spear into the side of the creature he's fighting. The others back off even as Haeden roars, a primal sound. I shake my burning blanket at them as they cringe backward, and one by one, they peel off and run away, dashing for the hills.

Just in time, too. The blanket's crawling flame has only been aggravated by my running and the wind, and it's licking at my hands. With a yelp, I toss the blanket to the ground and then blow on my stinging, burning hands.

"Jo-see?" Haeden's voice makes me turn. His big shoulders are heaving as he pants, and his vest is torn. There are scratches and gouges on his arms and one on his face from the metlak claws, but he looks fine otherwise. I face him, ignoring my throbbing hands for a moment, and wait for the lecture. Knowing him, it'll start with *females are weak* and end with something about me playing with fire. Oblivious to the emotion spitting between us, my khui hums a happy song in time with his.

He says nothing. Is he waiting for me to admit I'm sorry? Not gonna happen. I wave a hand at him, beckoning. "Go ahead and give it to me—"

Haeden puts an arm around my shoulders, and in the next moment, I'm pulled to his chest, my cheek squished against a broad pectoral, as he hugs me to him.

I freeze, because it's the last thing I'm expecting. His arms wrap around me and then he's holding me with both big, strong arms, as if I'm the best thing he's ever seen. I realize I'm not going to get a lecture—well, not yet—because he's *relieved*.

He's so happy to see me that he's hugging me. And okay, it feels really good to be hugged. His hand strokes over my hair as he holds me to his chest, and I close my eyes and bask in the warmth of his body against mine, and how wonderful it feels just to have someone touch me with simple happiness. I've never been hugged much, and I can see right away why some people are addicted to cuddling. Haeden's strong body holding me close is bliss. In his arms, I feel safe and protected and the worries of the world slip away.

But then one of my hands brushes against his clothing, and a shot of pain rips through me. I hiss and back away, gazing at them. My fingers and my palms are purple and starting to blister.

Haeden grabs one of my hands, taking care not to touch the injured spots. "Jo-see, what have you done?"

Ah yes, that's the Haeden I remember. "It's called saving your ass."

"You have saved more of me than my ass," he says, and I swallow the smart-ass comment bubbling in my head. He glances around and then retrieves his spear. With his other arm, he pulls me close again. "The metlaks will be back. We need to find shelter and build a fire."

Shelter's not a problem. "I know the perfect place." I point at the wrecked ship with its flashing light.

For a moment, it looks as if he wants to argue, but then he nods. "I will follow your lead."

Now there's a change.

Haeden

She's safe.

Overwhelming relief moves through me in waves, as if spurred by my khui. It has been humming its song loudly ever since she appeared on the horizon, waving a flaming blanket. To think that she risked her safety to protect me from metlaks? It is humbling. While metlaks are normally not a danger to hunters, these were younger and therefore more aggressive. Their attack caught me by surprise, as did Jo-see's rescue.

She came to rescue *me*.

I rub my chest, absurdly pleased by the thought.

My mate heads toward the flashing, strange light on the horizon, chattering. It's a ship, she tells me, even as she cradles her injured hands in front of her, palms up. It's a ship and she has found others inside and that is why she was returning down the trail because she realized she couldn't stay and do nothing and it's frustrating but she has to do the right thing because that is what others would want her to do if the *tay-bulls* were turned. I listen to her with half an ear, lost in the song of my khui. It is overwhelming me with her nearness, and I want to press her close to my body again. This is the first time I have been this close to her in days, and although I knew she was healthy, I cannot stop staring at her, at the sway of her hips as she walks, her graceful motions. She says something, and I grunt a response just in case she expects one. A moment later, she stops and turns to me, frowning.

"Will they be back?" she asks me.

Ah. "The metlaks? Yes. They will be curious and return once

they have their courage. If we have a fire once more, they will leave for good. They are not smart creatures."

She bites her lip and nods, squinting when the red light flashes bright into our eyes. "Don't touch that thing, by the way. I learned the hard way it's a little hot." She waves her damaged hands in the air.

"You did not have to do that," I tell her.

"I wanted to help. They were attacking you. Were you in danger?"

If I was at full strength? Not likely. But I am weakened by the khui's unfulfilled song and many days of travel. I nod.

She smiles brightly as if pleased by my feebleness. "Then I helped."

The urge to correct her rises in my throat, but she is so happy to be helpful that I bite the words back. I am still pleased by the idea that my mate sought to protect me. No one has ever fought for *me* before. And she hurt herself in the process. I am distressed by this . . . and humbled by it as well. I take her by the elbow and glance into the dark recess of the strange cave. "Stay here and I will check for animals."

"I've already been inside," she says, wrinkling her strange, flat, movable human brow at me. "Weren't you listening?"

Do I admit that I have ignored some of her chatter in favor of eyeing her body? I glance away, and then back at her seeking eyes. "My concentration . . . the khui . . . it is difficult." I rub my chest to emphasize my lame answer.

But she nods understanding. "I know what you mean." Her cheeks flush a bright pink and she glances away as if shy. "At any rate, it's safe in there. No live things." She shivers. "Just dead ones."

"Very well." I want to chide her for wandering blindly into a cave that could have any sort of creature nesting in it, especially in metlak territory. But we . . . are not yelling at each other, and I am reluctant to make her angry. Not when the relief of seeing her is still pouring through me.

I enter the mouth of the strange cave. It is much like the elders' cave with its odd smooth walls and floors. It makes me uneasy, but Jo-see needs shelter and a place to rest, so it will do. She clambers in after me and I reach out to help her, as she is favoring her hands. We move inside the large chamber several paces, and when we are far enough from the entrance, I gesture. "Sit," I tell her. "I will make a fire in this cave and then we will take care of your hands."

"I'm fine," she says quickly. "I can help—"

"Jo-see," I say, my voice gruff with irritation, and I watch her back stiffen. I choose my words carefully. "You are clever and you are brave, but you are still injured. I am not. Let me do this and we will take care of your wounds. The sooner we treat them, the sooner they will feel better."

And, greatly daring, I brush the backs of my fingers over her cheek. I should not, but I cannot help myself. I can no more resist touching her than I can resist breathing.

I wait for her to shove my hands away. I wait for her to scowl up at me. But she only gazes up at me, her eyes big in her round human face, and then she nods, wincing. "They do hurt."

"Then let me help." *Let me take care of you, my mate.*

When she doesn't protest, I throw my pack down on the ground and pull a few things out of it. My strikers, for starting a fire. My bag of collected tinder and fluff, and a few dried dung-cakes scooped up from the trail for future use. Then I close it again and gesture that she should sit on it. There are no comfortable sitting mats here, and my mate will not be forced to kneel on the cold ground.

She sits down heavily, and I realize how tired she is. I stroke her soft hair—again, unable to help myself—before I get up and begin to craft a firepit nearby. There are no rocks to encircle it, but the floor itself is of a stone-like surface so I clear it of deadfall and start my fire. My Jo-see needs warmth, a meal in her belly, hot tea, and a poultice for her burned hands. With no wind to hamper me, the fire starts easily and soon I have it stoked to a brisk flame. I feed it all the tinder in my pouch and then grab a handful of the debris I had shoved aside to stoke it higher.

"Can . . . can we move my seat closer?" Jo-see asks, getting awkwardly to her feet. "I'd do it but my hands are starting to sting pretty bad now."

"Yes," I tell her, and move the seat close enough so she can enjoy the fire. I set up my tripod and then head to the entrance to fill the water-sack with snow to boil. I sprinkle some herbs to make tea, and then glance at the entrance. Jo-see's things are spread out on the snow. It looks as if she scattered them in her haste to come help me, and I feel a surge of affection and lust for my mate. My clever, brave Jo-see. "Wait here and I will get your things," I tell her.

"Not going anywhere," she says faintly, staring down at her hands.

They are paining her more than she wants to admit. I hate that. I grab her things, gathering her furs and her supplies in my arms. Her pouch of travel rations is impossibly light, almost empty, and I feel a pang of unease. What if she had run out? I picture my mate starving as she plods endlessly on the trail, and frustration wells inside my breast. Now is not the time to chastise her. I fill her satchel with armfuls of snow and return with the things to her side.

"Here," I tell her, opening the mouth of her bag. "This is full of snow. Put your hands in here. The cool of the snow will help the pain. I must go and get more fuel for the fire and some liidi stalks for your hands."

"Lee-dee?"

"It is a plant that grows like a vine amongst the rocks. It is good for burns. Helps them heal faster."

She nods and sticks her hands into her bag, whimpering when the snow touches her skin. "Get me a whole bushel, then."

I will. "Do not leave the fire. If the metlaks return, they will not come close."

She looks up at me with worried eyes. "Will you be all right?"

My khui's song grows even louder, and I rub my chest, fighting the lust I feel. She worries for me? "I will be fine. Have no fear."

Jo-see nods. "Hurry back."

CHAPTER TWELVE
Haeden

Every moment away from Jo-see's side feels like salt water poured into a wound. Even though I know she is safe with the fire, I think of her with her hands pressed in the snow, of the pain she feels, of the metlaks returning and finding her unable to pick up a weapon. I must gather more fuel, though, or we will not be safe through the night. And more than anything, Jo-see needs the liidi stalks. I hurry, racing through the churned snow, following the trail of dvisti and scooping up their leavings. Once my bag is weighed down with dung, I race to the nearest cliff and pry apart the cracks in the stone with my knife, looking for the twisty, skinny roots that grow between them. When I find enough to satisfy me, I head back toward the cave. A hopper jumps out of the bushes a short distance away and I toss down my supplies to hunt a fresh meal for Jo-see.

When I return to the cave, she's sitting by the fire, her hands in the bag, resting on the melting snow. The fire is crackling, and I watch her nudge the coals with the tip of her boot every so often. Her eyes brighten at the sight of me, laden with a fresh kill and bulging pouches. "I'm glad you're back."

My face cracks into a smile. She is glad to see me.

Jo-see looks startled at my smile and hers widens. "I hope you brought plenty of that lee-lee root, because my hands are killing me."

"Killing you?" I rush to her side, dropping my burdens. "You are dying? Let me see them!"

"Wait, wait! It's a figure of speech," she says, and the words mean nothing to me. But she pulls her hands out of her bag and shows me the blistered skin. "It just means they hurt really bad."

"Then we will fix it now." I grab some soapberries out of my scattered supplies and go to the snowy ledge at the edge of the cave and wash my hands and the liidi roots clean. Then I return to her side and shove them into my mouth, grimacing at their terrible taste.

Her eyes widen. "I thought the roots were for me."

I chew, my teeth grinding the tough roots. "They are," I grit out. "The poultice must be chewed before it is spread."

"Oh." Her eyes widen. "You're going to spit that crap out on my hands?"

I nod. "I am going to spit this *crahp* on your hands, yes."

"That sounds awful, but they hurt bad enough that I'm willing to go for it," she admits, wrinkling her nose and watching me chew.

The roots are very fibrous and have a sharp, bitter taste to them. They also leave the lips and tongue numb, and by the time I spit the first mouthful out onto her palm, my stomach is turning at the flavor. She squeals in horror at the mushy greenish lump I left on her hand, but when I begin to gently spread it over her burns, her noises of dismay turn to a little sigh of pleasure. "Oh wow, it feels better."

And because it pleases her, I gamely fill my mouth with more of the awful-tasting root so I can ease her pain.

By the time her hands are covered, my lips and tongue are numb, the taste of liidi feels as if it is etched into my teeth, but she isn't making the tiny sounds of distress anymore, so it was worth every foul mouthful. I shrug off my now-tattered vest and tear it into strips.

"What are you doing?" she asks.

"We are going to cover your hands so you keep the liidi on them until morning." I take one thick strip and slowly wrap it over the poultice and around her hand. Her bones are so delicate that it worries me how easily she can be hurt. She does not have the protective bony plates on her limbs and covering her chest that the sa-khui do. She is all softness, softness that can easily be torn by a metlak claw.

"What about you?"

I tilt my head at her, pulled from my distressing thoughts. "What do you mean?"

Her cheeks are bright pink again. "You . . . you tore your clothes up for me. Won't you be cold?"

Ah. I grunt. "The wind does not affect me as it does you. I am fine."

She gives a little shiver. "I'm cold," she admits. "Can you put my fur cloak over my shoulders?"

I finish wrapping her hands in the makeshift leather bandages and then place the cloak gently over her, bundling her warmly. It fills me with pleasure to be able to do these simple things for her. "Shall I roast your dinner for you?"

"I can eat it raw," she says, a brave note in her voice. "But you might have to feed it to me."

I ignore how my cock reacts to that. Of course I will have to feed it to her. Her hands are useless. I am filled with an odd sense of pleasure at the thought of her needing me. She has worked very hard to fight our mating, so she cannot be happy with this turn of events. "I will," I say gruffly, and then pull my kill closer to the fire. I take my time cutting the choicest bits for her. The organs and some of the bones go into the pouch over the fire to make a tasty stew. We will need to make every bit of food count in case the metlaks return in greater numbers. I turn to her, a small chunk of meat in hand, and offer it up.

She opens her mouth and leans in.

I bite back a groan of need at the sight of her small, pink tongue. It is as smooth as the others have said, and my mind immediately begins to imagine it tracing lines over my skin. I shake my head to clear it and feed her the bit of meat. Her lips close over my fingertip and I feel her tongue brush against my skin.

This is . . . torture.

She chews, wrinkling her nose at the taste. I remember Jo-see is one of the humans that prefers her meat roasted. I bite back a smirk of my own. "Would you like me to cook it for you?"

Jo-see shakes her head and swallows hard. "I need to learn to like it."

Not while I am around to take care of her. But if this is how she wishes to enjoy her dinner, I will humor her. I feed her another piece, and cannot resist grazing my thumb over her full bottom lip as I do. She gives a little shiver, and her khui grows louder.

Seeing her shiver reminds me of the fire, but I cannot build it higher without burning through more fuel and I want to keep it going all night because of the metlaks. Of course, thinking of the metlaks makes me also think of how she raced toward me earlier, screaming, fire in her arms. She could have been hurt. "It was dangerous for you to attack the metlaks," I chide, and cut another square of meat to feed her.

"I'm not a wimp. And I couldn't let you die out there."

"I shall ignore the wound to my pride at the realization that you think a few adolescent metlaks can kill me." I shove the meat into her mouth and watch her chew frantically. "What kind of hunter do you think I am?"

"You didn't look like you were doing so well when I saw you," she says as she chews. "Scuse me for trying to help out."

"You could have been killed."

She rolls her eyes and continues chewing.

"You should have come back in here and stayed safe," I lecture, cutting my next bite smaller. My stomach growls but I ignore it. I will feed my mate before I will ever put a bite into my own mouth.

"It wasn't like I had a choice."

My eyes narrow as I offer her another piece of meat. I watch her take it from my fingers with her mouth and wait for her to chew for a bit before I speak. "Because I was being attacked?" I resist the urge to rub my chest out of pleasure.

"I didn't realize you were being attacked when I came out. I was leaving anyhow. Once I saw you, I couldn't just walk around you while you were being jumped."

I frown at her words and feed her another tidbit. She was leaving? "Where were you going?"

To my surprise, her lip trembles. She pauses in her chewing and closes her eyes, then opens them again only after she swallows. When I offer her another bite, she lifts one bandaged hand

and shakes her head. "I was leaving because . . . I have to save the others. I didn't even know you were there."

So she was not coming to save me? I am surprised—and irritated—at the sting I feel in my chest. She does not care for me after all. "What others?" I ask gruffly, shoving the bit of meat into my own mouth and swallowing quickly.

"The ones in the pods." She gestures with her head, indicating something over her shoulder. "Remember when you guys saved us and six of the girls—Nora and Stacy and the others— were in pods sleeping?" Her eyes get shiny but the tears do not spill forth. "I found more of them."

"More pods?"

Jo-see nods, the look on her face heartbroken. "And they're not empty."

"More . . . females?" The unmated men of the tribe will be ecstatic. "Why are you so miserable? We can save them."

"Because they shouldn't be here," she says angrily, jerking back. Jo-see won't look me in the eye, either.

"Lies. That is not what you are angry about. You are angry at me." As she glares in my direction, it dawns on me. "You are mad because you have to come back. Because you cannot leave them and you cannot free them on your own."

"Oh, I can free them," she says bitterly. "Free them to a death sentence. They'd die in a week, remember? I can't kill a sa-kohtsk on my own."

I watch her blankly, the realization that she does not yet care for me crushing.

If it were up to her, she would remain out here in the wild alone, forever. My wants and needs are nothing. The only reason she must return is for the safety of new human females.

Her mate is simply an annoyance.

Josie

It feels weird to realize I've hurt Haeden's feelings. He's silent as he moves around the cargo bay that we're using as a cave, tending to the fire, roasting the rest of the kill, and then scraping the hide clean with a bone knife. He melts more water, makes tea, and then hands me a cup, all without a word spoken to me. His face is devoid of expression, features tight, and as he works with his back to me, his tail flicks back and forth like he's pissed.

It's not a good feeling. My cootie purrs a happy song, but I feel pretty fucking miserable. I just made this journey for nothing, Haeden was almost killed by metlaks, and I'm still resonating to him. Oh, and my hands suck. A little sigh of misery escapes me.

His entire body tenses, alert, and he glances over his shoulder at me. "Do your hands hurt?"

"No, they're fine." They're numb and covered in goo, but they're fine for now. Tomorrow I imagine it'll suck to be me, but I'm trying not to think about that.

He grunts and turns back to poking at the fire with a rib-bone.

An apology springs to my lips but I bite it back. I'm not in the wrong, I tell myself. He should know that I don't want to see him.

But then I think of the way he held me close after the metlaks ran off, and he stroked my hair like I was the best thing since sliced bread. The urgent desperation in him as he gazed down at me, like everything was right in the world as long as I was safe. The way he fed me bits of meat with such intensity, like his entire world centered upon feeding me and taking care of me.

I squirm uncomfortably in my seat. He's made me the center of his world . . . and isn't that what I've always wanted? A mate who puts me before everything?

Except it's Haeden, and that makes things tricky.

"I'm sorry," I say after an uncomfortable length of silence once again. I don't think I'll be able to stand it if he doesn't talk to me all night. I haven't seen anyone else in days and that's why I feel a desperate need for him not to be mad at me, I tell myself. If it were anyone else, I'd be just as unhappy.

But then I think again of the way he looked just before he hugged me in against him.

He grunts acknowledgment of my words but doesn't turn around.

Clearly I'm going to have to say more. "This is just hard for me," I tell him, resting my hands palm-up on my knees so I won't hit them against anything. "I guess . . . sometimes I just want a say in something, you know? It feels like every time I turn around, the universe is deciding my fate for me, and it gets old." When he continues to remain silent, I add, "If you could go back and change things, wouldn't you rather not resonate to me? If you had a choice?"

"No."

"No?" I'm dumbfounded by his answer. Dumbfounded . . . and oddly pleased. I stare at his back, at his twitching tail, trying to understand. "Really?"

He nods slowly at the fire, but I know the nod is for me. "I would change nothing."

Oh. Warmth furls through my chest. I think this is the first time someone's picked me. Really picked me, not put up with me because they had to, or because the check for foster care wouldn't come in otherwise. "Thank you," I whisper. "That means a lot to me."

"Clearly it does not, because you would not have returned for me." He pokes the fire again, angrily. "It is easy to say words, Jo-see. It is another thing to mean them."

"I know. I know I'm making this difficult for both of us. I just . . . I need time, okay? I'm kind of gun-shy about not being wanted after my childhood."

"Eh?" He turns to give me a narrow-eyed glance over one shoulder. "*Guhn-shy*?"

"It's an expression," I tell him. "Skittish. Wary. Afraid."

He grunts again and the silence falls. Then, he tosses aside the bone he's been using to prod the fire and gets up. He picks up the cup of tea that I can't hold and brings it toward me. I drink a little with his help and he sets it down again, then crouches near me. "Why are you *guhn-shy*?"

I shrug and stare down at my bandaged hands, which look like the saddest mittens ever. "Just had a bad childhood. Happens to a lot of people."

He looks up at me expectantly. When I'm silent, he gestures for me to continue.

I wince. "Please don't make me talk about it."

The expression on his face grows wintry again. "How can I understand if you will not share?"

I swallow hard, my throat suddenly dry. "Because it sucks. Because it was a long time ago and I am determined to not let it control my life forever." But he's not wrong . . . he can't understand how much it means to me to have a real family unless I tell him why. "This isn't an easy story to tell."

Haeden grunts acknowledgment and, to my surprise, reaches

up to brush a lock of hair off my shoulder. "Neither is mine, yet I told you."

Fair enough. I nod slowly. "So . . . my parents gave me up when I was two—"

He interrupts, the look on his face intent, as if he must capture every single word. "I do not follow."

Oh boy. Yeah, I can guess that something like that won't make sense to him. In their small tribe, every child is welcomed with joy by everyone. "Well . . . there are a lot of people back where I come from. Hundreds and hundreds and hundreds. So many that your mind cannot comprehend it. And sometimes these people are not . . . responsible, I guess. The people that had me didn't want me and so they took me to a place called a state home and left me there. With strangers." At his frown, I add, "The state home is where people take the children they don't want and leave them for others to take care of."

His frown deepens. "This happens . . . often?"

"Not often, but enough that there were a lot of children there. And I was a pretty miserable kid. I had a lot of ear infections and so I was always screaming and crying. No one wanted to mess with me for long. I was older when I got my first set of foster parents and, well, they just wanted the checks." I realize a moment later that he's not going to understand what that means, and I explain to him. "That means that other people paid them in goods to look after me. They didn't want me. Just the goods. They had many children like me in their home so they could get many, many goods." It wasn't a great place, but it also wasn't the worst place. "I was there for four years. After that, I got moved again. And again. And again. No one wanted me. Some people would say the timing wasn't right, or I was too old and they were looking for someone younger. Or they had their hands full or were about to get a job transferred and so they'd send me back. And at a few places . . ." I swallow hard. "Um. A few families wanted me for the wrong reasons."

"What reasons are worse than taking care of a child in exchange for goods?" His lip curls, the expression in his eyes unfathomable.

Bless his heart, he truly has no idea. "Some men like to . . ." Oh gosh, how to say it delicately? "Take pleasure from small children. And I looked really young for a very long time."

His mouth parts, and then his fangs bare in a hiss. "Someone let your caretaker touch you? While you were a *kit*?" His words are an explosion of anger. "This is *done* in your world?"

More often than I like to think about. But I don't say the words aloud. I just nod, my skin crawling with old, bad memories. Memories that I don't allow myself to cry over. Been there, done that. "I usually didn't stay at those homes for very long. Just . . . long enough for someone to catch on."

Haeden jerks to his feet, raking a hand through his hair. Did I think his tail was lashing before? It's whipping furiously now as he paces. "You said 'homes.' This was done more than once?"

"A few times," I say faintly. "Sometimes there are bad people in the system. You kind of learn to spot the creepers after a while. Unfortunately, sometimes they're the only ones that want to take in a teenage girl."

The flat of his hand slams against the wall. He snarls and rages back and forth, muttering furious words under his breath. I watch him, a little amazed at his violent reaction. He looks as if he's about to truly lose his shit. He flings himself against a wall and slams a flat hand against it again, tail moving furiously. The entire bay shakes as he smacks the wall once more. He looks like he's trying to pound it into submission.

And call me crazy, but it makes me feel . . . good. Someone cares enough about me to get angry on my behalf. I've never had that before. I've had social workers that just give me pitying looks, or the wives that give me a "You Jezebel" stare like I've done something to entice their husbands. But I've never really had someone totally go apeshit at the thought of me being abused. I shouldn't like it, but I do. I like that he cares.

I would change nothing.

Strangely warm with pleasure, I get to my feet and move to his side. "Haeden," I call softly. When I get his attention, I wave a bandaged hand in the air in front of him. "Hey. Don't hurt yourself, okay?" I almost say *I'm not worth it* but I know, somehow, that would be wrong. To him, I am worth it. And that makes me feel even warmer. So I throw in a joke. "We can't both hurt our hands, okay?"

He takes a deep breath, nostrils flaring, and then closes his eyes. Nods.

"This is why I didn't want to tell you. I don't like to think about it myself. It's like your story with Zalah. It happened. It was bad. It's not something you want to relive over and over again. But do you understand now, why I'm scared? I can't . . . I can't live in a family with hate again. I can't live with someone that doesn't want me. I can't raise a child like that."

The look Haeden gives me is incredulous. "I do not hate you, Jo-see. How could you think that?"

I laugh. "How could I not? You're mean to me! You always say shitty things like 'Humans are weak' and 'Josie should stay home from the hunt because she will drag us all down.'"

His jaw grits. "Humans *are* weak." He touches my arm and then wraps his hand around it. "My fingers can go all the way around your small bones. You shiver in the warmest of breezes. One wrong footstep on a hunt and you will be ended. How can I not worry over you?"

Okay, so he's not entirely wrong on that. "But that doesn't mean I suck."

Haeden's brows draw together. "I did not say you 'suck.' But I fear for you. And ever since you appeared, with your leg broken in many places, I have felt . . ." He closes a fist and presses it against his heart. "Something. A connection that has worried me. It has filled me with fear for endless days."

Resonance? Maybe he felt it long before and I never did because of my stupid IUD? Well, that's not entirely true, actually. I felt a tug toward him, even when I didn't want to. I sought him out even when I was pissed at him, if only to rub it in his face. We've been drawn together like magnets since day one, sometimes attracting, sometimes repelling. Who can say that wasn't just thwarted resonance?

Maybe this has been going on for longer than I imagined.

Wait. Fear? "You're afraid? Of me?"

"Of losing you," he rasps. "Like Zalah. And you are so much smaller and more fragile than her."

Oh. I melt like butter at his words. My good feeling ebbs a little when I see the echo of stark terror in his eyes. He really is afraid I'm going to be so wimpy this planet will eat me alive. No wonder he freaks out when I leave the cave. No wonder he lost his ever-loving mind when I went alone to warn the tribal cave of the massive storm. He probably lost his shit when I disappeared on this journey, too.

I know his past, and it makes me realize that I've been unfair to him. All this time I've been flouncing because I haven't had a choice in things, and I've been tearing him apart.

"I'm sorry," I say softly. "I didn't realize. Can we . . . can we try to get along?"

He nods, and there's no smile on his face, but that's all right. It's going to take time for either one of us to get used to this situation. But I guess it's time for me to stop running.

CHAPTER THIRTEEN
Josie

The next morning, I wake up with the tip of a curved horn inches from my eyeball and my cootie purring happily. I blearily frown at the horn, trying to figure out where it's coming from when I realize where I am and who's curled up next to me.

Or rather, who's curled up against me.

I vaguely remember falling asleep sitting up near the fire before Haeden picked me up and carried me to bed. I also vaguely remember still shivering despite the furs and him pressing his big body against mine to share his warmth. I don't remember much after that, though, so I must have slept like a log.

My hands are still sleeved in the wraps, but my arms are tucked around his head. His face is pressed against my chest, where my cootie rumbles almost as loudly as his snoring does. His arms are wrapped tight around me and I have one leg thrown over his hip. We're completely tangled together and I remain still, wondering if I should wake him up.

I shouldn't be enjoying the feel of his body pressed against mine, I tell myself. This wasn't what I chose. But he's holding me as if I'm the best thing that ever happened to him, and I'm warm and cuddled and I feel . . . loved. And I crave more of it. My fingers twitch and my nipples harden, and even though I'm gloved, I can't resist using the inside of my arm to stroke his hair just to see what it feels like. It feels different than mine, I decide a moment later, each strand larger and somewhat coarser, but there's so much thick hair it feels healthy and smooth.

He makes a little grunt in his throat and nuzzles against my chest. My breath catches because his lips are inches away from my aching nipples. Or at least they *would* be if I wasn't wearing a leather tunic.

The spell is broken, though. He jerks awake and rears back, eyes blinking as he looks up at me and his gaze meets mine.

"Morning."

Haeden grunts and then rolls away. "I must have grabbed you while I slept." He doesn't apologize, though. Instead, he heads to the front of the cave, grabbing his spear, and then peers out into the snowy landscape. When he's satisfied that we're safe, he turns back to me. "How do you feel?"

Disappointed? "I'm cool."

He frowns. "You are cold?" He moves to my side and immediately starts to pile furs on my shoulders.

"I'm good. I'm good. 'I'm cool' is just an expression."

"Oh." He brushes his fingers over my cheek and then jerks his hand away. "I am going to scout the area. Stay inside until I come back."

I nod. I know it's for our safety, but as he leaves, I find myself wishing he didn't have to. That he could crawl back into bed with me, put his head back on my breast, and we could just . . . cuddle for another hour or three. I've never been held for long, and that small taste just has me craving more.

While he's gone, I head to the back of the cargo bay, where the door leads deeper into the ship. My hands have made using the bathroom a bit of a chore and so I'm not wearing pants, letting my thigh-length leather tunic act as a dress. Haeden helped me out of my leggings last night (in the most humiliating, unsexy moment of the night) after I'd refused to let him help me pee. Of course, thinking about it now makes me remember my leg wrapped around him this morning. My *bare* leg wrapped around him.

I finish my potty business in the hall, taking a dark sort of pleasure in doing it on the alien floor. It's like I'm saying "fuck you" to the dead aliens who stole me so many months ago. I could really use a bath, but my hands are still wrapped so that's impossible. I manage to close the door to the hall behind me and then head to the fire—mere coals—and grab the bone between my bandage mittens to nudge the coals into a bit more life again. It's weird—my hands aren't numb anymore but they also don't hurt. I'm a little worried about that.

After what feels like a really long time—but is probably only a few minutes—my cootie starts to purr. I look up from the fire I'm coaxing back into shape and Haeden appears, his big body silhouetted by the sunlight. I feel a funny little stab of attraction at the sight of him, and my smile is wide. "You're back."

He grunts and approaches, taking the bone out of my mittened hands carefully and stoking the fire with a few well-placed jabs. "Some tracks, but none too close to this place. They are wary of it."

"That's good, isn't it?"

He nods, still poking the fire and not looking at me. Is he feeling uncomfortable after our "sleeping" together? Why do I find that kind of cute?

"I don't feel any pain in my hands," I tell him, and hold them out toward him. "Is that a bad sign?"

"The liidi works fast. The khui will take care of the rest." But his fingers brush against my skin as he grips my wrist and then begins to unwrap one hand. "We will look to be sure, though."

"Okay."

I hold still as he carefully removes the leather bandages. I can't help but stare at his chest a bit, since it's bare. He sacrificed his vest so he could wrap my hands, and the thought makes me feel warm. He didn't even check to see if I had extra clothing, or suggest a blanket. Nope, he just whipped his vest off and took care of things. Like I'm far more important than his own inconvenience.

All right now, all these thoughts are getting addictive.

With careful touches, Haeden pulls the leather off of the sticky mess on my hands and then cleans them with a fresh bit of fur from his bags and some warm water. The skin underneath is no longer a bright, angry purple. Instead, it looks much better. It also looks massively blistered. But Haeden is pleased. He grunts at the sight and nods. "One more day with your hands covered in liidi, and they will be good."

"Really?" I wrinkle my nose at my hands. I'm glad they're not hurting, but they still look kind of bad to me, what with the whole "one massive blister" thing and all.

"Yes." He pulls the bandages off my other hand and cleans it. "Come sit by the fire. We will give your hands time in the fresh air and then we will apply more liidi. We will remove it tomorrow."

"Will it be safe for me to travel with my hands all gunked up?"

He shrugs. "It does not matter. We are not leaving until your hands are healed."

We're not? "But . . . the metlaks—the girls—" I gesture at the wall behind me, feeling strangely obligated to the two strangers sleeping in their pods. "Shouldn't we work on rescuing them?"

"If what you tell me is true, they have been there for many moons already. Another day or two will not matter." The look he gives me brooks no argument.

"All righty then." I wiggle my fingers and they feel weird. The skin feels a little bubbled for all that it doesn't hurt. Eek. I'm not sure I like that. "Er, can I use them?" I don't want them to touch anything, and yet my skin feels filthy and itchy from days of sweaty travel and I would kill to be clean right about now.

"Use them?"

"I wouldn't mind having some time to myself."

The idea makes him scowl. "No."

"What do you mean, no?" Just when I was starting to have a soft spot for the big lug.

"Whatever you need done, I shall do for you."

"What, are you going to give me a sponge bath?" I taunt.

His eyes flare and I can hear his cootie get louder. "Do . . . do you want to bathe?" His voice has a hoarse little hitch in it, and his gaze is locked onto mine.

Oh, lordy. I taunted the devil and now he's taking me up on it. I should say no, but . . . my own cootie's going a mile a minute and I'm getting all aroused just at the mental image of Haeden washing me. *Be strong*, I tell myself. *This isn't what you wanted*.

But what I wanted was thrown out the door a long time ago, wasn't it? And part of me wants to go with the flow, to see where it takes us. I know I should be thinking about the two girls nestled away in the pods, sleeping and unaware of their future. I know I should be thinking about the fact that I have to go home, and the tribe might try to prevent me from leaving again.

But all I can think about are Haeden's big hands skimming over my skin.

"Do you want to bathe?" he asks again.

"I don't know," I admit. I can feel my cheeks heating. I think of this morning, waking up to his head pressed against my breasts, my bare leg hiked up around his waist. For the first time, I feel a pang of regret that I've been fighting this so hard. *Why not just see where this leads?* a horny little voice inside my head asks. *Can't be any worse than where we've been before.*

Except that Haeden's gazing down at me with such simmering intensity. It's like bathing me clean of dirt is suddenly the only thing he's ever wanted.

"I'm scared," I admit after a moment, and then I feel stupid. I'm not scared of a sponge bath—I'm scared of where it might lead.

I wait for him to taunt me over my words. To mock me for blurting something so random. But he only touches my cheek. "We are both frightened of what this could mean," he says, voice husky even as his warm, callused fingers trace my jaw. "But that does not mean we should not explore it."

I want to lean into his touch, and the idea's shocking to me. It's almost as shocking as the realization that I'm going to say yes.

Haeden

Jo-see looks up at me with big, wary eyes. "If . . . if I say stop, we'll stop, right?"

I nod, because I do not trust my own voice. To think, she is going to let me bathe her—it feels like the greatest gift I have ever been given. "Always."

She nods. "I would like to be clean," she says in a faint voice, but the bright color on her cheeks tells me it is not the only thing she likes. I can smell her arousal, and her khui is humming in time with mine.

I feel a surge of triumph. She is yielding to me. Bit by bit, Jo-see is seeing that I can be a good mate to her. I want to shout my pleasure at the thought, but I force myself to only give a brief nod. Everything will be as she asks. I will push for no more than she will give me.

"Do you have extra soapberries?" she prompts, pulling me from my racing thoughts.

I nod and touch her cheek one more time, then move to the fire. I stoke it high. I want the water to be warm and pleasant for my mate. I quickly fill my stew pouch with fresh snow and add a few soapberries to it. "It will take some time for the water to heat." Perhaps during that time my lust will cool long enough that my cock will not ache as I touch her. The idea is . . . not likely, though.

"Okay," she says in a soft voice, and then moves to the opposite side of the fire.

We're silent as we wait on the water. She hums a small song under her breath, as she so often does, but I am quiet. My thoughts are focused entirely on the concept of bathing her. I have bathed others in my tribe, washed the backs of many, scrubbed a friend that was injured. It should mean nothing. Instead, I cannot stop thinking about it. It is just a bath, but this is Jo-see.

My Jo-see.

And I worry I will come in my breechcloth again.

A breeze rips through the shelter, bringing with it fresh snow and cold air. The fire flickers and Jo-see lifts her hands as if to rub her arms, and then stops. Her gaze meets mine and she flushes again, her cheeks wonderfully pink. And for some reason, I feel like smiling.

I get to my feet, ignoring my erection. I cannot hide it, just like I cannot hide the song my khui hums. I dip my fingers in the water. It is warm enough. "Come," I tell her. "Let us take your clothing off."

And my groin tightens in anticipation.

She makes a little squeak of anxious sound but gets to her feet. Her eyes are wide as she moves slowly toward me.

I get to my feet, and when she comes to stand before me, it takes everything I have not to crush her against my chest. I want to hold her, to feel her warm skin against mine. I want to protect her from the world. But for now? I will settle for touching her.

I can feel the tension between us, crackling like lightning. I reach for the laces at the neck of her tunic, and she shivers. "Cold?" I ask.

"Just . . . nervous." She gives me a faint little smile. "Silly, right?"

Not so silly. "I am nervous, too."

My confession startles her and her gaze flicks back up to me. "You are?"

I nod slowly. "I worry if I do something wrong, you will run . . . again." I pull at the laces, untying the loose knot at her neck. I am admitting too much, but if she is being honest and open with me, how can I not do the same for her?

Now she is all curiosity. "You mean when I left at the ship? When you were being a jerk?"

I indicate that she should lift her arms so I can pull the tunic over her head. She does so, obedient, and while her face is hidden, I admit my shame. "I was cruel to you because I was ashamed that I could not control myself."

Then the tunic is in my hands. I am careful not to look at her naked body as she steps out of her boots, though I want nothing more than to gawk at her. As my gaze meets hers, she gives me a confused expression. "Control yourself?"

I groan inwardly. Do humans not have a word for it? "My desire was so great I . . . lost control." I emphasize the last two words, not sure how much clearer I can make it. My jaw grits as shame washes over me. "I . . . should have done better."

Comprehension dawns on her face and her eyes go wide. "Oh. *Oh.* You . . . okay. I get it now. That's why you were a jerk?" A little smile curves her mouth. "I thought you were just being mean to me because I wasn't enthusiastic enough."

"Never. You are perfect, always." I move to the pouch of warm water and dig in my nearby bag for a cleansing cloth—soft, hairless leather that has been worked soft enough that it smooths over the skin easily and soaks up water. I dip it in and then turn to her, rubbing her small shoulders with the wet cloth. She shivers and I instinctively move between her and the entrance to this strange cave, to block the breeze.

"Haeden?"

I look down at her, meeting her eyes.

"I don't want you to be embarrassed, okay? It's a normal thing and we've both been pushing our cooties hard with this whole resonance thing. I don't want you to feel weird about it." She reaches out as if to touch my arm, hesitates before putting her palm down, then turns her hand and rubs the back of it along my skin. "It happens."

"It should not have happened to me," I say, irritated.

Her lips twitch and she pats my arm with the back of that hand. "I don't mind. It makes me like you more." At my scowl, she explains herself. "It gives me a reason why you were mean to me, and it's not a bad one. I thought you were just being a jerk."

I do not know what a jerk is, but I can guess it is not something pleasant. I smooth the wet cloth over her shoulders, frowning to myself at how thin she is, how pale her skin is. I will focus on that and not how creamy and soft she looks, or the delicateness of her bones. I will focus on how fragile she is and not how beautiful. "It was my first time. I wanted to get it right."

She gasps and stills. "Your first time?"

My gaze flicks to hers, and again, I feel the spark between us. My khui sings loudly, desperate for me to claim her. My cock presses against my breechcloth, but I ignore all these things. I focus on her small, round face, her big blue eyes that look up at me with such curiosity. "Of course. I told you, I did not claim Zalah."

"And she died when you were young . . ." Sympathy fills her expression. "Oh, Haeden. We've both had crappy experiences with sex, haven't we?"

"I have had *no* experience with sex," I grumble, and lean to the pouch of water to wet my cloth again.

"Fair enough," she says.

When I turn, she stretches, putting her arms over her head.

The cloth falls from my hand.

She is . . . beautiful. Her body is lean but curved in different places than the women of my tribe. She is all pink flesh and softness, and my hands itch to touch her. My gaze roams over her, hungry, and I focus on the pert breasts that jut from her chest, the nipples small and hard. Below them, her stomach is rounded and her hips swell out in a gentle curve leading to slim thighs. Between them, there is a dark patch of hair that matches her mane.

I groan, closing my eyes. One of my fists presses against the side of my cock, and I struggle to remain in control. "Jo-see, what do you do?"

"I'm just . . . stretching." But there's a sly little smile on her face that makes my heart race. "Keep washing?"

I nod, trying to regain control. I give her a heated look that tells her exactly what I am thinking.

She just gives a little wiggle, bouncing on her feet. "I'm cold. Can we hurry this along?"

Her breasts bounce enticingly and my nails dig into my palm. I force myself to nod, and then I pick up the washcloth and begin to bathe her again. I run it over her arms and her shoulders . . . and then back over her arms again. And then her shoulders. I fear for my control if I wash her any lower.

Jo-see makes a humming sound of pleasure and then turns around. "My back now?"

I grunt acknowledgment and swab her shoulders again. She now has the cleanest shoulder blades of any female ever born. In response to my movements, she squirms and arches against the cloth. "Lower?"

Drips of water slide down her back, gliding along her spine and down to her buttocks. I watch a droplet disappear between the cleft of her ass and close my eyes. This is . . . difficult. My cock aches fiercely, and I can feel the pre-cum slicking the head. I picture throwing her down on the floor and mounting her, her legs spread wide and that sly little smile on her face as I claim her.

But . . . then I picture her injured hands slapping on the floor, and that dashes my arousal. I would never cause her harm. While she is wounded, I will not touch her with anything but carefulness. Renewed, I clench my jaw with determination, kneel behind her and scrub her back as if she were any other sa-khui and we were not mated.

Jo-see gives a small sigh. "Thank you. That's much better. My skin felt itchy after all the traveling." And she turns around.

The cloth falls from my fingers once more.

As she turns, my eyes are level with her pink-tipped breasts. From here, I am close enough to see the dewy softness of her skin, and I can smell her. I can smell the faint sweat—not unpleasant in the slightest—and the hint of smoke from the fire that lingers, and I can smell her arousal.

She is death to my control.

"Now my front?" she says brightly, and gives another one of those ache-inducing wiggles.

I groan, my head dropping. "Why do you torture me?"

"Because it's fun?" she admits with a throaty little laugh. "I know it's terrible of me, but I like seeing the effect I have on you."

So she wishes to play games, does she? I should be angry, but I find that I'm more interested in touching her fascinating body . . . and inhaling more of her scent. I scoop the cloth up yet again, dunk it into the water, and then begin to wash her front. I slide the cloth over her breasts, and to my surprise, she shivers and her skin prickles in response to my touch.

The scent of her arousal deepens.

Pleased, I pull the cloth over her breasts again. Her nipples don't scrape against my hand, and I am surprised. They are as soft as the rest of her, unlike the women of my tribe. I am fascinated and want to touch one, but I do not yet have her permission. So I wash.

A soft noise escapes her throat.

I look up and her eyes are heavy-lidded as she watches me, her expression dazed. The smell of her arousal grows even more, until her perfume seems to fill the entire cave.

"You like it when I touch you," I say, fiercely pleased. If she wishes for us to be bold with each other, I shall join in her game.

"Mmmhmm." Her lips part, but her gaze is completely focused on me.

I lightly move the cloth down her stomach. "Shall I go lower?"

She bites her lip, her small, square teeth brushing over her full mouth, and then she nods, need in her eyes.

Another fierce surge of possessiveness moves through me. My mate is letting me touch her. Bathe her. Please her. There is nothing better. Already I'm addicted to the musky scent of her need in my nostrils. My cock is hard and insistent, but my focus is entirely on Jo-see.

The small tuft of hair that covers her sex is mere fingerspans from the cloth, and I slowly drag it downward. I wait for her to tell me to stop, to push me away and scream that she hates me. But she trembles and is silent, and all the while the scent of her perfumes the air.

As she gazes down at me, I touch her. The cloth brushes over her folds, and the sweet, hot scent of her arousal grows stronger. My khui hammers in my breast, insistent and wild.

Jo-see moans softly.

My grasp over my control is very close to breaking. Her hips are too close, the object of my desire within reach. One hand brushes over the rounded curve of her hip, and I close my eyes, then look up at her. "Tell me that I should not touch you, Jo-see."

Confusion flits over her face. "W-what?"

"Tell me that I should not touch you," I repeat again. "Tell me that I should not press my mouth to your skin and taste your cunt."

She licks her lips. She opens her mouth to speak—

And then closes it again.

Jo-see is giving me permission.

I groan and pull her close, burying my face between her legs. I barely hear her little gasp as I hold her hips, my tongue seeking out the folds hidden by the tiny thatch of hair between her legs. Wetness blooms on my tongue and then I have the taste of her in my mouth—tart, musky, sweet.

This is what I have *needed*.

I swipe my tongue over her folds and she cries out, leaning heavily against me. I do not want her to harm her hands, so I tug on her legs, indicating she should join me on the floor, but my mouth never leaves her cunt. I want to remain here forever.

Through awkward motions and tangling of limbs, I manage to get her on the floor, on her back, and from here, I can taste her to my heart's desire. I drag my tongue over the tender, wet folds, exploring her. She is soft here, so soft. The well of her cunt is scorching hot, and I dip my tongue there, unable to resist. She writhes against me, making soft whimpering noises and panting. I love the sounds, almost as much as I love her taste. I can feel her khui singing, all through her body.

I stroke my tongue over her folds again and then discover the third nipple that the other males have mentioned when discussing their human mates. She has a tiny nub, half-hidden in the slick petals of her cunt. When my tongue grazes it, she cries out. I do not know if it is a good cry or a bad cry, so I lick downward instead.

"Go back," she begs, frantic need in her voice. "I'm so close!"

So it *is* a good cry. I return and begin to work the nipple once more. I roll it against the tip of my tongue and then lick it, trying to determine the way she likes the most. Her little cries grow more frantic as I circle it with my tongue, so I continue to do so, lost in the pleasure of giving her this. My breechcloth is stuck to my body, and I am positive that I have come already, but it does not matter. Nothing matters except this.

Her body arches and she cries out, and more wetness floods into my mouth. She's coming. I groan and lap it up, my khui singing with fierce intensity. It will have to wait for another time. For now, my Jo-see is pleasured and I am content.

I continue to taste her and nuzzle against her folds as she rocks against my face, her movements slowing. Finally, she gives a gusty sigh and then all of the tension seems to leave her body. When I lick her again, she squirms. "You can stop now, Haeden. I came."

Stop? I never want to stop. I could live with my face buried between her sweet thighs. But I lift my head, because pleasing her is more important than what I want. I sit up next to her and lick my lips. And then lick them again, because I can taste her on my skin and already I crave more.

She presses the back of a hand to her forehead and a small laugh bubbles up inside her. "I think we forgot about bathing."

"We did not forget," I say. "You were distracted."

She kicks at me playfully.

I cannot help the grin that curves my mouth. She's smiling, some of the tension that she carries vanished. Her naked body is a glorious sight to see, and I drink it in, still hungry for her.

Her gaze slides to me. "Thank you."

Why is she thanking me? I gave her a mate's due. But I don't want to argue, so I simply nod.

"What . . . what about you?"

"I finished as well." If we are being honest, there is no sense in hiding it. Oddly enough, I feel no shame this time. Is it because she clearly enjoyed my tasting her? And when she nods and dismisses it as if it is nothing, I realize there is no shame to be had, only pleasure between us.

I pick up my cloth and dip it into the water, determined to complete my mate's bath.

CHAPTER FOURTEEN
Josie

I curl up in the blankets near the fire and watch Haeden as he works. I'm sleepy, clean, and well pleasured, and my hands are tightly bound again with more numbing cream. Behind me, deep in the ship, there are some old dead bodies, and in the wall are two strangers who are waiting for their chance to be freed. These things are important, I'm sure, but I'm more interested in watching Haeden's movements and contemplating our situation.

I might be obsessing—just a little—over the oral sex from earlier. And who can blame me? It was amazing. What he lacked in experience he more than made up for in enthusiasm. I came so hard my toes curled. And maybe I'm sending mixed signals all over the place, but I couldn't help it. The way he was looking at me made me want to push the boundaries.

So I'd pushed. And I'd gotten rewarded with the most intense orgasm ever.

I tuck the blankets closer around my body and watch him as he bends over the fire. He's doing a myriad of things—smoking some meat for travel, sharpening his blades, and making sure the fire stays nice and hot. He's got hot tea warming in the pouch, and off to one side there's a freshly scraped skin rolled up, waiting to be finished. I'll say one thing for Haeden—he's not lazy. Nor does he expect me to do anything. If it were up to him, I'd sit around and let him pamper me all day while he works.

It's kind of nice. It's also kind of messing with my head.

I don't hate the guy anymore. I can't. Not after hearing the reason why he's been so standoffish. He's been afraid. I can't even blame him for that—he's been living in a state of fear, worried that what happened to his last mate is going to happen to me. And haven't I been doing the same thing? I've been worried sick about bringing a child into the world and forcing it to grow up unloved and miserable like I did.

I think now we're starting to realize that both of us are wrong. Maybe, just maybe this thing between us can end up working out. I'm cautiously optimistic.

I'm also an utter horn-ball because as he leans over the fire, I think about him being a virgin. I think about him making sure I orgasm and taking nothing for himself. I want to turn the tables on him and do the same for him, actually. I want to see how he reacts if I touch him. If I lick him the way he licked me. The thought makes me give a little shiver and my cootie starts up again. I might not be ready to seal the deal on this resonance thing, but I'm down with exploring a little.

Of course, I can't do anything right now with my hands like they are, but I can use my imagination.

He looks up and catches me staring. His eyes narrow. "What?"

"Nothing. Just thinking."

He grunts a response, and when I don't say anything, he looks over at me again. "Well?"

"Well what?"

"Are you going to tell me what you are thinking?"

Oh. I don't want to tell him I'm thinking about giving him a blow job, so I cast about for another topic. "Do you like children?"

Haeden looks at me like I'm asking the world's stupidest question, and okay, I can't blame him. I just asked a man who comes from a slowly dying tribe that had very few children prior to the arrival of humans. Of course children are prized.

"I just . . . I want a lot of kids," I said. "When I settle down, I want a big family. I never had one, you know? So I always dreamed about having tons of babies and just filling my house with them. Like five or six or even eight kids. I'd be down with that. You?"

"That is a lot of mouths to feed."

I feel weirdly crushed at his response. "I . . . guess it is."

He scrapes at his knife, not looking me in the eye. "Then it is lucky for you that I am an excellent hunter."

Warmth blooms in my chest. "That *is* lucky."

For the first time, I let myself picture Haeden as my mate. He'd come home after a long day of hunting and I'd have a baby—or two!—at my feet. He'd set down his spears, head in, and give me a kiss, then scoop up a child in his arms. We'd talk about his day, I'd feed my family, and we'd enjoy our time in our cozy cave. After the babies were put to bed, we'd spend the night snuggling and making more babies.

I imagine Haeden with a baby in his arms and feel curiously melty. He'd be a good dad, I decide. Firm but fair. And doting,

I add as he picks up a teacup and brings it to my lips so I can sip at it without hurting my hands. When I'm done drinking, I think about the mental image again. A kiss. We haven't kissed yet. Before, I thought it was because he didn't care, but I suspect it's because he doesn't know how.

I add it to my list of things to practice, and for the first time in what feels like forever, I have something to look forward to.

We spend the rest of the day in pleasant idleness in the cave. Haeden stays busy with chores, but he also introduces me to a game called "story spinning" that he says they play with the kits back home, when the snows get too high. The game works with someone being given a topic, and the story-spinner must come up with a story line to go with whatever words are offered to him. It's kind of like a verbal Mad Libs, and we spend a lot of time trying to trip each other up. To my surprise, Haeden's got a sharp wit and even my goofiest stories manage to make him crack a few smiles. I teach him "I Spy" and we play that long into the afternoon, until the suns set and the cold sucks all the fun out of the evening and even the fire can't keep me warm.

Then, Haeden crawls into the furs with me and pulls me against his chest, and I spend the rest of the evening cuddling with him. My cootie hums urgently, wanting more, but I do my best to ignore it. I won't think of the bath, either. Tomorrow will be the day, I tell it. Be patient until tomorrow.

I fall asleep with my head on Haeden's chest as he strokes my hair, and really, I could get used to this. Maybe it's just the extreme horniness brought on by the cootie, but when he holds me? I feel . . . loved. Adored. Cherished. Like I'm the best thing that's ever happened to him.

Maybe I am.

I . . . kind of like that thought.

When we wake up the next morning, the weather is colder. I shiver despite the furs Haeden piles onto me, and even he shrugs on a warm tunic over his chest. "It is because we have gone north," he says. "The air is not as pleasant here as back at the tribal caves."

I frown to myself. "North? I was trying to go west. Toward Harlow and Rukh's cave."

He snorts. "You are several days away from it, then."

Am I? Drat. "Well, that sucks."

"You were likely turned around. The big salt water is close to here, but the cave is not." He pokes at the fire to stoke it, and then his tail flicks with frustration. "We are low on fuel for the fire. Stay here and I will go scout the area."

"Okay." I tug the blankets closer. "Hurry back."

He picks up his spear and nods at me. He doesn't smile, but that's Haeden. He devours me with a hot, possessive look and then turns and marches out of the "cave" entrance, and I decide I'll take a steamy glance over a friendly smile any day.

I flex my hands and they don't feel too bad, so I gingerly try to do a few chores around the cave while he's gone. I keep the fire stoked, put on some water for tea, and do my best to straighten up without using my hands too much. The meat he was smoking overnight looks done so I put it into one of the many pouches and tug the drawstring shut with my teeth. Then, there's not much to do but wait.

Haeden returns a short time later, a frozen hopper in hand

from one of his traps. He kicks the snow off his boots and un-wraps his furs, then moves immediately to my side. I think he's going to hand me the kill—maybe he's forgotten my hands are jacked—but instead he comes over and presses a fierce kiss to the top of my head.

And again, I melt. Why did I think this guy was a douche? Hard to get along with sometimes, yes, but loving? Absolutely.

"Everything okay?" I ask, worried. "Any sign of metlaks?"

"All over," he says, and squats by the fire. He looks surprised to see that it's burning strong and there's a pouch of tea on. He glances over at me. "Tea?"

"I thought you might be cold when you came back."

He grunts in that way that I've come to interpret as his "ap-proval" grunt and dips the cup into it. Haeden drinks it down quickly and then dips the cup again and offers it to me.

"I'm good. So . . . more metlaks?"

He nods. Instead of butchering his kill, he wraps it in one of the furs and begins to pack his things. "Tracks everywhere, young and old. They know we are here, but they are scared to come after us with the fire. We must be deep in their territory."

Goose bumps prickle my arms. "So what do we do?"

"We leave the moment your hands are better." He turns to me. "I will not put you in danger."

I ignore the giddy rush of warmth his words give me and focus on the problem at hand. I need to think, not be all giggly because he's saying all the things I've been dying to hear. "Will we be safe if we go?"

"The metlaks usually do not come after sa-khui. If we leave their territory, they will not follow."

"But they attacked you."

He nods thoughtfully. "We will rub ourselves with ash from the fire. If we smell like smoke, they will stay away. They are not smart enough to realize we are not on fire; they only recognize the scent."

"Okay." I hold my hands out. "Shall we check these, then?"

Haeden moves to my side and I do my best to stay still as he begins to gently unwrap my hands. He's always so careful with me, even though I know his cootie must be making him as crazy as mine is making me. Right now it's singing up a storm, and his is matching to thunderous effect. I'm kind of surprised we haven't kept the metlaks away just with the noise our chests are making.

When my bandages are unwrapped and the gunky liidi washed away, my hands are smooth with no sign of blisters. I flex one cautiously, and when it doesn't hurt, I beam at Haeden. "I can't believe it's already fixed. You're a genius."

He grunts, but I can tell he's pleased. He unwraps my other hand and doesn't look me in the eye. "The liidi takes care of the pain. The khui takes care of the rest."

"Well, I still appreciate the help."

"You are my mate. Of course I would do this for you." The look he gives me is challenging, as if he's waiting for me to protest that he's my man. But I don't say anything. *Let him chew on that for a while.*

As he wipes my hands clean, I turn to gaze at the wall, where the green lights dance and I know there are at least two women sleeping. "Do you think they will be okay?"

"They have been here for many moons. As I have said, what is another day or two?"

"Yes, but . . . what if the metlaks come in and damage the walls? Or somehow pry them loose?"

"That will not happen. And we cannot take them with us. We are not prepared to bring two weak humans—and they will be weak—over the mountains to take back to the caves. We cannot bring down a sa-kohtsk on our own. We will wait and bring a hunting party back here with the proper gear."

I nod. His words make sense. I know he's right; I just feel guilty at the thought of leaving the others behind. But the rest of the ship has been mostly undisturbed over the last year and a half, so I know he's being logical—there's no point in opening them up right now. Not when we barely have enough furs to keep me and Haeden warm. We could all snuggle together at night, I suppose.

I picture two strange human women curling up against Haeden's big, brawny form and I'm shocked at the violent stab of jealousy that moves through me. I don't want anyone else touching him. He's . . . mine. I'm still coming to terms with that concept, but it sticks in my head. Mine. Mine mine mine.

"Do your hands ache?" he asks, interrupting my thoughts. His fingers brush over my palm.

"They're good," I say and flex them to prove it. "So we leave . . . today?"

"As soon as we pack our gear." His hand smooths over mine again and he rubs it. "A few days' hard travel and we will be back at the tribal caves."

Back, and I'm probably going to get my head bitten off for leaving on my own. I'll have to endure the pitying looks of the others, and the smirks of those that realize we haven't completed our resonance yet. I'm reluctant to go back. I love the tribe but right now it's touchy for me.

So I grip Haeden's hand. "If the girls are safe in the wall for a bit longer . . . would it be okay if we go south instead of directly back to the tribe? Take a few days for ourselves? To get used to this thing between us?"

I expect him to protest, but he studies me and then nods. He gets to his feet and presses a quick kiss to the top of my head again. "It shall be as you ask."

CHAPTER FIFTEEN
Haeden

I push Jo-see hard for the first day of travel. I am not comfortable with the amount of metlak tracks that I see all around the cave or covering the trails. This place is thick with the wild, unpredictable creatures, and the sooner we leave, the better. Because she walks slower than I do with the snowshoes, I carry her pack. And as the hours on the trail creep from morning to late afternoon, she begins to slow. She does not protest the bruising pace I set, but I can tell she is tired.

So toward the end of the day, I carry her, as well. She doesn't want me to, but I ignore her words and her small slaps and bend over so she can climb onto my back. She does and I hoist her higher, her arms around my neck, and we continue.

Eventually the metlak tracks disappear and we move into sa-khui territory. These are the fringes of hunter lands, but I know these places. I know where the caves are and where caches are hidden to freeze extra kills when the traps are plentiful. We stop as the twin moons come up into the sky and I take my mate to the closest hunter cave. It is a small one, but well stocked with fuel for a fire and warm furs for bedding. I set her down gently and then sling the packs off my front. "I must scout the area to make sure we are safe," I tell her. "But let me start a fire first so you stay warm."

"I can do it," she says, and pulls out the firestarter she keeps on a thong at her neck. "You do what you've gotta do. I can help where I can."

I nod slowly, rubbing my chest as my khui vibrates in response. That she would help me prepare our camp despite her exhaustion means much to me. It makes me feel as if we are in this together for the first time. That she is acknowledging that we are one. I grab her in a fierce hug and kiss the top of her head again before she can say anything, and then head out of the cave to scout before she asks questions.

I track back on our trail, looking for signs of metlaks, but there is nothing. If we were followed, they gave up many hours ago. Pleased, I return to the cave and my mate, where she has the fire blazing. I am proud that she is not complaining, though she is clearly tired. Instead, she busies herself in the cave and looks up from the fire when I arrive, her eyes brightening.

It has taken many torturous nights to get to the point where her eyes light up with pleasure at the sight of me, but I would trade not a single one. This moment has made all of them worth it.

"Everything okay?" she asks, crumbling a few dried herbs into the stewing pouch to make tea.

"No tracks," I agree. "The metlaks have abandoned us in pursuit of easier prey." I did not see much prey at all, which concerns me. Normally these hills are crawling with game.

"That's great," Jo-see says, smiling. "Will we be at Harlow and Rukh's cave tomorrow?"

"If we travel all day, perhaps." I do not point out that this will be unlikely.

She nods slowly, a frustrated look crossing her face. "So no, then. I'm sorry I'm slowing us down. It's difficult to keep up with you."

Does she think I chastise her? "Do not apologize. We are not at our full strength." I rub my chest, thinking of the khui that has been the bane—and hope—of my existence recently. "We will simply go as fast as we can and not worry about anything else."

"I feel guilty you had to carry me today—"

"That was because we were in metlak territory. We are safe now." I lean forward and touch her chin, tilting her head up so she gazes at me. "And I would carry you for days on end without complaint, and be glad to do so."

She blushes and ducks her head. "Let's hope it doesn't come to that or I'm going to have bruises on the insides of my thighs from trying to hold on to you."

I picture her thighs gripping my hips and lust roars through me. If it came to pass, I would not mind her sweet thighs clenching around me endlessly. The only things I would mind are the bruises she would wear. "I will be more careful with you."

Jo-see just shakes her head at me, amused.

We pass the dark hours companionably, talking about the weather and drinking tea. I offer Jo-see tidbits of the meat that I roast. Even though her hands are better, I enjoy feeding her. She does not protest the treatment, and after the meat is gone, she starts to yawn.

"Sleep," I tell her. "There will be much traveling to do tomorrow and you will need your strength."

She nods and glances over at the blankets, then shivers. "Will you join me? You're my *fur-nus*."

"*Fur-nus?*"

"You provide warmth," she teases, all smiles.

I nod. I will gladly *fur-nus* for her. I settle into the furs and she moves her body against mine, tucking her smaller form under my shoulder. She gives a little sigh and her cheek rests against my chest, her fist over my heart. My khui sings pleasantly and I close my eyes, content to ignore the hum coursing through my body, demanding that I claim my mate. For now, this is enough.

"Your khui is loud," Jo-see murmurs softly, and her fingers pet my chest, stroking the hard ridges over my heart.

She is not wrong. Though the song is pleasant, it is throbbing loudly. I grunt acknowledgment. "Ignore it."

Jo-see says nothing, but her hand continues to stroke the ridges on my chest, and my cock—already ready—grows achingly hard. I keep my eyes closed and my body still, determined not to react. If she wants to pet me harmlessly as she goes to sleep, I will welcome it without protest. Her every touch is a gift.

Moments pass and her fingers continue to stroke my chest.

Then, her hand slides lower, away from my heart and down my belly.

My mouth goes dry. My cock jerks against my breechcloth, stabbing at the air. Perhaps . . . she does not realize what she is doing? I wait in rigid silence, my hand fisted at my side as her fingers glide over my belly, teasing at the edges of my breechcloth. I listen to her breathing to see if she is sleeping and her hand is simply wandering.

But then I smell her arousal in the air, faint but growing stronger.

The groan I have been biting back escapes me. "Jo-see?"

"Is it okay if I play a little?" Her voice is hushed and soft, and her fingers *stroke stroke stroke* my belly. Over and over. "Do a bit of exploring?"

I give a jerky nod. As if I would refuse this? No male could.

Her hand moves lower. "I never thought about you being a virgin," she confesses in a hushed voice. "I admit it changes my perspective on things."

"How . . . how so?" My voice cracks as I speak, and I clear my throat.

"It's weird, but I feel like I understand you now. Why you're so scared of me being 'weak.' And it makes it feel like, well, like you're all mine. Funny how that's so appealing, isn't it?"

It is not strange to me. The thought of another male touching her fills me with helpless rage. "I belong to no one but you," I tell her through gritted teeth.

"I know," she says softly. "I kind of like that."

And then her hand slides over my leggings and cups my shaft.

I choke on my own breath, my fists tight against my sides. Part of me wants to pry her hand away so she does not torment me further . . . and part of me wants to grab her by her small wrist and have her pump my cock until I spurt all over her fingers.

"You're really hard." She sounds fascinated. "And big. I'm impressed."

"You . . . have seen me . . . unclothed . . . before." It is difficult to get the words out when she is touching me. My mind cannot concentrate on anything but her hand, gently stroking.

"Yeah, but seeing and feeling are two different things, you know?" Her voice is breathless with wonder. "And I'm definitely feeling something impressive." Her hand leaves my cock and I could cry out in frustration—but then I feel her fingers move to my leggings. The knot in the waist-cords gives and then the material loosens.

And she pushes it down, exposing my cock to the air.

"Can I keep going?" she asks, sitting up.

The breath gusts out of me. As if I could stop her? Pre-cum slicks the head of my cock and dribbles down the ridges on my length. My sac is tight. At any moment, I feel ready to explode. At the same time, I do not want to come too soon, not before she is finished.

She takes my silence as permission, because her hand returns to my cock and she lets her fingers lightly dance along my length, tracing the veins and ridges. It feels better than anything I have ever imagined, her hand on my cock, and I close my eyes and think of hunting and tracking and metlaks and snow—anything to keep from losing control.

"Your skin is so warm." Jo-see's voice is soft. She leans closer, and then I feel her breath on my cock. "And you're so thick."

A groan escapes me. How can I think of metlaks when her lips are less than a fingerspan from my length? How can I think of *anything*?

"And these ridges," she says with a little sigh, tracing her finger over one. "I think you might have the perfect dick, Haeden. I can't believe I'm the first woman to touch it."

"Only," I grit out, voice ragged. "You are the *only* female that will ever touch me." Because I am hers and hers alone.

Instead of being afraid of my words, she gives a throaty little chuckle that makes my sac tighten even more. "Just me," she says, and the tease is back in her voice. Her fingertips lightly stroke up and down my length. "Only me."

Then, she leans in and presses her mouth to the flat of my belly.

The breath hisses from my throat. I am in agony. Pure, perfect agony, and it has been created by my mate's soft mouth.

Her tongue lightly touches my skin. "Haeden?"

"*What.*"

"I need to ask a favor," she says, and then licks my lower belly again. Her mouth is so close to my cock that obscene, fascinating images scroll through my mind, faster and faster. I do not dare to hope that her mouth will go lower. It does not seem like something she would enjoy. And yet . . .

"Anything," I rasp. She could ask for my arm and I would gladly remove it from my body.

"I need . . ." *Kiss.* "You . . ." *Kiss.* "To hold off . . ." *Kiss.* "And not come until I'm done playing, okay?" *Kiss.*

And then her mouth—her soft, wicked mouth—goes to the head of my cock and she presses a small kiss to it.

Fire ignites my body. I clench at the blankets, sweat breaking out on my forehead. What she asks is impossible, yet I hunger to please her. "I . . . *will try.*"

Her sultry giggle at my response makes my skin prickle with awareness. Her breath is on my cock, her hand gripping my shaft. My belly is wet from the touches of her tongue and her lips. My khui is throbbing an intense beat that seems to have settled itself into my cock.

Do not come? With her mouth so cruelly, wonderfully teasing? Surely a hunter would be more likely to be struck by lightning.

But my Jo-see wants to play, and I will do anything for her.

So I lie very still, my nails digging into my palms as she lowers her head. My tail thrashes wildly against my thigh as she moves closer, and then she presses another kiss to my cock head. Her other hand seeks out my spur—the hard length above my cock—and she rubs it, dragging her fingers back and forth. Pleasure bursts through me, and I hold my breath.

Metlaks.

Metlaks hunting outside the cave. Jo-see in danger.

Metlaks with their tearing claws—

Her mouth closes over the head of my cock and her tongue swirls against the tip.

The breath I've been holding explodes. My hand goes to her hair, as if I am no longer in control of my body. When she raises her head to laugh again, I push it back down, dying for more. I am so close to coming that fire burns in my belly, and I can feel my seed rising in my cock, the throb of my khui making it unbearable. And I need her hot mouth, her tongue, her lips on my cock again.

She makes a small humming noise of pleasure and her arousal spikes the air around me even as her mouth closes over my cock again. Then she pulls, sucking with her mouth and taking me deeper even as her fingers play with my spur.

I thrust my hips, unable to stop, and push deeper into her mouth. She makes a noise of encouragement and sucks harder, and then, despite my vow, I spill my seed violently. I can feel it spurting into her mouth, her tight, hot mouth that feels like nothing I have experienced before. My entire body trembles with the force of my release even as she makes small humming noises and waits for me to finish.

Shame grips me as she releases my cock and gives it a final lick. I let go of her hair and close my eyes as she sits up. "I . . . am sorry. I failed you."

Her sweet laugh fills the cave. "Haeden, I was just teasing you. Don't be so serious." She moves to my side and curls up against me. "I was deliberately trying to make you come."

"But you said—and I grabbed your hair—"

"Which was sexy," she agrees and settles in next to me. Her arm goes around my waist. "Unexpected but sexy."

I am utterly confused by her. Confused, but also oddly pleased. "So I did not disappoint you?"

"With that cock? I'd have to be crazy to be disappointed." She pats my chest. "We'll work on your stamina. Tomorrow." Her fingers brush over my skin, and she's still feeling, still touching. Her aroused scent still lingers in the air, and I realize she has not come herself. This was all for me.

I am . . . humbled by such a gift.

"You know what else I'd like to practice?" She muses. "Kissing. Mouth kissing. Let's put that on the schedule for tomorrow, too."

I want to please her. I want to hear her come. I want to see her come. I want to taste it. My arm goes around her and I stroke her shoulder and her soft, soft skin. "We can practice tonight."

"My mouth is tired," she teases, but I feel her thighs squeeze, as if she's pressing them together.

An idea strikes me and I roll to my knees, then pull her thighs open. If she has done such for me, can I not do it for her? "Lucky for you that your male has a strong mouth and an even stronger tongue."

She sucks in a breath and then falls back on the furs, a moan escaping her throat. "I *am* lucky."

Her thighs part eagerly, and I bury my face between her legs, pleased.

CHAPTER SIXTEEN
Josie

I wake up the next morning with Haeden's head between my legs as he licks me into another rippling, shivering orgasm. God, the man does have a strong, amazing tongue. And apparently he loves giving as well as receiving.

Clearly I've been giving this resonance thing too hard a knock.

"Good morning, my mate," he murmurs between licks, then goes straight for my clit.

I moan something that might be a response, and my hands go to his horns. I hold them like handlebars as he goes to town on my pussy, feasting like he's starving and licking as if I'm the center of a Tootsie Pop or something. Who could hold out against such enthusiasm? No one—and I come within a matter of minutes.

Once my body is reduced to nothing but a quivering mess, he licks me one last, lingering time, and then nuzzles the inside of my thigh. "We must start our journey soon."

"Right. Journey." I pant. "Got it." I'm pretty boneless at the moment, my cootie purring pleasantly. It seems to be eating up all the endorphins I've been sending its way, because the need has been less urgent in the last few days—or maybe it realizes I'm inches away from giving in to this whole resonance thing.

Heck, after a morning greeting like that, I'm having a real hard time remembering why I ever fought against this. Haeden's caring and sweet and devoted. Sometimes cranky, yes. Sometimes surly and overbearing, but when it comes to me? I'm his world and he lets me know it.

Which . . . I'm not hating. I'm not sure if I'm ready to bend yet. I'm not ready to say no, but I feel like I need a little bit more of a push in the "yes" direction, and I want to see where things take us. I'm having fun with him right now, and while the resonance feels inevitable, I also just want to enjoy the moment.

He gives my thighs one last nuzzle and teasing lick, then gets up and moves toward the dead coals of our fire. "Do you require fresh tea this morning, my mate, or shall we drink cold water and move out earlier?"

Mate? Eeep. I want to tell him to ix-nay the ate-may thing because I'm terrified of jinxing it. But he seems . . . so happy this morning. So pleased with himself. And as he glances over at me, he gives me another fierce, possessive look of pride.

Yeah, I can't deflate that right now. I slide my tunic lower over my splayed, naked legs and stretch a little. "Cold water's fine. I want to get to Harlow's cave. The sooner the better, I think."

Because there, I think we'll seal the deal.

We're maybe an hour out from the cave when Haeden stops abruptly, and I run into his back and then nearly fall over in my snowshoes. "What the fuck—"

"Hsst," he says, waving a hand in the air to indicate silence. I cling to his back and try to peer around his shoulder.

To my surprise, he grabs my arm and half-steers, half-drags me away to the nearest cliff. "Haeden," I protest, trying to walk as fast as I can in the snowshoes. "What's going on?"

"Quiet!" The asshole is back in play. He pushes me against the rock wall of the cliff and pulls my small bone knife from its sheath and shoves it into my hand. His eyes are narrow, his face tight with wariness. "Wait here and do not move."

"What is it?"

"With luck, it is nothing." He gives me one of those devouring looks and then turns away, holding his spear at the ready.

I clutch my knife in my fur-mittened hand, blinking. He's crouching low in the snow, his movements slinking. It's almost like he's hunting something, but I don't see any game. He didn't hunt yesterday when we were traveling, and said it was because he wants me to be safe, and even a wounded dvisti can be dangerous. So why is he hunting now? I gaze up ahead of him and see something dark splashed in the snow. A short distance away, there's a lump that seems to be out of sync with the rest of the environment, like a pimple on one of the snowy hills.

Haeden crouches low near the darker splashes and touches one, then lifts his fingers and sniffs them. I realize what I'm looking at. "Is that blood?" I call out.

He turns and gives me a furious shake of his head, indicating I should be silent.

Oh crap. I'm annoyed at his mood but I'm also not stupid. If he's freaking out, this is bad. I clutch my little knife tighter and wait for him to come back.

His tail thrashes against the snow as he studies the whatever-the-hell-it-is and then gets to his feet. Instead of heading back toward me, he moves toward the lump up ahead. I realize when he picks up something long and stiff and turns the thing over that it's a body. It's gray and furry and . . . I think it's a metlak.

Oh, shit. What killed it? Who else is out here? I try to think of any sorts of predators big enough to eat one of the tall, skinny metlaks. The snow-cats are fierce but not much bigger than bobcats. The dvisti are grass eaters, and the sa-kohtsk? Well, I don't know what they eat, but they're too slow to be predators. I rack my brain as Haeden studies the carcass and then returns to my side, a grim expression on his face.

"What is it?" I ask, worried. The look on his face makes my blood freeze. "What killed it?"

"I do not know." His mouth is drawn into a grim line. "There are no tracks, only blood."

I swallow hard. "Maybe . . . maybe it snowed?" But I've been here long enough to recognize fresh powder and the snow we're walking in is slightly crusty. That means it's been on the ground long enough to melt slightly in the sunlight and then ice back over again. More than that, the weather is clear, with barely a breeze.

He grunts acknowledgment, though we both know I'm wrong. "We must be careful. Stay on alert as we walk and keep safely behind me." He takes my pack from my shoulders and slings it over his front. "If you get tired, let me know and I will carry you."

"I'll be fine." If things are as bad as they seem, I don't want him to be weighed down by carrying my sorry human ass.

Haeden nods and starts walking again, his strides big and ground-eating. "Stay close."

Oh sure. The tiny human woman in snowshoes will somehow manage to "stay close" to the seven-foot-tall alien who walks like it's a spring day. Sure. No problem. But I don't protest, because it's clear he wants to get out of this area. Whatever it is that happened to that metlak, it's rattled him.

I take a gander at it as we pass by. The blood spray is everywhere and the thing . . . well, I'm surprised I can tell it was a metlak. It looks as if it's been chewed up and spit back out again.

I shiver and pick up the pace behind Haeden.

We keep a murderous pace through the day, and I do my best to keep up. It's clear to me that the easy-but-brisk travel of yesterday is gone, and in its place, we're marching at a breakneck pace. It sucks. It sucks even more that he's picking a twisty trail instead of an obvious one, keeping us near the trees or walking in the shadow of a rocky cliff instead of out in the open. That means the drifts are higher, the wind is colder, and all of the travel is just garbage and a half. Even though it's taking everything I have, I manage to keep up (well, relatively) and Haeden doesn't carry me.

By the time the twin moons are directly overhead and the snow is lit up with the night, Haeden steers me toward a rocky outcropping. "Hunter cave in there."

Thank God. My legs feel ready to fall off and my toes went numb with cold hours ago. My cootie's too tired to sing even, and all it manages is a half-assed purr when he gets near.

So not scoring tonight.

The cave is clean of any occupants, and by the time Haeden strikes up a fire, I've barely managed to peel my wet furs off my body. Exhausted, I let him help me undress but I don't have the energy to do more than crawl into the freshly unrolled bed furs and collapse.

When I wake up the next morning, he's holding me against him, his cootie purring happily, and his finger strokes my cheek. I yawn and raise my head to look at the entrance of the cave. There's sunlight pouring in, which means I've slept a good long while.

Doesn't feel like it. I'm still exhausted.

"Sorry," I mumble at him, and then set my head back down on his warm shoulder. "Guess I passed out."

"You are tired." He traces my jaw lightly. "It is understandable."

He seems more relaxed today, and I'm too tired to think about sexytimes, so I broach the subject of yesterday's "problem." "What killed that metlak?"

"Stop asking, Jo-see."

I ignore his sourness. It's a ploy to shut me down and I'm wise to him now. He gets cranky when he doesn't want to answer. "That's not an 'I don't know.' That's an 'I know but I don't want to tell you.'"

He snorts.

"But you do know, don't you?"

His hand slides to my arm and he brushes tickling little circles on my bare skin. I'm naked. Oh. So is he. Didn't realize that until just now, but weirdly enough, it doesn't feel sexual. I suspect he just wants to hold me. "There are . . . stories."

Doesn't sound like a good start to me. "I'm listening."

"My father used to say that when it grew too cold, it was a bad thing. That the sky-claws would appear and hunt in sa-khui territory."

"Sky . . . claw? I haven't heard of that." The words sound strange in the sa-khui tongue.

"There are many reasons why the sa-khui do not live near the great salt waters. The creatures in those waters are very large and aggressive, with many fangs."

"So I've heard." Harlow has shared some hair-raising stories of the stuff she's seen. Makes me think of all the documentaries I watched on dinosaurs as a kid—the ocean here is experiencing some primordial soup or something. "And the sky-claw things live in the water?"

"No. They come from above. They snatch their prey from the ground and swallow them whole. And they are big enough to eat a kit the size of Farli."

I feel sick. I'm the same size as Farli. In fact, I'm pretty sure I have one of her old tunics. "You don't say."

"I do not know for sure if it is the sky-claws," he says, rubbing my arm as if to comfort me. "But if it is, we would do best to keep an eye on the skies."

Weirdly enough, I think of the big shadow I saw flying overhead a few days ago, when I had my spyglass and was scoping out the island. I wasn't able to find out what it was. The thought that it could have been some sort of gigantic flying predator that eats people for breakfast fills me with fear. "So the sky-claws hang out on the coast? How come Rukh and Harlow never said anything?"

"They come down when it is cold."

"It's always cold!"

"Ah, but this bitter season is much colder than the last one."

Well, goody. "Do you think they're coming from the island?"

"Eye-land?"

I sit up and look at him. "There's something out in the water. If you stare out at it far enough, you can see a smear of green. I think it's an island. With trees."

He snorts derision. "Trees are pink. Like you." His hand smooths down my arm and he gives me a hungry look.

My nipples harden and I remember that I'm naked and giving him some full-frontal action. I tap his chest with my hand, because he's starting to look distracted. "Pay attention, Haeden. Trees are green on my planet. Chlorophyll or some shit. Anyhow, I took this glass thing from the elders' spaceship and it lets you see long distances. I promise I saw a bunch of green and I'm pretty sure it's an island. Do you think the sky-claw things are coming from there?"

He shrugs. "Does it matter? This area is not safe. We need to avoid the coast and head inland, toward the tribal caves."

"All right."

"Which means we should leave soon."

I groan and flop on the blankets, facedown. I'm a heavy sleeper and I need my rest, and I feel like I need a heck of a lot more of it. "How soon is soon?"

He chuckles. "*Very* soon."

And then the bastard rips the blankets off of me, leaving me bare-assed in the cold.

I'm dragging.

I can't help it. I'm exhausted. Haeden's trying to be understanding, but he wants to go faster. He's set another bruising pace today and I'm doing my best to keep up. But every time he wants me to walk nearer the trees, I find myself edging out a bit farther. I can't march like a soldier and somehow plow through the thick drifts *and* somehow keep up with him. Something's got to give.

As the day wears on, Haeden's temper grows shorter. "Hurry," he snaps at me. "Do I need to carry you?"

"I'm hurrying!" I yell back at him, doing my best to drag my happy ass through the snow. The suns are high in the bleary sky, which means we won't be stopping anytime soon. Harlow and Rukh's cozy seaside cave is no longer an option—Haeden's taking me deep into the mountains . . . which means more snow. Which means it's even more difficult to keep up. And do I bitch? No. I shut my mouth and walk faster, or try to. I'm covered in sweat, though, and my furs are freezing against my skin. My poor cootie is thrumming, but I'm pretty sure it's expending most of its energy trying to keep me from being a human Popsicle instead of getting me pregnant. Priorities and all. Meanwhile, Haeden just storms through the snow ahead of me, faster and faster, like it's nothing.

I glare at his back and his twitching tail. He's carrying my pack and his, and I should be grateful, but I'm so stinking tired. I just want to rest for a day or three. There's no rush, I tell myself. There's no clock to beat. The girls in the tubes are safe for another week or three or even a year. We can camp out in the next little cave for a while and relax. The idea sounds like heaven, and my frozen feet slow even more. I'm exhausted. Maybe he does need to carry me for a bit this afternoon, because I don't know—

A shadow moves over the ground and glides over me.

I freeze. "Haeden?" My voice is a mere whisper. I clutch my stupid little knife—the one he tells me I need to keep out at all times—tight in my hand. "I think I just saw something."

He doesn't turn, too far ahead of me to hear my words.

"Haeden," I call, louder. This time, he turns. "I think I saw—"

A screech.

The shadow falls over me again.

And then I'm plucked from the ground and something hot and wet surrounds me like a vise. There's a horrible stink and something hard and pointed drags against my bared skin. Teeth. The vise flexes and then it grows completely dark.

Oh my God. My thoughts are in an utter panic—I've just been eaten alive.

"Jo-see!"

CHAPTER SEVENTEEN
Haeden

"JO-SEE!" My mate's name is ripped from my throat at the sight of the sky-claw as he descends on her and his pointed mouth plucks her from the snow as if she is nothing, a mere tidbit of meat.

My heart stops in my breast. I stagger to my knees.

My mate.

My everything. She's gone.

No. No. No.

"NO!"

The life crushes from my chest as I watch the sky-claw flap its wings and lift into the air again. It begins to soar, all wing and sinew and massive, massive jaws.

My mate.

I let out another anguished cry of her name, staggering after the creature even though I know there is no way I can catch him. I cannot fly. Even if I could, my Jo-see is gone. *Gone.*

I am in agony. I watch the creature soar away and turn my knife to my breast. I will not live without her. I cannot. There is no world if it does not have her smile and her bright, sparkling eyes in it.

"I have failed you, my mate," I say, placing my knife over my chest. The plates protecting my heart will not let me stab directly; I shove the knife against one and watch as blood wells against my skin. All it will take is one solid thrust and then I will join her. My gaze seeks out the loathsome sky-claw in the distance.

The creature is a black spot growing smaller on the horizon.

Then, it wobbles in midair.

Dips.

Falters.

The wings begin to beat erratically. It struggles to climb higher in the air, only to plummet farther.

Fury rushes through me. I chase after it, moving swiftly over churned snow. It disappears over the next ridge and I race after it. I will cut out its heart with my knife and offer it to scavengers. I will hack out its eyes and flay the skin from its filthy body for daring to eat my mate.

Another anguished cry rips from my throat as I find it on the ground, the delicate wings flapping against the earth. It's writhing in front of me, unable to fly. The creature is unlike any other bird I have seen—the face is a scaly, pointed triangle, with thick, tufted brown fur on its throat and body. The wings are naked and stretched thin between finger-joints like fine leather stretched tight over a privacy screen. The entire thing is longer than some caves I have seen. It is hideous.

But it is on the ground.

Now's my chance.

I give another cry of anger and stab at the thing's throat. My knife sinks into the throat, and hot blood splashes over me. With a vindictive howl, I drag my blade through the throat until it the thrashing head goes limp and I am covered in its lifeblood.

That was for Jo-see.

I stab my knife into its side, just under the wing, unsatisfied. I do not know why it landed, but I will take the opportunity to avenge my mate. I will carve it into pieces and enjoy every stab of my blade. Another howl of anguished loss escapes me. My face is wet with blood and the tears that must be streaking down my face. In one moment, I have lost everything.

Everything.

"I had a mate," I snarl at it, stabbing my knife into its side again. "And I *loved* her! You took her from me!" Over and over, my knife sinks into it. Then, I rest a hand, my heart pounding, against the creature's large belly.

The belly moves.

I recoil backward, staring. Is it pregnant? Are more young about to spill forth from the creature? But the belly moves again, and then something sticks out of the center of the belly . . . something small and hard and pointed, wet with red blood. A tooth—

Or a knife.

My khui, silent until now, bursts into song.

Another howl escapes my throat, and my movements become frantic. "Jo-see! Jo-see!" I slam my knife in next to the other and then begin to slice at the creature's thick stomach, trying to carve a hole. The thick, blubbery hide over the stomach fights me, and I snarl as I put both of my hands on the handle of my blade and use all of my strength to cut deeper, wider.

A bloodstained hand emerges, human fingers reaching and frantic.

Joy blasts through me, and I continue cutting. My mate! *My mate! She lives!*

When the creature's abdomen is hacked open, I grab the reaching hand and brace a foot against the belly of the creature and heave with all my might. The wound makes an awful sucking sound, and I pull harder. A growl of fury escapes me and then I pull again, determined. It will not keep her. *It will not.*

Then, the creature's stomach gives way and Jo-see, wet, covered in gore, and gasping for breath, slides out of it and into my arms.

My mate.

My everything.

I shout her name and pull her against me, no matter that she is soaked and covered in filth. My hand goes to her wet hair and I cradle her head—her sweet, sweet human head—against my chest.

My mate.

"C-couldn't b-b-breathe," she chokes out, shuddering against me. Her sticky hands work against my chest and then she curls them into fists. Her breath gasps from her lungs. "I couldn't see. I couldn't move—" She bursts into tears and then begins to sob hard, burrowing against me. "Oh my God."

"I know," I tell her, stroking her blood-slicked hair back from her face. "Shhh. I have you, my mate." I press my mouth to her smooth brow, not caring that she is filthy and I am not much better. She is mine, forever. The agony of the last few minutes surges through me and I stagger. The only thing that keeps me upright is that Jo-see sags against me. I press my mouth to her skin frantically again. "I thought I had lost you."

She just sobs, pressing her cheek to my chest.

My poor mate. I want to clutch her against my chest forever and never let her go, but she is shivering and upset. I throw my pack down on the ground and tear it apart, pulling out the bed-rolls. I wrap her in the furs, not caring that she is filthy. She must be warm. "Do not cry, my mate. I will take care of you."

"S-says the g-g-guy that wasn't just s-swallowed fucking whole!"

"I know," I murmur, kissing and touching her everywhere. I cannot stop reaching for her. I will never stop seeing that awful vision of the sky-claw swooping low to scoop up my mate as if she were nothing.

I will protect her with my life.

Once she is bundled in the furs, I pick her up and begin to run. I do not care how long it will take to get her to the next hunter cave; I only know that she is not leaving my sight again.

The suns are close to setting behind the horizon when I stagger into the cave. A quill-beast yips and scurries out, and I mentally curse myself for not checking first to see if the cave was occupied. My mind is a whirl of scattered thoughts, all of them focused on one thing—keeping my mate safe.

Jo-see has been quiet for some time, and I set her down gently inside. "Wait here."

She shivers and nods, but does not speak. When the shadows move over her face, I see a blank look there. It worries me.

So I work quickly. I scoop up the offal left by the quill-beast and sweep the cave clean with a dvisti-tail whisk broom left by the last occupant. I left many of our supplies out on the trail in my haste to clothe Jo-see in our furs, but they do not matter. I can make new hooks, new knives. I can collect new fire-making supplies. All that matters is her.

I build a fire and soon have water melting in the pouch. My tea is gone, left back on the trail. It does not matter—the water will be used to bathe her first. After that, I will worry about tea.

Jo-see is quiet in the firelight, but her entire body still trembles.

"Come," I tell her, and wince when my voice seems unnaturally gruff in the silence. "We are going to bathe you and then we are going to eat something."

"I don't think I can eat," she whispers.

"You can, and you will." I ignore the fact that we have nothing to eat and I left my travel rations back a way. One problem at a time.

"Don't tell me what to do," she snaps, turning to glare at me.

I will take her anger. At least she is not staring vacantly ahead. I narrow my eyes and give her an irritated snort in the hopes of riling her temper. "I am your mate. I know best."

"We're not mated," she cries out, and then bursts into new tears. "I almost died and you almost lost a second mate again because I'm a selfish asshole!" Her raw sobs fill the cavern.

I sit, frozen in shock. She was worried about me? All this time? Here I have been frantic with worry over her, how small she is, how shocked she must be, and she is thinking of *me*?

My chest aches. I rub it, ignoring the small nick at the top, where my knife dug into my skin. To think I almost killed myself while she was still alive in the sky-claw's belly, working to get out. The thought makes me ill.

I crouch in front of her. When she avoids looking at me, I cup her face in both my hands, ignoring how filthy she is. "Jo-see," I say, waiting for her eyes to meet mine. When they do, I continue. "You were mine the day you landed in this world. I felt a connection the moment I saw you, and it frightened me. When we resonated, I realized that you were always meant to be mine. And I will keep you safe."

Her eyes shimmer with tears and she opens her mouth to protest.

"I will keep you safe," I repeat. My thumbs smooth over her rounded cheeks. "You are mine. That is all you need to know. If you are taken, I will come after you. If you are sick, I will never leave your side. If you leave, I will follow. You will never be without me, because I will come after you. Know this." I brush my fingers over her breast, where her khui thrums. "Feel this and know it to be true."

"But we're not—"

"And when you are well," I tell her in the same firm voice, cutting off her protest before it starts, "I will lie down with you in the furs and take you as mine. We will mate until you carry my kit. Then, resonance will be sated. But do not seek to tell me that you are not mine yet. Because you have *always* been mine."

Her wounded eyes blink, and then she nods slowly. "Yours," she whispers.

"Always," I growl back.

CHAPTER EIGHTEEN
Josie

I must have passed out at some point, because I wake up a while later to find the fire crackling higher than normal, and I'm naked on top of the filthy furs. Something warm and wet rubs my arm, and I look over to see that Haeden is carefully bathing me with long, smooth strokes of his hand. There's a look of intense concentration on his face and I realize for the first time in a while that I am totally, completely safe. He's not horn-dogging on me; he's not doing this to score points. He's doing this because he wants to take care of me. Because I'm important to him.

And I want to tell him that I could kiss him for that, but my brain is still all shocky from earlier and I fall back asleep, letting him take care of things. For once, it's good to let my guard down and realize someone else has my back.

When I wake up again later that night, Haeden is gone. The fire is crackling and the cave is cozy and warm. New furs that smell a little musty and that must have come from somewhere in the cave are piled on top of me, and I drift back to sleep. Haeden must be hunting. Or something. Strangely enough, I'm not worried. I know he wouldn't leave me if there was a chance something bad would happen. I sleep on.

I wake up the next morning with Haeden's arms wrapped tightly around me, and his naked body is under the furs next to mine. We're spooning and his cock is hard against my butt, but I can hear how deeply he's asleep. I roll over slowly, my body moving inch by slow inch so I do my best not to wake him up. Every muscle in my body aches, and I don't know if it's from the endless hiking or from, ugh, being swallowed whole. Just the thought makes my gorge rise and I spend the next few minutes doing my best not to freak out all over again.

Haeden, however, is warm and strong and wonderful, so I snuggle closer to him and his arms tighten around me reflexively. My cootie is purring loud, joined by his, and the ache between my legs has returned. We need to fulfill resonance, and soon. I lift a hand to smooth it over his chest and realize there are deep scratches down my naked arm. I frown at them, trying to figure out where they've come from. The creature's teeth must have gouged me as I went down its throat.

I shudder hard. It's going to take me a long fucking time to get over that. If I close my eyes, I can still feel the awful clench of its throat as it swallows me.

"Hush," Haeden murmurs, his hand brushing over my shoulder and down my arm. "I am here. I will not let anything else harm you."

I want to tease him about his confident words, but they make me feel better. I relax next to him. "Where did you go last night?"

"Hunting. I ran back to pick up our packs, as well." His fingers brush my cheek. "Were you scared?"

"No. I knew you wouldn't let me get hurt." I trace my fingers over his pectorals, just because I like touching him. "I'm a bit banged up, though."

His eyes remain closed even as his hands roam over my body possessively. "Mm. It will heal soon enough. Do you hurt? Shall I get liidi to numb your aches?"

I wrinkle my nose at the thought of more of that goop. "No thanks. I'm just sore and a bit scratched." My fingers glide across a deep cut directly over the center of his pectorals and I frown. "Did that thing get you, too?"

"No. I did that."

I sit up. "You cut yourself? Why?"

He pulls me back down into the furs, all without opening his eyes. Man, he must be wiped. "I did it because I placed my blade there. If you had died, I wanted to follow you."

"That is so fucked up," I whisper, shocked. "I mean, don't get me wrong, it's also the sweetest thing I've ever heard, but it's seriously fucked up."

"You are my mate. There is nothing for me if you are gone." And he pulls me back down against him and fits my head against his shoulder. "Rest now."

I relax against him because I know he needs his sleep. I can't drift off, though. Not while thinking about him grieving and upset at the idea of losing me. I think hard, and then because I'm insecure, I poke him in the chest to wake him up.

"Did you try to do that after Zalah?"

He struggles awake, blinking at me. "Do what?"

"Did you try to kill yourself after Zalah died?"

He snorts as if amused by the thought. "No. Go to sleep."

For some reason, this pleases me. I'm more important to him

than Zalah was. I shouldn't care about something so petty . . . but fuck that, I totally care. And it makes me happy.

If we both weren't so tired, I'd totally nail him right now.

Haeden sleeps on for hours, and I drift off again, too. When I wake up the next time, it's (sadly) not to my man nuzzling between my thighs but to the scent of cooking meat. Okay, I'll take that.

I sit up and rub my eyes, yawning. He's crouched near the fire, slowly turning a spit, his tail flicking back and forth. He's also naked, and I can see his ball sack hanging between his strong thighs from behind. Most people wouldn't be able to make that work, but I can't stop staring at him. He's so damn sexy.

Remind me again why we've been fighting this? I ask my brain. The ache between my legs increases and I have to physically keep myself from pressing a hand between my legs and masturbating at the sight of him. I must be feeling better.

My cootie's increased hum alerts him and he glances over his shoulder at me, black braid spilling down his back. "Awake?"

I nod and sit up, letting the covers slide to my waist so he can get a good look at my nudity. "Very awake. How long have we been sleeping?"

He grunts acknowledgment and turns back to the fire, which is disappointing. "It has been a day since . . ." He coughs as if he cannot say the words, then concludes gruffly, "A day."

I slide a little closer to him. "Is that all? It feels like longer."

He nods. He doesn't look at me.

For some reason, that hurts. "What is it? Why won't you look at me?"

Haeden glares at the fire. He rubs his chest absently, his khui purring so loud that just the sound of it makes me wet with need. "Because I nearly lost you, and it is taking all of my effort not to throw you down onto the furs and ram my cock into your cunt to claim you."

Oh. That should not turn me on nearly as much as it does. I squeeze my thighs tight together. "Because . . . your body hurts?" I guess. "You're still exhausted?"

He snorts in derision. "Not me. You are not well. You are fragile and need more rest."

Oh barf, more of this "fragile Josie" shit? Does he think now I'm going to break into a million pieces if he touches me? Because some bird the size of a bus tried to have me as a snack? Because seriously? Yes, I'm traumatized. But the best solution for that would be for him to hold me, not ignore me.

Clearly I'm going to have to take matters into my own hands.

I want to move forward, not backward. I want us to become one.

I *want* to become his mate.

I reach out and grab his swishing tail. It immediately curls around my wrist, feather soft and smooth. He glances over at me then. "Hi," I say, smiling. "Remember me? Your mate?"

His brows furrow in confusion, not getting my joke.

"You promised you'd practice kissing with me. We can at least do that, right?" I bat my eyes at him, doing my best to look innocent. My plan is an evil one, though. I figure if we start with kissing, he won't be able to stop.

And really? I think it's long past time we consummated this thing.

Haeden scowls in my direction as if I've just suggested we go for a naked morning jog. "You want to practice kissing? Now?"

"What's wrong with now?"

"You are tired and ill—"

"I'm not!"

He tries again. "You have had a bad time of things—"

"But you saved me." I bat my lashes again.

Haeden moves forward, peering at me, and cups my face. "Is there something in your eye?"

God, he really sucks at flirting, doesn't he? "Nothing," I say sourly, then change tactics. He wants to play nursemaid? All righty. "Though I do have something that hurts."

He stiffens, all alarm. "What is it?" His hands smooth over my skin, checking me. "Where do you hurt?"

Aw, man. He's so worried about me that it takes all the fun out of my idea of cupping my pussy and saying *Here, big boy. I hurt here.* He's so sweet—and so determined to protect me from everything that could harm me. How did I ever think he was a dick? I pat his chest. "I'm just teasing, Haeden. But I do want to practice kissing."

His ridged, thick sa-khui brow wrinkles. "Are you sure? I do not want you to exhaust yourself—"

I sit back in the blankets and pat them encouragingly. "I'll be very careful."

Haeden gives me a wary look and then nods, joining me in the furs. He moves with grace despite his big body, and I can't help but stare at the fact that he's got a raging hard-on already. Is he denying himself for me? How sweet. How misguided. I'd love to help him with that little problem.

Or not so *little*. His cock is impressive and my girl parts give an anticipatory little squeeze. We're doing this tonight, come hell or high water. I've fought long and hard not to be his mate, but it's funny how things work out. I can't imagine anyone but

Haeden for me. Even his gruffness is just a show, and I realize that now. He's crabby because he cares too much and it scares him.

And if that doesn't make a woman turn to goo like a marshmallow, I don't know what does.

Haeden thumps onto the furs next to me, his face close to mine. I give him a little smile to let him know that things are fine, that I'm not tired, and that this is gonna be great. I decide to start off slow. "So I know you're a virgin—"

He scowls. "You keep bringing that up."

"I bring it up because it's sexy, big guy." I shift a little closer to him and put my hands on his chest, letting my slight weight lean against him. "But what I was *going* to say was . . . how much do you know about kissing?"

As if to show me, he leans in and presses a peck to my mouth. It's quick, and polite, and like something a stranger would give.

Yeah, that won't do. I know he knows kisses are filled with emotion—he presses his mouth to my face in almost-kisses all the time, and I get the impression he knows it involves lips but not the depths behind it. Oh, this is going to be fun. "That's how you start out, yes. But there's a lot more to it."

His eyes narrow as if I've told him he's doing something wrong. "My kiss does not please you?"

"It pleases me," I say quickly, stroking his chest with my hand. "But there are things you can do with mouths and kissing that are even more pleasing."

The look on his face gets smoldering. "Like when you put your mouth on my cock, or when I lick your cunt?"

Oh, mercy, did it just get warm in here? I half-fan myself. "Like that, yeah. Except we do it to each other's mouths."

He looks intrigued. "Why?"

"Because . . . because." I've never thought about why people kiss. We just do. I slide a hand up his chest and move it to the back of his neck, moving closer to him. "Because it feels good. Because it's wet and slick and tongues feel amazing." My words become husky, and I'm getting aroused just talking about things.

"Your tongue felt . . . amazing . . . on my cock." His gaze drops to my mouth. "It is very smooth."

"Yeah, I thought you'd like it if I tried that." I can't help but smile.

"Did you enjoy doing that to me?" His voice has dropped to a husky note. "I could smell your arousal when you licked me . . . and I smell it now." His hand moves to my thigh. "Do we skip the kissing then, Jo-see? I can lick your cunt until you scream. I enjoy doing so." He runs his tongue over his lips in anticipation. "Very much."

Oh, dear lord, such an offer. I'm tempted, but I want to seal the deal with my man, and the incident yesterday has made me crave becoming one with him. I want this. I want all of this. "We'll get to that later. For now, let's focus on mouths." I tap on his lower lip, and then lightly rub it with the pad of my finger. "There's a type of kiss that we call French kissing."

"Fransh-kay-seeng?"

"Close enough." I tease my finger against the seam of his lips. "It's where I put my mouth on yours—or you put yours on me—and our tongues mate."

Recognition dawns on his face. "I have seen this."

"You have?"

He nods. "I never thought to try it. We always seemed too . . . far from that." The look on his face gets hungry with need and his gaze moves to my mouth again. "I want to try it, Jo-see."

"I want that, too."

His hands go around my waist and he pulls me forward, and then my breasts are pressed against his chest, my legs straddling one of his thick thighs. Our mouths are inches apart . . . and then he pushes his lips to mine. Not a gentle press, but an awkward push of his face against mine.

I remain still, waiting for him to feel his way through things. It's a little odd, but I don't want him to feel like he's not doing it right. To encourage him, I part my mouth, and when he doesn't swoop in, I take the initiative and flick my tongue against his.

A groan escapes him and I feel his arms tighten around me. His tongue rubs up against mine and it's full of ridges and strange creases . . . just like his cock. I moan as they drag along my tongue and set my nerve endings on fire.

"I like this," he rasps between licks of his tongue against mine.

Oh boy, I do, too. I'm not able to do much more than whimper along with each thrust as he experiments with kissing. He tries moving his tongue in different ways, slicking along mine and trailing along my teeth. When he's satisfied he's got the thrusting-tongue part down, he teases my lips with his. The deep, licking kisses turn to light, playful nibbles that make me ache just as much as the others.

He's entirely too good at this for a beginner, and all I can do is cling to him and enjoy the ride. Over and over he kisses me, mouths melding, tongues teasing, until I'm a quivering lump of woman in his lap. His mouth on mine is doing crazy things to me, and it's like I can feel my cootie vibrating through every inch of my body right down to my spleen.

Haeden nips at my lower lip, and he's careful despite those big sharp teeth. They graze over my lip softly and I feel his tongue flick a moment before he lifts his head and gives me one of those laser-focused, intense looks. "Jo-see."

"Hmm?" I'm floating in a sea of arousal and the man wants to make *conversation*?

"I want to *frankiss* other parts of you." He garbles the two words into one and then nips at my lip again.

"O-oh?" I've never been propositioned quite so sweetly and yet so dirtily. "I thought you said I was fragile?"

He moves lower, nips at my chin, and then begins to trace my jaw with his tongue. "I will do the work. You can rest and I will kiss you."

I giggle. Is this the sa-khui version of *just lie back and enjoy it, baby*? Doesn't matter—I'm glad I've convinced him that it's playtime instead of *Jo-see is fragile and needs bed rest*. "I will do my best not to interfere, then," I say playfully. And I set my hands on his shoulders with every intent of leaving them there and doing nothing to interfere.

He gives me a scorching look that makes my thighs quiver, and then puts a hand to the back of my neck and gently maneuvers us until we're lying in the furs. I'm on my back underneath him and he's looming over me, all blue-suede skin and muscle, his horns casting shadows in the firelight. He looks a bit like a demon from this angle, hard face cast in shadow except for his glowing blue eyes, and I shiver again because it shouldn't be half so sexy as it is.

"You are shivering," he points out, a look of concern on his face. "Shall I stoke the fire?"

"It's sexy shivering."

He snorts, not believing me. "No such thing."

"Sure there is. I'm shivering because you're so hot."

In typical Haeden fashion, he misunderstands me. "I am too warm?" His body immediately lifts off of mine, his fists pressing in the furs on the sides of me. He looks frustrated and disappointed.

"No, no," I tell him and grab at the long braid of hair that hangs over one shoulder and tug it forward. I love Haeden's hair—he shaves the sides of his head short and braids the rest of it into one long braid that hangs down his back. All of the sakhui have thick hair that they plait in different ways (some just to keep it out of the way) but I like Haeden's the best. I wrap his braid around my hand and pull him toward me. "It is a human expression. We say something is 'hot' when it means we find it pleasurable or stimulating. Arousing. To me, you are hot. Perfect. Sexy. Wonderful."

His eyes gleam and I realize it's been forever since he's had that dead look in his gaze. It's been gone from the moment we resonated, and for some reason it makes me feel like crying with happiness. It's like this resonance between our cooties is saving us both. I do get a little weepy and sniff.

The sexy look on his face dies, replaced by worry. He cups my cheek. "Now, why do you cry, my Jo-see?"

"I'm just emotional," I say, blubbering a little. I wipe at my eyes with his braid and try to give him a cheery look. "I'm happy."

His scowl returns. "You were nearly eaten by a sky-claw yesterday. How does this make you happy?"

"You big ding-a-ling, you make me happy. Here. This moment. You and me. I just looked at your smile and realized that you've been sad for far too long. Me, too. I think I've been sad and lonely for a long time. And I'm not sad anymore." I pat his chest, putting a hand over the plates covering his heart, where his khui thrums a song in time with mine. We resonate to each other so much that it feels normal now, like the constant low-pitched vibration is just a thing, like breathing. "This makes me happy. You and me together."

Haeden nods slowly. His nostrils flare and the tense look crosses his face again before he slides an arm under me and tugs me against his body. I try to figure out what he's doing but it's clear a moment later when he lowers his body onto the furs that he's holding me against him. He's holding me tight. "I nearly lost you—"

"But you didn't," I say, stroking his braid to soothe him. "It's okay."

The growl that escapes his throat as he buries his face against my neck tells me that he doesn't quite believe me. That's all right. If he wants to hug it out for a few, we totally can. I'm in no hurry and I love cuddling with him. So I let him hold me close and my hands play over his arms, brushing over hard muscle and enjoying the soft velvety feel of his skin against mine. One of his horns presses against my cheek and rubs there, and it's a little awkward and achingly sweet at the same time.

"You've got me," I tell him when he remains silent. "You always have me. I know I'm safe when I'm with you because you won't let anything happen to me."

"Never," he growls against my throat. "*Never.*"

Just hearing that turns me on a little more. He's so possessive. Funny how that's never turned my crank in the past but now it makes my nipples hard. Funny how it's *Haeden's* possessiveness that makes me so wet with lust. I never thought I'd fall for the guy in a million years, and yet . . . my cootie sure knew what was up.

Good cootie. I'm totally listening to you from now on.

While I'm lost in thought, Haeden nuzzles my throat again.

Then, I feel his tongue rasp against my neck, in the sensitive spot between collarbone and throat. Oooh. I moan.

He licks it again and then begins to press frantic, quick kisses and tiny bites along the line of my shoulder. It's like he can't get enough of just touching me, and I stroke my hands over his arms and down his chest, doing my best not to interrupt him. Because really? I want more of this. I want more of his mouth on my skin, his body pressing mine into the furs.

I want more of everything.

He licks at the curve of my shoulder again and then nips at the skin with his pointed teeth. It stings, just a little, and I gasp. He makes a tsking sound under his breath and then licks the wound, and another moan escapes me. All right, I'm down for biting if it means I get more tonguing. "I like this *frankissing*," he breathes against my skin. "You are so soft everywhere. It is a pleasure to touch you."

"Pleasure's all mine," I tell him, and it's true. I'm not doing more than touching his arm and grabbing at his braid—he's making this all about me. "You do whatever you feel like."

"I want to *frankiss* all of you, Jo-see." He moves back to my throat, nipping and kissing and then dragging his tongue over my skin. "I want my tongue all over your body."

Oh boy, I want that, too. My cootie's practically throbbing in my chest, it's so excited. "I'm all yours."

He nuzzles his way down my front, heading toward my breasts. "Your teats are so full," he murmurs as he explores the valley between my breasts with his lips.

They . . . are? I've always been a pretty flat-chested girl, but I suppose compared to the sa-khui women, I'm downright busty. They have flatter pectorals unless they're nursing. Come to think of it, Maylak the healer is the only one I've seen that fills out a shirt, and she's both nursing *and* pregnant. Oh. I never thought I'd be considered busty. "You like?"

"Love," he growls, and licks along the slope of one small breast. He moves to the tip and then runs his lips over my nipple. "So soft, here."

I squirm, moaning with need. "Soft?" My nipples feel pretty dang hard.

He lifts his head, and his eyes are glowing a fierce, bright blue. His cootie's humming like a freight train, too. "Soft," he repeats. Haeden takes one of my hands and guides it to his breast, placing my fingers over his nipple. "Not like me."

I touch his nipple and it's as he says—hard as a rock. It feels a lot like the ridged, rough plates covering his breast, actually. Huh. I stroke it and glance up at his face. "Does it feel good when I touch it?"

He shrugs his big shoulders. "It feels like a touch. All of your touches feel good."

Big, sweet man. "But I guess it doesn't feel like when I touch your cock?" I slide my hand lower, between us, and brush against the length of it.

Haeden's gaze darkens and I can hear his sharp intake of breath.

I'm going to take that as a "no, not the same."

"It feels that way when I touch your nipples? To you?"

I nod. "It feels almost as good as when you touch my pussy."

"Pooh-see?"

I am so not explaining that word to him. I point primly.

He grins, looking smugly pleased. "Your cunt." And he reaches between us and cups it, because he's a bold son of a bitch. "Your wet, warm cunt."

A little hitching moan escapes me. "That's the one."

"I will get to it soon, Jo-see. But first I want to finish *frankissing* your teats."

"Go right ahead." I'll even ignore his repeated use of the unsexy word "teats" if it means he's going to tease my breasts some more. I arch encouragingly, thrusting my breasts out in an invitation.

Haeden notices and his gaze drops back to my breasts. There's a fascinated look in his eyes as he leans in and very carefully, very slowly licks the tip of one aching breast and watches my face to see my reaction.

I nearly come right then and there. A little whimper escapes my throat and I wriggle under him. "Oh, do it again, Haeden."

He does, and then growls low in his throat. "Say my name as I lick you, Jo-see. I want to hear it on your tongue."

I moan. That's so damn filthy . . . and so sexy. "Haeden," I say breathlessly, and then whimper again when he gives my breast another teasing lick. "God yes. Just like that, Haeden. My big, sexy mate."

My big, sexy mate growls again and takes my nipple between his teeth, lightly nipping and then licking away the hurt. My pussy clenches hard in response, and I gasp. I swear I'm going to come if he continues this, and that's a first for me. Normally it takes a lot for me to get into sex—my past hang-ups have left me with a lot of unpleasant memories. But with Haeden? None of that exists anymore. It's like he touches me and I'm instantly in the zone. And I love it.

He moves to my other breast and begins a thorough, leisurely exploration of it with lips and tongue, as if it's a fresh new part of my body to discover instead of a twin to my other much-loved breast. His enthusiasm makes me quiver hard, and I cry out his name again as the intensity builds. "Haeden! Please." I'm

panting, my cootie singing desperately. "Please, I need more."
My pussy's clenching around empty air and I'd be stoked if he
gave up on the foreplay and we went straight to the fucking.
"Please."

Haeden moves over me and cups my cheek, worry mixing
with the heat in his eyes. "What do you need, Jo-see? Tell me
and I will give it to you."

"I need to come," I tell him, grabbing his braid and tugging
on it. "I'm so empty. I need you to fill me up."

"Fill you . . . here?" His hand cups my pussy again.

I moan loud and spread my legs, eager for his touch. "Yes!
Put your finger inside me."

He captures my mouth with his again, and I moan into his
mouth. His ridged tongue slicks against mine and I can taste
him, all delicious, musky male. Our khuis throb together even
as his finger glides through my folds, and I nearly come off the
blankets when I feel the thick length prod at the entrance to my
core.

"Please," I pant again, utterly shameless.

"You want to ride my hand?" he growls, nipping at my
mouth and then kissing a line along my throat, making his way
to my ear. "You wish me to fuck you with my hand?"

I shiver, because I want everything and anything he's willing
to give me. I worry that he might be offended somehow, though.
He's a virgin—will it feel wrong to him to use his hand instead
of his cock? It's not like I don't want his dick—I'm greedy. I want
everything.

But then he pushes into me and I shriek, my arms clenching
tight around his neck. I'm coming, my pussy clenching around
his thick finger as he gently bites my earlobe. It's the hardest I've
ever come, and wave after wave of intense orgasm washes over

me. My legs quiver and jerk as he slowly pushes his finger in and out, and then another moan escapes me when he licks my earlobe and begins to thrust into me with his finger.

Did I say I was greedy? Because I want him to stop, and at the same time, I want more. Rippling aftershocks flutter through me with every pump of his finger, and my hips rise off the ground to meet the thrusts. It's like the orgasm train hasn't stopped—my cootie's going a mile a minute and the quivers it's sending through my body are only amplifying the pleasure. It's like I've got a vibrator in my chest and in my pussy, and I wrap a leg around him, digging my heel into his ass as I start to come again. His tail thrashes against my leg as I cry out, another orgasm ripping through me with brute force.

"Jo-see," he groans into my ear, and I feel his body rubbing up against my side. A moment later, I realize it's wet. He's come against my hip, unable to help himself.

And for some reason, I love that. I wrap my arms around him and kiss him fiercely even as he continues to stroke his finger into me with hard, rocking thrusts. "You came while making me come?" I kiss his mouth lightly and then suck on his lower lip. "That's so sexy."

"My need . . . too great." He sounds as out of breath as I am. His finger strokes deep into me again, sending a new quiver through my body. Haeden kisses me again, a quick press of his mouth against mine. "My cock still aches for you, though."

I don't doubt it. I've come twice in the space of about a minute and my cootie's still revved up. It's ready for more. It's like, now that we're close to the finish line, it's not going to let us back away. I tug on Haeden's braid again and rub my foot against his buttock. He's so muscular it's a bit like rubbing against a velvet-covered bowling ball, but even that thought turns me on. He's rock hard, my mate. "Do you want to stop playing?" I ask him.

The look he gives me is one of derision. "I have not finished *frankissing* my mate everywhere."

"Oh?" A new little quiver rips through me.

He pushes his finger in and out, a little more slowly. I'm not ashamed to say that I'm so wet from coming twice that every motion of his hand is making wet sounds. I've never been so slick from arousal before, and I love it.

Haeden nods and sits up in the furs, his hand leaving my pussy. I'm a little sad about that but the naughty gleam in his eyes is making me anticipate what comes next. I admire his body as he rests back on his knees, because there's not an ounce of fat under all that velvety blue skin. He's nothing but rock-hard muscle and abs that go on for miles. And a big dick. Can't forget that part.

He grabs one of my legs by the ankle and carefully lifts it into the air.

I can't help but giggle. "What are you doing?"

He frowns down at my laughter and gives me a serious look. "I told you. I am *frankissing* my mate in all her places."

"Oh, sorry," I say, teasing. "I won't interrupt again."

"Good," he says, voice sharp. "This requires all of my attention." For a moment I think he's suddenly in a pissy mood for some reason, but then I see his mouth twitch and I realize he's fighting back a smile.

Another peal of laughter escapes me, especially when he holds my foot close and then licks the bottom of it. I squeal, wriggling at the ticklishness. "Don't lick my foot!"

"Silence, female. Your mate is pleasuring you." He licks my foot again and then nips at my toes.

I can't stop laughing. It's ticklish and silly all at once.

But then he kisses the side of my foot, and all of the laughter dies in my throat because that one tender little action just made me melt. And then I'm no longer laughing as he kisses my ankle, and then drags his tongue over it. When he moves on to my calf, nibbling at my skin, I've gone from finding this amusing to finding it terribly arousing. My cootie agrees, humming loudly.

He continues to make his way forward, ignoring the outside of my leg in favor of inner knee and then inner thigh. He glances at me every so often, as if wanting to make sure that I'm watching. Like I could turn away? I'm utterly fascinated by his mouth on my skin. When it parts and he licks at the inside of my thigh, I feel myself getting all wet again, and my hand reaches down between my legs to start touching myself.

When Haeden sees that, though, he pushes my hand away. "That is mine."

"Pfft. I can touch myself if I want." And I put my hand there again, my fingers seeking out my clit.

He pulls my hand away again. "Do I need to show you that it's mine, female?"

Oooh. Now I'm all hot and bothered, especially at the sly gleam in his eyes. "Maybe?"

He grunts acknowledgment of my response and presses one last kiss to my inner thigh before putting a hand on the opposite thigh and pushing it wide. He leans over the juncture of my hips and his braid falls onto my leg. "This is mine," he growls low in his throat, and that's the only warning I get before he pushes his face between my thighs and begins to kiss my pussy.

And oh God, I almost come again right then and there.

Like he promised, he kisses my folds and then licks them with his tongue. This isn't exploration as much as it is sheer determination to torture me, and he's doing a really great job at it. I moan as he drags his tongue over my sensitized clit.

"So wet," he rasps between licks. "Your taste is like nothing I have had before. It makes me only want more."

I grab the braid on my thigh, feeling desperate to anchor myself to something, but when that doesn't satisfy the urge, I take his horns instead. He holds my thighs spread apart and licks me with long, slow, leisurely strokes of his tongue and each one makes my hips buck and rise. I want him to go on forever, even as I want him to stop and fill me with his cock. It's torture, all right, but the best kind. "Haeden," I moan. "I need you."

"I need you to come for me," he replies in a husky voice, and then licks my clit with that delicious ridged tongue of his. "I want to have my tongue inside you when you do."

Another moan rips from me at the visual image, and I push his head back down for him to continue licking.

"My mate," he murmurs between licks and nibbles. "I have waited so long for you. To taste you. To pleasure you."

"You have?" His words are melting me more than his tongue is. "I hope . . . I hope I'm not a disappointment." I've fought him so hard and I'm feeling guilty that I've pushed him away for so long.

"Never a disappointment. It is everything I have wanted and more."

For some reason, it makes me weepy. Maybe it's all the emotion barreling through us, courtesy of our cooties. Maybe it's because it feels like, for the first time, I'm loved and cherished. Whatever it is, a sob escapes my throat.

Haeden tenses, and a moment later, he's up in my face, frantically kissing me. "My mate, my heart. What is it? Why do you cry?"

I shake my head. "I'm just happy. Emotional, but happy. You're giving me everything I ever wanted."

"We have not fully mated yet," he reminds me with another kiss. I can taste myself on his lips, and it's a weirdly erotic flavor.

"So what are we waiting for?" I slide a hand to his hip and wrap my legs around him, trying to maneuver him into the perfect spot. "An engraved invitation?"

"A . . . what?" His brow furrows.

"That's human for 'stick it in already.'"

Haeden's eyes narrow. "It is?"

"Close enough."

He hesitates over me, and then leans in to press another kiss to my mouth. "I do not want to hurt you, my Jo-see. Human females are not as strong or large as sa-khui females. What if I am too much?"

I pat his shoulder. "That's sweet, Haeden, baby, but there are eleven other women who are very happily mated to your tribemates and not a single one has complained that her man broke her in bed. We'll be fine."

"There are eleven other females, but I do not care about them," he says, and strokes my hair gently. "I only care for my mate. And she is small and fragile."

"She can take it, I assure you." I'm torn between frustration at the delay and giddiness at his sweet words. "We'll go slow and I'll let you know if it's too much, all right?"

Like hell I will, but if he thinks I'll sound the alarm, at least we can get things moving. And I'm getting desperate for things to get moving. The deep ache inside of me urgently needs filling.

He gives me another look of concern, but then kisses me, because he knows kisses are awesome and they don't hurt me. I return the kiss with urgency of my own, dragging my tongue against his in what is hopefully an enticement for more. He pulls his mouth from mine and groans, eyes closing, and I realize just how difficult this is for him. He's already come once, and if I'm sensitized, I'm sure he's in agony.

And yet he's stopping because he doesn't want to hurt me. God, that's sweet. I caress his cheek. "I love you, Haeden."

He grunts acknowledgment and thrusts his cock against my pussy. It slicks against my folds, dragging along my heated, sensitive flesh. I moan encouragement. He thrusts against me again, and his cock barely stabs at my entrance. I'm not sure if this is foreplay, stalling, or him just not entirely sure what to do next, but it's time to take matters in hand, it seems.

I reach between us and take his cock in my hand. The breath hisses between his teeth and his body stiffens over me. I wait, just in case he's going to come, but when he doesn't, I realize he's just trying to hold out. "You're doing awesome, baby," I whisper, and then guide him to the entrance of my core—my cunt, as he crudely calls it—and set the head of his cock against me. Then, I place my hand on his butt and urge him to push forward. "Take your mate," I tell him. "Claim her."

A roar begins in his throat, soft and growing louder. His body shudders and then he thrusts—hard—into me.

I gasp, because it's an onslaught of sensation all at once. He's big—really fucking big—and thick, and when he pushes in, I feel every ridge on his cock, every twitch of his muscles. His spur pushes through the folds of my pussy and rubs against the side of my clit, like a big extra bonus that I never knew I wanted until this moment. His tail lashes back and forth, like an angry cat's, and it sends little motions through our joined bodies. Our khuis hum in time, synced up, and my entire body feels like it's vibrating, which only enhances the sensations ripping through me.

And his cock inside me? God. It's a strange cross between pleasure and pain with his initial thrust, but as he stiffens over me and his body freezes, it slowly morphs into a bone-aching pleasure.

"Did I . . . harm you?" Haeden strokes my hair again. "You made a sound."

I reach up—and boy, that seems like effort because I feel a bit like a butterfly pinned to a cork board, except, well, a sexy version. It's like I'm a bundled mass of nerves that are centered around where he's impaling me against him.

It's amazing.

"Jo-see?"

Oh, shit. He wants an answer and here I am, all dopey with endorphins. "I'm wonderful," I breathe, a blissful smile curving my mouth.

"I need to . . . move," he says in a strangled voice. His hips grind against mine, just a little, as if he's trying desperately to hold back from going to town on me.

"Then do it," I encourage. I move my hands to his big shoulders and squeeze my legs tighter around his hips. This close together, the sheer size and bulk of him against me is emphasized, and if it were anyone else, I might have a real concern for my safety in his arms. But this is Haeden, and he would absolutely *die* before harming me, so I know I'm safe. "I trust you."

It's like my words cause the dam to burst—and his control flies out the window. He groans loudly and then his hips surge against mine. It's a strong, hard thrust of his cock deep inside me, and then I'm groaning just as loud as him, because when he moves? Not only do I feel every ridge drag back and forth inside me, rubbing against my walls, but his spur glides against my clit, brushing against the hood. It feels incredible.

Then he's moving again. And again. Each thrust seems to grow in strength until he's pounding into me. And it feels amazing. My groans have turned to little cries, and I'm lost in the whirl of sensation. The entire world has boiled down to just this moment, just this place where our bodies are joined and all pleasure seems to be exploding through me at once. As he fucks me, it's like every sensitive spot in my body is being teased at the same time, and it's too much. Another blistering orgasm rockets through me and I scream out his name, my nails digging into his shoulders. I can feel my pussy clenching tight around him like a vise, and somewhere in the blur of pleasure, he's shouting my name in a hoarse voice, and my cootie is singing with his so loudly it's like a freight train is barreling through the cave. And I just keep coming through all of this cacophony of sound and bliss. Over and over, orgasm after orgasm wallops me.

I'm pretty sure I pass out at this point.

At some point, my senses come back to me and I realize I'm flat on my back on the furs, still gasping for breath. My body is wet with sweat, and the warm velvet that is Haeden's skin is stuck to my own. His big body is crushing mine into the furs, but strangely enough, I like it. And my mate? He's pressing kisses to my neck, our cooties purring gently in our chests.

"Wow," I breathe. "You might have boned the consciousness out of me."

"Eh?"

"Nothing." I pat his shoulder absently. "Was it good for you, baby?"

He exhales deeply and props up on his elbows to gaze down at me. I realize that I might still have his long braid wrapped around one hand—or what's left of it. I think there's more hair loose than in his braid at this point, and this is the most mussed

198 • RUBY DIXON

I've ever seen Haeden. He's sweaty and flushed and his long hair is everywhere and it makes me grin. "It was . . . enjoyable."

Wow. Faint praise much? I frown up at him, and I realize that I blabbed about loving the guy mid-bone and all he did was grunt at me. Maybe he didn't hear me. "I love you, you know."

Haeden narrows his eyes at me as if I've said something puzzling. "Of course you do. We are mates."

I shove a hand at his shoulder. "Are you serious? I just confessed love to you and you're all 'duh' about it?"

"I am what?"

I start wriggling out from under him—no mean feat, given that his epic cock is still buried inside me and feels amazing and still a little hard—and try to get away. "Get off of me. I am so done here."

"What?" He grabs me and holds me down under him, and all my squirming just seems to make all my sensitive girl parts get all turned on again. "Why are you mad?"

"Why am I mad? Because I told you I loved you and you act like it's nothing!" I smack a hand on his shoulder. "You're all 'mates love each other' and all I have to say to that is bullshit! I've seen Asha and how she treats Hemalo! She can't stand him. I wouldn't be surprised if she was screwing someone else just because she wants to piss off her mate! Or how about Zalah, huh? Did she love you? Did you love her? Because you resonated to her just the same as me!"

He looks at me with surprise and stiffens. I see a flash of anger cross his face and then that awful dead look returns to his eyes. He gets off of me—and I feel an ache of emptiness when his cock slides from my body—and moves to the fire. He pokes at it with a long bone and won't look at me.

I should be mad, but instead, I feel like I fucked up. I feel guilty and awful, like I just crushed whatever we had under my foot. I threw Zalah in his face, and that's a low blow. I wouldn't like it if he threw my past in my face—the foster dads that snuck into my bed, the guys I slept with in high school when I was desperate for anyone to love me, the alien that raped me on the ship. I have a very long history with sex, all of it bad. And yet here I'm lashing out at the one person that made me feel wanted and adored, all because he didn't say the right words back to me when I wanted to hear them.

I look over at Haeden. His back is stiff, his tail still except for the small flick of the end of it near the furs.

I pull the blankets up around my chest. "I'm sorry. I shouldn't have said that. I just . . ." I exhale deeply. "I have a real need to be told that I'm wanted and loved. I never was as a kid and now I guess it's still a sore spot with me. I shouldn't have lashed out at you, though."

He slowly puts down the bone and turns to me. Haeden's eyes are narrow, the look on his face tight. I wince, expecting him to give me an earful of how pissed he is.

But he only moves toward the furs and sits down next to me. We're both silent for a long moment, and then he says, "When the sky-claw pulled you into his mouth and flew away, I thought my world was over. I put my blade to my breast and was ready to follow you to the next world."

I swallow, then nod.

"I did not do that for Zalah." His voice is achingly gentle. "I would not do that for anyone else. But you, Jo-see, I would follow."

My eyes brim and hot tears start to slide down my cheeks. I nod again, because what else can I say? He's right—I was looking for words when, all along, he's been a man of actions. Words are easy to say, but actions are everything.

He reaches up and gently brushes the tears from my face. "I have never had a mate before, Jo-see. I will not always do the right thing. I will not always give you the words you feel you need." He cups my chin and forces me to look up at him. "But make no mistake—if you leave this world, I will not be long behind, because I cannot live without you."

I burst into tears and fling my arms around his neck.

Who needs a few love words when you have a guy like Haeden?

CHAPTER NINETEEN
Haeden

ONE WEEK LATER

It takes many, many days for the resonance to sing through our systems. Perhaps it is because we have both denied it for so long that it is now insisting upon regular matings to feed its need for Jo-see to carry my kit. I am glad to comply. Mating with my female is a joy, and filling her with my seed seems to fill my heart as well. We explore each other over the days, learning what makes the other aroused. I learn that Jo-see's ankles are very sensitive, and so are her bountiful teats—which she insists are quite small. I learn that when she starts repeating my name over and over, her cunt will start to milk my cock hard, and the pleasure doubles. I learn that she loves to wake me up with her mouth on my cock.

I shamelessly enjoy that, as well.

But after two hands of days in which Jo-see and I do nothing but sleep, eat, and mate, I am ready to leave the cave and turn homeward. This hunter cave is sufficient, but it is cramped and the winds blow right through late at night, which sets my small mate to shivering against me. The furs need a good airing after our repeated matings, and we are low on rations. I can always go hunting, but I worry about leaving my mate alone for long periods of time. Every time I think of leaving her behind, I see the sky-claw swooping low and snatching her away, and I head back into the cave and hug my female tight against my chest.

And then we mate frantically once again.

Jo-see and I must return to the tribal caves, though. If Harloh and Rukh have not yet sent hunters out in search of our trail, the tribe will eventually wonder why we have not returned from visiting the elders' cave. And I must warn them about the sky-claws that have appeared. Raahosh takes his mate, Leezh, out hunting with him, and they must be careful.

Above all, we must rescue the females in the cave. Jo-see reminds me of this daily, but I have not forgotten. I just will not put her in danger to save them.

So as my mate sleeps against me, her cheek pressed to my chest, I lie in bed with her and think as I stroke her soft mane. I contemplate ways that I might travel back to the tribe with my mate safely at my side. She cannot walk back; I still have nightmares of her being snatched away again. I consider a sled, but she can be plucked as easily from the top of a sled as she can from walking. And I cannot leave her alone in the cave as I head back. We are still two or three days of slow travel from the tribal caves.

So I ponder.

She makes a soft waking noise and then nuzzles at my chest. My cock gets hard and my khui awakens in my breast. The painful urgency is gone, and I hope it means that my kit is even now growing inside Jo-see's body. The thought fills me with pleasure and terror both. She *must* be brought safely back to the caves. My own safety is nothing compared to hers.

"Is it morning?" Jo-see murmurs. She doesn't get up, only flings a small arm over my chest and hides her eyes in the crook of my shoulder. She clings to me like a kit. Amused, I imagine standing up and seeing if she would crawl atop me and hold on, her arms around my neck so I can carry her.

My eyes widen.

That is the solution.

"We're going to what?" Jo-see's mouth opens in shock as I pack her things into my backpack and then hoist it over my shoulder.

"I am going to carry you," I tell her. She's shrugging one of her furs around her, preparing to travel. One end trails on the ground because the fur was made to fit my larger body, and so I move forward and tuck it around her. "Like a kit. I made a wrap."

Her mouth drops open again. "You're going to carry me like a baby? Why?"

"Because you are small and easy to carry." I pull the fur forward, making a hood for her mane. "And while you are strapped to my chest, I will not have to worry about a sky-claw pulling you from the ground and devouring you."

"But . . . carrying?"

I nod and loop the full waterskins over my neck, settling them against my belt. Then I take the long length of fur that I have sewn to another and offer her one end. "I am going to put this around you and tuck it into my belt."

"Oh God, you even made a baby carrier!" She holds one end with a look of horror on her face. "You're not joking about any of this."

"I am not."

A short time later, Jo-see's arms are around my neck, her legs are around my hips, and the fur is wrapped tightly around the both of us, strapping her to my chest. Her cheeks are bright red and she wriggles against me in a way that makes me wonder how far we will manage to travel. I can feel her cunt resting against my cock through the furs, and my khui starts a humming song.

But she is safe this way, and her weight is nothing. I can walk with my cock aching in my breechcloth—have I not done so for more than a turn of the moon?

I take a few steps and she sucks in a little breath and clings to me tighter, her teats pushing against my chest. "This is . . . very personal," she says, a quiver in her voice. "I'm not sure if this is the best idea, or the worst."

I am not certain, either, but it will keep her safe.

We start out from the cave, my gait awkward but sure. A fresh snow has fallen and my steps crunch with every landing of my boots. All of this just confirms that my decision is a good one. The air is crisp and refreshing, but Jo-see shivers against me. It is colder than usual, which means the sky-claws will be hungry and seeking prey. Not my mate. Not this day.

I walk faster, one arm resting against her bottom to hold her in place. Her face is pressed up near mine, but she is silent. She does not seem happy with me carrying her, but I am pleased with my decision; now I can walk as fast as I need to, and she is safe. This is best. I jog a little, eager to get home and take my mate into our cave.

Jo-see's hands grip my leather vest tightly and she moans, burying her face against my neck.

I stop. "Jo-see?"

"I'm fine," she mumbles. "Carry on."

Her words are confusing. Her body is tense against mine—I can feel it—but she pretends otherwise? It concerns me, but we must leave the safety of the small hunter cave and start our journey home. She cannot hide in it forever and I will not leave her. So I press a hand to the small of her back, my other supporting her tailless bottom, and continue forward.

We walk, continuing on. The flat, open snow changes to spindly trees, and a distant cliff lines the edges of a valley. On the horizon, there is a herd of dvisti, and the churned snow here tells me that they came from this direction. I move to follow the herd, as it will be easier for a sky-claw to pick off a dvisti kit than a human, but I will not let my mate walk, regardless.

Her arms clench tighter around my neck and she moans again. I feel her thighs quiver around my hips, and a surge of lust grips me. A moment later, I smell her scent on the air.

She's aroused?

"Jo-see?"

"I know," she mumbles against my neck. "I'm sorry. I just . . . this position is really wild. Every step you take pushes me against your dick and I thought I could just kind of quietly endure it but why did you have to be so sexy?" Then, her small tongue flicks against my skin.

I nearly stumble. My cock is achingly hard at once, and my khui—quiet until now—begins a loud, insistent song. The need to claim my mate overwhelms me once more. We will not be able to travel if this continues, and it is a problem I am all too eager to resolve. I look around for something to lean my mate up against, and finding nothing suitable, I reach between us and begin to undo the waist-tie of my leggings.

She gasps and wiggles against me. "What are you doing?"

"I am going to pleasure my mate," I tell her. "Keep your arms tight around my neck."

"Oooh, we're stopping?"

"We are not stopping," I tell her. At least, that is my hope. I free my aching cock and my leggings slide to my thighs.

She notices this and a breathless giggle escapes her. "We're not going to get far with your pants around your knees."

"Hush," I tell her, nipping at her earlobe. I rather like having her against me like this—I do not tower over her this way. Our faces are close together, like in our furs at night. I fumble under her tunic to find the tie to her leggings, and her hand pushes mine out of the way so she can free herself. She shoves the material down, but not very far—her spread legs gripping me will not allow the leather to give much.

It does not matter; I can feel her warm cunt, smell her perfume on the air. I lick at her soft neck even as I take my cock in hand and guide it into her warmth. I sink into her easily—she is wet and eager. Jo-see cries out when I enter her, arms tightening around my neck. Her thighs squeeze against me and she moans my name. It is a tight fit like this, but thrilling. The smallest rocking motion of my hips makes her slam down on my cock, and my spur glides through her folds, hitting the third nipple that makes her cry out with such excitement.

"Damn," she breathes into my ear, and tries to raise her hips in an awkward bounce. She wants more.

I grip her body, anchoring her to me, and begin to thrust. Not deep strokes, but small, quick motions, my hands pulling her down onto my cock with each surge of my hips forward.

She cries out again and clings to my neck as we move together. She doesn't last long; I don't, either. The khui makes us desperate with our need, and once she comes and her cunt begins to squeeze around me, I thrust harder, releasing inside her with a ferocity that surprises me.

Every time with my Jo-see, it is better. It does not matter how fast or how slow we go, we burn hot for each other and it is always, always good. I wrap my arms tight around her, holding her against me as I pant to catch my breath.

"Whew," she says after a moment, giving me a dazed look. "That was intense." She leans forward and presses a kiss to my mouth. "But awesome. Maybe there's something to being carried after all."

"It is not that," I say. "It is that my female is insatiable for her male."

She gasps, then giggles and mock-slaps my shoulder. "Don't turn this around on me, you *show-vuh-nist*!"

I do not know the word, but her meaning is plain, as is the smile on her face. I give her an affectionate nuzzle and then reach between us to lift her off my cock. We are both sticky with our release, and I grab a handful of snow from the ground and clean us off, despite my mate's squeals of protest. Then I tie my laces again, one handed. The knot is not as tight as it could be, but it doesn't matter. I suspect, due to the pleasant hum of our khuis, that this will occur more than once. I leave Jo-see's leggings unlaced.

Once the leathers are secured around us, I heft my light mate back into my arms and on we go.

By the time we crest over the next valley, Jo-see shifts against me and I hear her khui begin to sing again.

"My mate?" I ask. "Do you need your male again?"

"What? No!" she squeals. "I'm fine! Ignore me."

Very well.

We continue on.

"Oooh," Jo-see moans again a short time later.

"Do you need your male?" I ask again. My cock is already ready for her.

"Not yet!" I continue on, and then she adds, "Maybe."

When we crest onto the next ridge, her "maybe" turns into a yes.

We do not travel far that day. But it is the most enjoyable travel I have ever had, and my mate is well pleased by the time we stop for the night.

Josie

"I see the cave in the distance," Haeden murmurs in my ear as I drowse against his chest. "Do you wish to walk in or shall I continue to carry my female?"

"I need to walk," I tell him, stifling a yawn. I'm exhausted. Between the marathon of five long days of travel, we've been stopping regularly to have sex, thanks to the awkward-but-delicious position that Haeden carries me in. I'm pretty sure we've had more sex in the last week than I've had in my entire life. No complaints here, but as I yawn, I think I'm ready to have a break from travel at the very least. It'll be good to be back in the cave, where others can help out when you're too tired to do everything yourself. Where there are other women to talk to when the guys disappear and go hunting. Where there are a bajillion babies to hug and kiss on.

And soon I'll have one of my own. Warmth floods through

me at the thought, and I squeeze Haeden's neck tightly and press a kiss to his check.

"Eh? One more time before we reach the caves? Insatiable female." He reaches between us and begins to undo the knot on his leggings.

"Wait, that wasn't what I meant," I protest. But when he nips my ear in that sexy way, I figure one more romp won't hurt matters. "Just a quick one," I amend, tugging at my own clothes.

He sinks into me and we work quickly. I've figured out that grabbing the front of his vest to anchor myself and letting him do all the heavy lifting works out best. Gravity does the rest, and within a span of a minute or two, I'm biting my lip and coming so hard that I'm seeing stars.

"My mate," he hisses into my ear possessively. "My Jo-see—"

"*Ho,*" calls out a distant voice. "Haeden? Jo-see?"

I squeal in horror and shift against Haeden, just as he comes. Oh my God, someone's going to see him nailing me and then it'll be all over the cave. "Babe," I say in his ear. "They're going to see us—"

"*I need a moment,*" he bellows.

My ears ring but I'm glad he said something. I bury my face against his neck as his entire body shivers with the force of his orgasm. He bucks one last time and then nuzzles my cheek. "I should put you down."

It's sweet that he sounds strangely reluctant to do so. I press a kiss to his face and then slowly peel off of him. "Love you, baby."

He still doesn't grasp my human need to say what he thinks is obvious, but when he grabs a handful of my hair and gives me another fierce, breathtaking kiss, I know he means it just as much as I do.

Then we straighten our clothing and Haeden tucks me under his protective arm—even though I'm assured that no sky-claws come this far over the mountains—and we go to meet the hunter waiting for us. To my relief, the big blue shape on the horizon has given us some space and headed back down the track-covered paths leading toward the tribal cave. There's a plume of smoke in the distance and I feel a strange pang of happiness at the sight of it. To think I wanted to leave and never come back. A lot has changed in a few weeks.

I touch my stomach, wondering if even more has changed than I imagined. I really, really hope so. I think of Haeden's baby in my stomach. I think of us as a family and it makes me shiver with happiness.

He pulls me closer and tugs the furs over my chest closed. "Cold? We will be home soon."

"I'm good." I loop my arm around his waist, reaching for his tail. "I promise."

"Are you anxious?"

I consider this. I am returning home failed in my mission to defeat my cootie. But I'm also really happy the mission didn't work. I know everyone's going to be watching us like hawks to see how we react to each other. Ideally I'd like another month alone with my man, maybe get a bit more of the frenzied fucking out of our systems and settle into being a couple, but I keep thinking of those two girls in the pods back in metlak and sky-claw territory. They need a rescue. And really, I can handle a few people smirking because I finally got laid. "Not nervous," I tell him. "You?"

He snorts as if the question is ridiculous, and I grin.

"Ho," the other calls again as we approach, raising a hand. I can tell from the long, smooth hair and the shade of blue that it's Salukh, Tiffany's mate. I'm suddenly eager to see my bestie. Up until she mated with Salukh, she'd been my roomie from day one on the ice planet and I've missed her more than anyone else.

I wave back.

He jogs toward us and I see his eyes widen a bit at the sight of Haeden's arm around my shoulders. I guess it is a little surprising to see us so snuggly. I'm not even bothered by that, strangely. I don't care. I'm happy and no one's going to burst my bubble.

"It is good to see the both of you," Salukh says as he approaches. He leans over to clap Haeden on the shoulder and smiles at me. "Many have been worried. I think if you were not back in another moon, the chief would have sent us to find you."

Haeden makes an irritated sound in his throat. "Jo-see is safe with me. Vektal would not send anyone because he knows I am a good hunter. There is no need for a rescue."

Salukh just gives us a calm smile and takes Haeden's overloaded pack from his shoulder, slinging it onto his own. "Of course." That's just how Salukh is—he's chill. Nothing bothers him.

"How's Tiff?" I ask as we head down to the cave. "She have morning sickness?"

"She is very good," Salukh says, grinning over at me. "No sickness at all."

"That bitch. It figures." I smile. Tiffany is like perfection come to life. She's beautiful, smart, talented, and nice to boot. I'd hate her if I didn't love her like the sister I never had. "She's probably going to be the most perfect pregnant person ever."

"Not in my eyes," Haeden says, his tone a little surly as if the very thought irritates him.

And that just makes me even happier. I give his tail a little squeeze (which, okay, probably arouses him).

We make it into the cave, and the scents of smoke and roasting meat, the chatter of people, and a baby's cry fill me with a happy pang of homesickness.

"Oh my God," someone squeals. "It's Josie and Haeden!"

A moment later, we're surrounded by people determined to hug and greet us. I'm smothered in a wave of people as Nora, Stacy, Ariana, Megan, and Georgie take their turns hugging me. Liz shows up next and plops her baby into my arms. "Because you'll want to see Raashel before her mommy, right?" She smirks. "Get that practice in?"

I blush. "Maybe."

"Oooh, someone sealed the deal!" She leans in and puts a hand to her ear. "I don't hear your cootie humming like a freight train anymore."

"Jeez, Liz, why don't you be obvious about it?" I say, but I'm smiling. Raashel looks bigger than the last time I saw her, a thick shock of black hair sticking up and pulled into a tiny leather bow atop her head. She's so stinking cute.

"Didn't you know? Obvious is my middle name!" She gives me a half-squeeze. "I'm glad you're back and everything worked out."

"How are you sure it all worked out?" I ask, curious. I haven't even had a chance to say much of anything.

"Because you're all goofy grins?" Georgie butts in, shifting her baby on her hip.

"And Haeden keeps looking over here like he'd like to snatch you by the hair and drag you back to his cave, Neanderthal style?"

I glance over, and sure enough, Haeden's giving me a scorching hot look even as the other hunters greet him and chatter his ear off. I blush again.

Then Tiffany appears, and Kira, and Harlow, who's come to the main cave for a few weeks in the hopes that I would return. I'm handed babies to hug and I admire Megan's baby bump. She's so close to giving birth, and Claire is just now starting to show, and everyone can't stop talking and hugging me. It's wonderful.

I realize we're a family after all, the twelve of us. I never had a family in the past, and it's like fate has handed me a brand-new one full of eclectic people.

I'm so happy I could cry, but that would upset Haeden, so I just beam at everyone and hug the babies.

"So what made you run?" Harlow asks, handing over her little Rukhar for his turn at having my attention. "And did you bring back my glass disc? I need that for the next rock cutter."

"It's in my bag," I tell her, and press a kiss to Rukhar's little blue cheek. Of all the babies, he's the smallest but also looks the most sa-khui. "As for the running, it's a long story. Look at you, Rukhar! You're getting so big!"

As if to prove that he's not going to fall for my clumsy attempt to change the topic, Rukhar grabs a handful of my hair and yanks, burbling. I wince and detangle it from his little fist.

"I'm glad you're back, though I was starting to wonder if you'd ever return. You can be a little . . . stubborn."

I grin, even though Rukhar's bobbing fist just yanked out several strands of hair by the roots. "I wasn't planning on it at first."

"What changed your mind?" Kira asks.

Oh shit. No one else knows about the other girls yet or that I found the crashed ship. And Kira . . . if she finds out there were other pods, broken pods—she'll be devastated. She brought down the ship by destroying the crew, and while I haven't shed a tear for the kidnapping, rapey, murderous bastards, it's different when you realize there were humans on board. "Um, it's a long story and one I should probably tell the chief first."

Georgie steps forward and hands her baby to Liz. "I'll get Vektal. Meet me in my cave?"

I nod and give Rukhar another kiss before reluctantly handing him back. My stomach is in knots. It's a dual-edged sword, the finding of two more girls. On one hand, there are still many, many unmated men in the tribe who would love the chance at a family. On the other hand, I wonder at how this will affect poor Kira. And I think of the recent fighting over Tiffany's attention—these poor girls are going to be mobbed.

But that doesn't mean we shouldn't rescue them, of course.

I glance around for Haeden. He's standing a short distance away with three other hunters and they talk quietly. He turns the moment I spot him and gives me another possessive look, as if he's already done with all this "reunion" stuff and can't wait to drag me back to our cave. Boy, Liz wasn't wrong about that.

I step away from the others, heading toward the cave that Georgie and Vektal share. Haeden immediately comes to my side and I feel warm with pleasure when he joins me. I lean in close to him. "I told Georgie that we need to talk to her and Vektal privately about the ship and the girls. I worry it's going to upset Kira."

He nods thoughtfully. "And the unmated males will be eager to set out in the hopes of claiming one of the women. Some of them are without hope now that you are mine." He rubs a knuckle on my cheek. "They will have to wait long seasons for Farli to come of age, or even longer for Esha, Talie, and the others."

Considering that Talie's a newborn and Farli's probably thirteenish? Yeah, that's a long time. "So what do we do?"

"We take it to our chief and let him handle it," Haeden says. "It will be his responsibility, not ours."

Maybe it's selfish, but I'm glad of that. I'm tired of all the burdens and the drama. I just want to curl up with my mate by the fire and relax. I nod and lean against his arm as we head into the cave.

No one's inside, which means Georgie's still out hunting down her mate. Haeden's big hand smooths my hair, as if he desperately needs to touch me. I get that. It's weird being back surrounded by all these people after weeks of being alone. I know that there will probably be a celebration tonight for our mating. I know that people are going to be watching us and asking questions for the next while, because they're nosy. I know Haeden and I are going to have to go back out to the ship to rescue the girls, because we're the ones that know where it is. All of this just makes me tired.

Haeden's fingers lace through mine, and even though it's a little strange since I have more fingers than him, it's still really nice. And as long as he's by my side?

I'm down for whatever.

CHAPTER TWENTY
Haeden

I let Jo-see do the telling of the strange ship and the pods she found inside. It is her discovery, and so it is hers to share. Even if it was not, I am content to remain at my mate's side and simply watch her talk with her friend Shorshie. She is enthusiastic, tucking a strand of her soft mane behind her ear as she gestures with her hands. Her voice grows loud as she speaks, as if, if she is louder, the words will come out faster. It does not bother me as it did in the past. I find it . . . amusing. I touch her leg to let her know she is loud, and she casts a smile in my direction and lowers her voice, and I am filled with pride at my mate.

She is perfect.

"Two more females like you and Georgie? I am pleased. The males without mates will be pleased." Vektal gives Jo-see a curious look. "Why is this a problem?"

"Because everyone on that ship was killed," Jo-see says, glancing over at me again. "And I don't know how Kira will take it."

He shrugs and rubs his chin, glancing at me. "She will be pleased we can save two females, will she not?"

My thoughts are the same as his, but Shorshie looks to her mate. "I think it's more complicated than that. I can talk to her. Maybe she will want to go with the hunters on the journey. Make penance for her crimes, though I can't say that I'm sorry they died, considering what they did to us. But Kira might feel differently."

Jo-see nods. "That's a good idea. I'll go, too."

I speak up. "No."

Everyone turns to me.

"No? What do you mean, no?" Now, Jo-see is frowning.

I ignore her show of temper. "I mean no. You will stay here in the safety of the cave. I will go."

She sticks her tongue out at me and makes a *thbbt* noise. "You're not the boss of me."

"I am your mate," I tell her evenly, doing my best to be stern and failing. A smile curves my mouth when she sticks her tongue out again. "Your mate that pulled you from the belly of a sky-claw—"

"Wait, what?" Shorshie says.

Vektal's expression darkens. "Sky-claws?"

I nod. "The cold has driven them over the mountains."

"Then no females go," Vektal says staunchly. "We send hunters, and only the biggest and strongest."

"What the heck is a sky-claw?" Shorshie interrupts. "And how did Josie get in the belly of one?"

Jo-see shoots me a frustrated look and gives a short explanation of the sky-claw and how she cut forth from its belly and fell into my arms. She shudders as she tells it, and I caress her back to comfort her. I understand her bad memories; I still wake up at night with nightmares of my mate snatched from my arms.

"I realize it's dangerous," Shorshie protests. "But—"

"No," says Vektal, crossing his arms over his chest. He looks at me and I nod slowly. On this, we are agreed. It is too dangerous to send a female out, especially one of the small humans.

"You didn't even hear what I had to say," Shorshie snaps.

"I know what you will say, my resonance." He looks at his mate. "You will tell me that a human female must go. I will say no. You will say I am wrong. But I am not wrong and it is too dangerous. If what they say is true, we nearly lost Jo-see. I will not lose another, not a mother with a kit."

"All right then, if you've got this all figured out," Shorshie says, anger in her voice. "Who are you sending?"

He looks over at me. "Haeden will go."

I nod at my chief. Of course. It will be frustrating to leave my mate, but she wants the females rescued, so there is no choice.

"We will send the unmated males, since they will give us no rest unless we do. So Hassen, Bek, Rokan, Taushen, Harrec, Vaza if he wishes to go."

Shorshie's brows go up and she nods as if impressed. "And which one of those men is going to open the pods and get the women out?"

Vektal opens his mouth to respond, and then scowls at his mate.

"Exactly," she says. "You need a human to go. Not just because it will be less scary for the women if another human is there and can talk to them—"

"We can speak human—"

"You can speak English," she corrects. "What if they're Spanish? French? Marlene is French, remember? We're just lucky she knows English, too. Anyhow, that doesn't matter. What matters is, if you get there, you need someone that can open the pod. You need a human. Is it dangerous? Yes. Does it need to be done? Absolutely." She crosses her arms over her chest, mimicking his glower. "Oh, and you can't send all the single guys, because they are going to scare the ever-loving crap out of those poor girls."

His expression hardens as he watches his mate. After a moment, he looks over at us. "We will need to speak privately."

I nod and get to my feet. "Tell me when I shall go, my chief. I am ready."

"You are *not* going without me," Jo-see protests. She stands and lets me lead her out of the cave.

I head for our cave at the back of the new tunnel, letting her speak her thoughts. She is unhappy at the thought of being parted from my side, and I am pleased by that, even if it does not override my need to keep her safe. She will stay here, and that is the answer.

People watch us curiously as we head to our cave, Jo-see bickering at me as I hold her hand. I am smiling, and I think several in the tribe are as surprised by that as they are that I am listening to Jo-see's endless stream of angry words. In the past, we did our best to ignore each other.

But in the past, she was not my mate. I did not try to know her like I do now.

"You're not listening to me," Jo-see says as we enter our cave. I have made it a cozy home for us even though she would not stay there with me. The bed is thick with furs, enough for a sakhui and a small human mate to curl up at his side. The firepit is lined with perfectly spaced rocks, and my supplies are neatly stored in woven baskets. Someone—likely Salukh—has set my traveling pack down in the corner.

"I am listening," I tell her even as I move the privacy screen in front of the mouth of our cave. With it up, no one will disturb us.

"I have to go—"

"No, you do not. The chief will send another female, but it will not be you." I move to my mate's side and peel her worn furs from her shoulders. She is wearing several layers, and I remove the first one and toss it aside.

Jo-see puts her hands on her hips. "I'm an adult. You can't control me, Haeden. This is bullshit."

"I am the mate that almost lost you." I finish unwinding the thick furs from around her body and peel away her second cloak of shaggy dvisti fur. "I am the one who will cry over your body if I lose you. And I will not let that happen."

She gives me an unhappy look. "I should have some say in this, you know."

"Whatever say you have does not matter, because you have my kit in your belly." I put a hand to her flat stomach and meet her gaze. "It would destroy me to lose you, Jo-see. I cannot imagine losing you both."

Her lower lip thrusts out slightly, and I sense victory. "It's going to take days for you to get there, and days for you to come back. Longer with the new women. I don't want to be apart from you for that long."

I pull her close and nip at that full lower lip of hers. "Knowing you are here will bring me back faster. I will make them run through the snow. I will insist the human females be carried like fresh meat."

A small reluctant giggle escapes her at that.

I kiss her cheek, then her jaw. My soft, sweet Jo-see likes to be kissed everywhere, and I am all too happy to please her. "And we will not take Vaza, because he is old. We will take young, strong males and whatever human woman has the longest legs. And every night after a long day of running, they will complain that I drive them too hard, but it will not matter, because the only thing that matters is coming back to my mate."

She sighs and wraps her arms around my neck. "All right, but you can't go explore the island without me, okay?"

"I will go nowhere that I do not have to." I pull the laces of her tunic free. "And for now, I wish to go nowhere but to bed with my mate."

"It's the middle of the day, Haeden!"

"An excellent time to enjoy resonance, is it not?"

Her hand cups my cock through my breechcloth, and it seems that we both agree.

Josie

The group gets ready to leave the next morning. It's been decided that Hassen, Taushen, Bek, Rokan, and my Haeden will go. Raahosh will accompany them because he is the best tracker. The human selected is Claire, initially, but Kira has put up a quiet stink to Georgie, and when the party gets ready to leave in the morning, it's Kira and Aehako who join the group. Claire and her mate will stay behind.

Kira brings Kae to me. "Can you watch over her while I'm gone? Stacy will feed her, and she's starting on solids with a not-potato mash, but I don't want Stacy to have to juggle two infants." She presses a kiss to her baby's head and she looks upset, but determined.

"Of course. Hurry back."

Her smile is grim. "Oh, I'm going to make them rush. I can't bear the thought of leaving Kae behind for longer than I have to."

"You don't have to go," I protest.

"I want to see," Kira says quietly. "I need to know."

I nod and hug Kae close. Poor Kira's been silently distraught. She wants to know just how many girls she might have accidentally murdered. I get that. I do. So I volunteer to go again. "I'm perfectly fine with going and reporting back."

"Absolutely not," Claire says at my side. She sets her pack down on the ground, ready to stay. "You're preggers."

"So are you!"

"I'm also half a foot taller than you," Claire points out. "And stronger."

I stick my tongue out at her because everything she says is the truth. Claire's always been a quiet one, but since mating to Ereven, she smiles a lot more and seems a lot more lighthearted. She looks pleased even though she's not going on the journey. Pregnancy hormones, I guess.

And okay, I'm a little excited about the whole preggers thing. Because she's right—I've missed my period. Granted, it might be due to the recently lost IUD. Or it might be that all the stress of the traveling caused me to skip. Whatever it is, I haven't had it and I'm hoping desperately that I'm pregnant, too.

But . . . I still want to go with Haeden and the others. "What about . . . what about the sky-claws? I bet they can snatch Kira just as easily as me. We probably weigh the same."

Kira looks over her shoulder at her mate. Aehako moves forward and ties a thick rope cord to her waist as a belt, and then ties the other end around his hips. Tied together. Of course. If one gets snatched, the other will be dragged along. It's a smart solution, and I kind of wonder if Haeden deliberately didn't do it because he wanted to carry me.

Carry me, that is, and then pause to fuck me every half hour. I press a hand to my heated cheeks. "It's still not fair," I protest.

"It'll be fine," Claire says, smiling encouragingly at me. She pats me on the shoulder. "I know you're disappointed but I'm sure they'll go as fast as they can."

I grumble a response but then Haeden emerges from our cave and my gaze goes to him. The man is positively mouthwatering as he strides through the central living area, his spear in hand. His movements are graceful but strong, and the fur cloak over his shoulders is lightweight, as the snow doesn't bother him like it does me. It barely hides his strong chest and I think of the next two weeks and how I'm not going to be able to sleep with my head pillowed on that rock-hard chest or wake up holding his tail. For the next two weeks, I won't be able to have sex with my man, to hear that wicked little snort he makes when he's amused by something, won't have his touch.

It is going to be a long freaking two weeks.

I give him a mournful look as he approaches and, to my chagrin, the waterworks start. I sniff, wiping at my eyes as I jiggle the baby.

He pulls me against him, mindful of Kae, and tosses his spear aside so he can wipe away my tears. "My Jo-see. It is a long trip but it is a worthwhile one. Do not weep."

"Of course I'm going to weep," I say crankily, leaning into his touch. "I miss you already and you haven't even gone yet."

"But I will be back," he says in a low, husky voice. "And we will start our life together."

"I suppose I do have reunion sex to look forward to," I say, trying to make him smile. He looks so somber, like he's just as bummed to leave me as I am to have him go.

"And lots of *frankissing*." He leans close and nips at my ear, then whispers, "All over. Even your ankles."

I smack at his chest but my cootie, the most obvious cootie on the planet, is purring loud and happily for all to hear. Someone nearby snickers. Screw them. This is my mate, and he's leaving me for two weeks. I curl my fingers in the front of his vest and press a kiss to his mouth. "You hurry home fast or I'm tossing you aside."

He snorts. "Bring someone else to your furs and I will ram my spear up his nethers."

That shouldn't amuse me nearly as much as it does. His jealousy keeps the smile on my face even when we say our goodbyes and the tribe members left in the cave linger at the entrance to watch them go. The group begins up the snowy hills and finally heads off over the horizon. One big, familiar body remains on the ridge for a long moment after the others disappear. He raises a hand, and I raise mine back.

Then, Haeden's gone and I'm left in the cave with the rest.

As if on cue, Kae starts to cry, wailing in my arms. Yeah, I know how that feels, Kae.

I turn around and Liz is right there, holding her baby. She takes one look at me and bursts into tears.

My eyes widen. "Liz? You okay?" I'd hold out my arms for Raashel but I've got a wailing Kae on my hands already.

She wipes her face with a corner of Raashel's blanket. "God, I'm glad I held in all the bawling and snot until they left, or I'd never live it down." She sniffs hard.

I give her a wary look, perching Kae on my hip and giving her a bounce. "Is everything okay?" Liz is normally the cut-up, the wise-ass that nothing gets to. Her mate is leaving with the others, and I admit I'm a little surprised Liz didn't volunteer to go with them. Sure, she has the baby, but she's left Raashel with Nora or Stacy before for a day or two. "Are you and Raahosh . . . you know, good?"

Her face crumples and she swipes at her nose again, then presses a kiss to the baby's bumpy little forehead. "Yeah, we're awesome. I'm just . . ." She sighs and leans in. "If you tell anyone, I'm going to skewer you like a quill-beast and roast your ass over the fire."

"I won't say anything."

She wipes at her face again and forces a smile to her lips. "It's just hormones. I resonated to Raahosh again. Bun number two is officially in the oven."

CHAPTER TWENTY-ONE
Haeden

As I promised my mate, I set a bruising pace over the mountains. The others do not complain—Raahosh is just as eager to return to his own mate, and the unmated men are eager to see the new human women. The only one that seems displeased is Aehako, who watches his human mate carefully and snarls at me when she needs to rest. Kira never complains, however, and is grimly determined to continue on as fast as she can go.

I miss Jo-see fiercely. As one day crawls into the next, I obsess with thoughts of her smile, her laugh, the soft feel of her skin against mine. The small sounds she makes when her cunt clenches around my cock. My khui is silent for the first time in forever, and I hate it. Now that I have her, there is no going back to the half-dead state I existed in before. Even though we are parted, I know I have her to return home to, and it spurs my steps.

There are signs of both metlaks and sky-claws the closer we get to the abandoned ship. More half-eaten dvisti litter the landscape, and a few metlak carcasses. We see nothing in the skies, but Kira draws closer to her mate for the rest of the day. We are somber that evening as we crowd close to the hunter cave. It is not big enough for most of us to sleep in, so Kira and Aehako sleep inside with a small fire and the rest of us keep watch at the mouth of it.

We sit around the small fire and the talk is constantly of the women. What color mane do we think they will have? Will they have the attractively dark skin like Salukh's mate or the strangely speckled skin like Rukh's mate Har-loh? Will someone resonate immediately or will there be a wait? Over and over, the men ask the same questions. They irritate me, because it makes me miss my sweet Jo-see even more. I realize how lucky I am that my khui chose hers. I picture her back in our cave, taking care of Kira's kit. My chest aches with pleasure at the thought and I rub it absently.

There is a long pause around the fire as the conversation dies. Then, one speaks up.

"Do you suppose there are more than two humans?" Taushen asks, eagerness in his voice. When the group is silent, he continues. "I hope that one will resonate to me."

"I am your elder," Harrec protests yet again. They have had the same argument for days. "If anyone is to resonate to a human female, it is me."

"But I am a good provider," Taushen retorts. "What do you think, Haeden?"

"I do not care."

"But—"

With a snarl, I get up from the campfire and stalk away. It is the same questions, over and over again, and they look to me for answers. I have none, but it does not stop them from asking. Do they not realize that I do not care a bit for new females? That I would gladly abandon them for season after season if it meant more time with my mate? The only thing that keeps me on this journey is the knowledge that Jo-see wants them rescued.

"What has crawled up his tail?" Harrec grumbles as I grab my spear and decide to patrol the area.

"Resonance," says Taushen.

"He misses his mate," cuts in Raahosh. "He is not the only one. The longer this goes on, the longer we are all away from home." I glance back in time to see him give a sour look to the men. "I expect you all to hike a little faster tomorrow."

I snort with amusement and go off to patrol the area.

The next day, the weather is blustery and colder than usual. Kira shivers despite the number of furs piled on her, and I can see the displeasure on Aehako's normally smiling face. His mate has risked her safety to come see this done. Snowflakes fly on the wind, and the drifting snow grows deeper by the hour, the skies grayer. Raahosh, always ahead of the group scouting the trail, comes back to meet us midmorning. He heads straight to me. "There is something you should see."

The others remain with Kira, and I jog ahead through the snow with him, over the next ridge. There, half-buried in new snow, is the strange cave. The blinking red light has burned a cave into the snow around it.

Scattered bodies of sky-claws litter the ground before it.

I frown down at the sight, an uneasy feeling churning in my gut. "Dead?"

"Freshly dead. The snow is falling thick, but there are many small hills on the ground." He gestures at the area near the cave. "Those might be more." He looks over at me. "What are your thoughts?"

I rub my jaw, gazing down at the dead sky-claws. They litter the ground like dung chips after a dvisti herd. "I am thinking I am glad I did not bring my mate on this journey."

He nods. "And I, the same. I do not like this. Are they drawn to the scent of the humans?"

"I did not smell anything, and I was there for many days with Jo-see."

"Metlaks, then?"

I squint at the dead corpses. Their wings are spread in the snow, and there is very little blood. Most of the bodies seem to be piled close to the red blinking light. "I do not think so? They do not seem smart enough to kill so many sky-claws. How do they pull them down to the earth?"

He shrugs. "It is not normal. I do not like it."

I do not like it, either, but we are wasting time. "The sooner we get the human females, the sooner we leave this place and return to our mates."

Raahosh grunts agreement, and we return to the others to tell them of the strange discovery. Aehako pulls his mate under his arm, clearly worried. But we are close, and I will not allow us to stop now, not when it means we are this much closer to returning home. I grip my spear and shake it at the hunters. "Follow me. Everyone watch the skies and remain alert."

It is a short walk to the strange cave, but it feels much longer. Our group, normally full of trail conversation and the musings of the excited unmated hunters, is silent. Raahosh pokes at a few of the sky-claws as we pass, but they are frozen with cold, the bodies unmoving. There is very little blood, which is strange. If metlaks were truly hunting something as large as the sky-claws, there would be blood everywhere. They are not clean hunters. It adds to the worry I see on all faces.

But when we get inside the cave, it is just as I left it. The remains of the fire Jo-see and I left are undisturbed, and the hides I had intended to scrape sit in frozen bundles by the cave mouth. There is a fine scatter of snow that has blown in, and no tracks.

"No metlaks," Rokan says, and sniffs the air. "Storm will get worse before it gets better, though."

"Where are the females?" Hassen demands, looking around the cave-like room. He turns to look at Kira. "Can you find them?"

"My mate needs a fire and to rest," Aehako says, the look on his face protective. He keeps his arm locked around Kira's shoulders. "Once she is warm again, then we will look for the human females."

Taushen moves forward to protest. "But—"

"They have been here for seasons," Raahosh bites out. "What is one more day? One more hour? Calm yourselves."

"It's okay," Kira says, but she's shivering, her jaw clacking. "I c-can look. B-but it's really c-cold and I think they will n-need a f-f-fire to warm up, too."

Immediately, the hunters scramble to build the fire.

Raahosh gives me a sour look.

I just shake my head.

A short time later, Kira has warmed up by the fire, the snow on the floors has melted, and we watch as she runs her mittens along the back of the cave. It is the strange flat black stone like the other walls, but small lights are flashing in patterns. Two of them are green, the rest are red. Kira studies them and then presses her forehead against one, her shoulders sagging.

"What is it?" Hassen demands, frowning fiercely.

Aehako hovers by his mate, stroking her hair and murmuring. After a few words, he looks up and glances over at the nervous hunters. "Two pods," he says. "There are only two. The ones marked with red are empty."

"How does she know?" Taushen asks. "Maybe they are marked wrong?"

"I learned the language back on the other ship—the elders' cave." Kira's soft voice fills the tense cavern. She points at one of the bubbles, with red scribbles across the top. "They all say they're empty. All but these two." And she swipes at her cheek.

I remember my Jo-see's worry that Kira would be upset that more girls were in the ship and did not live. It is good that there are only two. I will tell her and she will smile with relief, much like Kira is now.

"Are the others well?" Rokan asks. "Will there be a problem freeing them?"

"I can do it," Kira says after a moment, and runs her hands over one of the dark, hard bubbles. "It's just finding the *releez hatsh*."

"What—" someone says, but then a hissing noise fills the cave. We grab our spears. Two rush forward while I watch the entrance. The hiss happens again and I realize it's behind me. I turn again and the cave wall is moving. Steam fills the air and then a form appears to fall forward. Kira extends her arms to catch the female, and Aehako rushes to help her.

The female looks like nothing but a blur of dark mane and pale, pale skin. She twitches and shivers, and her thin clothing sticks to her skin, outlining her form. I suppose she looks healthy enough, but she does not appeal to me. Not compared to my Jo-see. But one of the unmated hunters groans at the sight of her.

I snatch one of the furs from the fireside and move to cover the female up even as Kira pats her cheek and tries to wake her. I push the fur over her body and glare at the other hunters, who are watching her like, I imagine, the sky-claw watched my Jo-see before snatching her away. I do not like the desperate look in their eyes, especially Hassen. I recognize that feeling of despair; how many times did I go to sleep feeling the same?

The human females will need watching. "Is this one well?" I ask Kira.

"I think so," she says, and pats the human's cheek again. "Wake up. You are with friends."

The female's eyes flutter open and they are green circles floating in a sea of white. I shudder at the sight. She has no khui and it is a repulsive thing to see. The female whimpers at the sight of us, her gaze flicking with confusion and horror as she looks between us.

"Hold her, Aehako," Kira tells her mate. "Let us get the other girl out, too."

As they switch positions and the female continues to make frightened whimpers, I stand guard so the unmated males do not rush her and try to force resonance. Raahosh hands me a second fur and we stand guard as Kira opens the second pod and the other female falls forward. This one is pale-haired, like Leezh, and thicker and stronger-seeming than the other, though her movements are equally feeble.

She has the same dead eyes, though.

As I see them, I realize that returning back to my mate will be a longer journey than I imagined. The females cannot live long without a khui, which means tracking and hunting a sakohtsk. The enormous creatures are rare this far out of the valleys, so we must drag the sickly humans along with us, which will make things slow. Even then, I do not know if they will travel fast. They have been in the cave wall for a long time and they seem weak.

I exchange a look with Raahosh and it seems we are thinking the same thing, judging from the grim look on his face. Two frightened, squealing human females in need of a khui, sky-claws and metlaks in the area, and our band of hunters looking as if they would steal one of the females for themselves at any time?

It is going to be a long journey back.

CHAPTER TWENTY-TWO
Josie

THREE WEEKS LATER

I raise a knee and a fist in the air at the same time, then switch them, and begin to do the "Single Ladies" dance while humming the song under my breath. It doesn't matter that Kae is too young to know the lyrics—she's a fussy little turd of a baby and nothing quiets her other than a bit of singing. And since she watches me dancing with big, fascinated eyes while she sucks on her fist? Well, she's getting a little Beyoncé today. Sometimes I wish the dang kid liked Adele or something.

As I start into the second verse, Kae's face crumples and she begins to wail louder.

Well, shit. No singing today, it seems. "I know," I tell her, abandoning my song and scooping her up into my arms. "I miss your mommy, too. I miss my hunny-bunny. But crying doesn't bring him back faster. Trust me, I tried that."

I've been a shitstorm of weeping for the last few weeks, me and Liz both. Even with Kae to distract me, though, it's not enough. I miss my mate. I miss Haeden.

I want to tell him that I'm pregnant. I want to see the joy on his face when I tell him. I want him to hold me close and stroke my hair.

I want him to hold me down and fuck the daylights out of me.

I sigh and hitch Kae onto my hip, abandoning my cave in search of Stacy. Maybe a meal will calm the crying baby down.

But Stacy isn't in her cave. Nora isn't in hers. We're the three at the back of the new tunnel and they're normally at "home" due to the fact that they have small children and there are always more chores to be done. It's weird that they're gone. "Hello?" I call out, curious, and head down toward the main cave with Kae wailing in my ear. When I get there, though, the fire is un-attended and the space is mostly empty, except for Farli, who's dashing across the cave. "Where is everyone?"

She skids to a stop at the sight of me, her eyes wide. Bouncing behind her ankles is her pet, Chompy, and he grabs at her leather tunic and tugs on it. "You did not hear?"

"Hear what?" I ask, cranky. I move forward with Kae, rub-bing the baby's back patiently. It's not Kae's fault she misses her mommy. "I can't hear anything over—"

I stop, because a familiar hum starts in my breast.

I'm resonating. That means . . .

I look up at Farli in wonder. "They're home?"

She nods eagerly and waves me forward. "Come! They are heading down the ridge!"

I trot after her, trying not to jostle Kae, but with a squealing, angry baby in my arms, I can't move very fast. I settle for a power walk and head outside after Farli. It's brutally cold and I pull the blankets tighter over Kae's head, even though I doubt the cold bothers her as much as it does me.

Sure enough, there are a ton of people outside, and several

shapes on the horizon. I push through the crowd, looking for a familiar pair of horns, pale blue velvet skin, and a long, long braid. One smaller form breaks off from the group and races forward, but it's too small to be my mate. I realize a few seconds later that it's Kira, her arms out, and I hold Kae up for her.

She reaches me a few moments later, scoops the baby into her arms, and frantically presses kisses to Kae's tiny, horned little forehead. "Thank you," she tells me between kisses, and I'm not in the least bit surprised to see that Kae's stopped crying.

"Of course," I say, and try not to sound impatient as I peek behind her. It looks as if a few people on the ridge are arguing. Angry gestures are being made, and I'm pretty sure I recognize Haeden's big form up there. I want him to come down and greet me. I miss him so badly. I press a hand over my heart, where my cootie is purring with excitement. "How did it go?"

Kira nuzzles Kae's downy head. "I'll let Haeden tell you. It's been a long trip and I'm glad to be home."

I nod, keeping the smile on my face even as Aehako joins her, murmurs a greeting to me, and then they head for the cave. Kira looks exhausted and I know it's not an easy trip. But now I'm free of baby duties and can seek out my mate. I head up the ridge.

The cootie in my breast gets stronger as I approach . . . but so does the argument. An arm flails and then a fur hood is pushed back and I see a human woman, a stranger.

Just one?

I study her. She's got blonde, tangled hair and she's a little chunky. And she looks super, super pissed. Her nostrils flare with anger as one of the men standing near her tries to calm her. "This is bullshit!" she bellows, arm flailing. "I don't give a crap if you tell me that you guys are friendly. My sister is gone! I don't want to rest at the cave! I want to go fucking find her and the bastard that stole her and—"

"Let us be calm," Rokan is saying, and Taushen hovers near the woman, a concerned look on his face. Haeden's arms are crossed over his chest, as if he's sick of all the bullshit already.

As I approach, Haeden turns.

"Hey, buddy, I am talking to you," the woman yells at my mate. "Don't turn away! My sister—"

Haeden raises a hand in the air, indicating silence. To my surprise, they all go silent. He turns away from them and starts to stride toward me. I'm pretty sure romantic-movie music is playing in my head at this moment, because he's so handsome and so wonderful and all mine and oh God I've missed him so much.

I burst into happy tears.

He doesn't stop as he strides toward me, just grabs me in his arms and hauls me against him, like he carried me back when we were traveling. I wrap my legs around his hips, my arms around his neck, and start kissing the hell out of him. He smells like smoke and sweat and travel and he tastes better than anything. My tongue slicks against his frantically, our cooties purring in time.

"Where's he going?" the woman cries, desperate. "What about my sister?"

"He is busy," Rokan says with amusement as we leave. "He has a resonance mate to tend to."

Haeden and I continue kissing as he carries me back to the cave. Around us there are people celebrating, the chatter of happy voices, and dozens of people talking all at once. My Haeden doesn't stop, just continues to carry me through the cave and back to our own private den. There will be a celebration tonight for the new woman—and her sister, though I'm not sure why she's missing—but Haeden and I will likely not be there.

Can't say I'm disappointed.

By the time we make it to our blankets, I'm so aroused I'm wiggling against him in anticipation. God, this has been the longest wait, and if he doesn't "mate" me in the next minute, I'm going to lose my ever-loving mind.

But my man, bless his heart, raises his head when we enter the cave and sniffs, surprised. "It smells like kit in here. Kit dung and sour milk."

I press frantic kisses to his jaw, his neck, everywhere I can reach. "Kae's a bit of a fusser when her mommy isn't here." And a pooper. And a barfer. It's been a long three weeks.

He grunts. "It stinks."

"Well, get used to it," I say, grabbing one of his horns and tugging him forward playfully. "Because you're going to be experiencing it yourself soon. Well, okay, not soon. More like fourteen months. But it sounds better the other way."

Haeden's eyes widen and his grip tightens on my hips. "You are with kit? You are sure?"

I pat my chest, where my cootie's vibrating. "Would this thing lie to you?" When he continues to stare at me in shock, I add, "And I haven't had my female, er, time of the, uh, moon." You know, I've never asked what the heck the sa-khui call it when a woman has her period. "Red tent. Aunt Flo. Whatever."

He pauses, and then a moment later, he sets me on the ground, then hugs me against him in a crushingly tight embrace, his face against my breast. "My Jo-see," he whispers, and his voice is choked. I can feel his face on my purring chest, and I have a sneaking suspicion that his eyes are wet.

And hey, he's not the only one. I sniff hard and stroke his long braid. "This is what we wanted, right?"

He lifts his head and gazes up at me with shiny eyes. "All I wanted was you."

Oh shit, now I'm really going to bawl. I swipe at my eyes. "But you want a baby, right?"

He presses a kiss to my flat, clothed stomach. "Almost more than anything."

And that's incredibly sweet. Almost, because he wants *me* more than anything. "I'm just warning you, though, if we don't have sex in the next five minutes, I'm going to lose my mind."

Haeden tugs at my tunic and begins to unwrap me like a present. Every inch of skin he exposes, he kisses and flicks his tongue over—more *frankissing*, as he likes to say. "There will be a celebration for the new female," he says. "Her name is Mad-ee."

Maddie? "Don't care." I stroke his horns lovingly. "They can celebrate without us."

"And a hunt for the missing female. Li-lah." He reveals my boobs and grazes his lips over one nipple.

"That's nice," I say dreamily, pushing him toward our furs. "I don't want to go. You don't, either. Let someone else go find her."

He lifts his head and gives me a heated, playful look. "I am surprised you want me with you, Jo-see. I thought you would be glad to have your leave of me after so many days of being my mate."

"Are you kidding? I missed you like crazy." I lie back in the furs and he crawls over me, tugging at the drawstring of his leggings.

"Even though I am unpleasant and surly?"

"That's just you being you. And I like you," I tell him, smoothing a hand over one big arm. His cock is freed from his leggings and he's pushing mine down. "You can be surly all you want to everyone else as long as you're good to me."

"I will always be good to you," he says solemnly, all traces of playfulness gone from his hard face. "You are my life, my heart, my everything."

I wrap my arms around him as he pushes into me. If I'm his heart, he's my soul. We're one, and we're together.

Nothing else matters. Not babies, not strangers, not endless snow. As long as I have Haeden in my arms, life here on the ice planet is utterly perfect. I couldn't ask for more. I've always wanted to be loved, to be the center of someone's universe. It took traveling halfway across the universe to succeed, but I'm exactly where I need to be.

"I love you," I tell Haeden as he begins to thrust into me with hard, possessive strokes.

And it makes my cootie purr a little louder to hear him say it back for the first time.

ICE PLANET
HONEYMOON

HAEDEN & JOSIE

Josie

A whimper escapes me as my mate thrusts deep, hitting me in just the right spot. My ass is in the air, and I'm on my knees, my cheek against the blankets. His big hands are on my hips and he's pumping into me with a single-minded determination that takes my breath away. My toes curl with delight as he pushes me across the furs, because how is it so damn good with Haeden every time? Every stinking time?

I'm so close. *So* close. I mean, sure, I've already come twice, but now I really, really want this third orgasm. I curl my fingers in the furs and moan as he shuttles into me, fast and precise, his spur tapping against my back door. I don't even mind that, and I've never liked anal in the past. With Haeden I might, though. The thought excites me. Nothing's off-limits with my soul mate, and I'm greedy for everything. "Harder," I pant. "Harder, Haeden."

He grunts, hands tightening on my hips, and slams into me from behind, nearly stealing my breath away. Even his "harder" isn't enough to hurt, and I sense he's being careful anyhow. It'd kill him if I came out of our bed-play with a bruise. I might not mind it if it's gotten in the right sort of scenario. He drives into me again and I gasp once more. So close.

I just need . . . a little more . . .

"Harder," I whine. "Harder!" When his thrusts grow ragged, I know he's about to come, and I blurt out the first thing I can think of to make us both come fast. "Punish me! I've been such a naughty girl."

Haeden thrusts . . . and stops in his tracks. "Eh?"

"No, no, no," I pant, gesturing at him behind me. "Please, finish me, Haeden. Please!"

He doesn't, of course. My mate pulls out of me instead, leaving me aching and hollow, and I want to scream with frustration. "Why would I punish you, Jo-see? What is wrong? What troubles you?"

Well, now I just want to cry. "Nothing is wrong." I wriggle my ass in the air. "Let's just keep having sex, okay? Please?"

"Not until I find out why you wish to be punished." Haeden's broad face looks troubled. He's panting, his cock thick and erect and so close that I want to just fling him down into the furs and mount him, but I recognize this concerned look on his face. "What did you do?"

I turn around and crawl over to him, kissing his dear face. "Nothing's wrong. I misspoke, okay? It was just a heat-of-the-moment thing. I love you. I really, really want to come. Can we please just finish having sex?"

He studies my face intently, and then cups the back of my neck, holding me in place. "You would tell me if there was a problem? I am your mate. I want to help."

"Nothing's wrong other than my pussy needs to be filled," I

tell him, kissing him again and nipping at his lower lip. "Please, Haeden, give me your seed."

My mate groans and falls over me, and I automatically lock my legs around his hips. This time he enters me oh-so-carefully, and I want to cry at how tender and thoughtful he's being. He watches my face as he strokes into me, slow at first and then with greater speed. His spur strokes against my clit as we mate, and the orgasm I'm chasing isn't long in returning. I cling to him as I come again, and hold him tightly as he comes a moment later.

It isn't until we're cuddled against each other later that he starts petting my cheek and hair with an almost desperate fervor, and I realize he's still thinking about what I said earlier.

"Be honest," I tell Tiffany the next day, pulling my tunic tight around my waist. "Do I look pregnant yet?"

We're seated in Tiffany's cave, which she shares with her mate, Salukh. It's a blustery day, which means that while the men are out hunting, it's a good time for the ladies to sit by the fire and sew. I'm working on a lightweight tunic for Haeden, since taking care of my mate is a pleasure and I want to help out. Or at least, I should be working on a tunic for him. Instead, I'm putting my hands on my waist and wondering if it's changed any at all.

Tiff looks up from the leather cloak she's working on hemming and gives me an "are you for real" look. "Jo, it's been a month. You're not going to show for a while."

"We don't know that!" I rub my flat stomach, excited. "Georgie got morning sickness early and Nora showed way earlier than we thought she would. Maybe I will, too."

"First of all, you do not want morning sickness earlier, because it means you're going to have it that much longer," Tiffany says in a reasonable voice, pushing her awl back through the leather and making a neat stitch. "And second of all, I would *not* say that to Nora."

Hmm, good point. I hitch my tunic tight against my waist again, adjusting. I wish we had a mirror, but it's probably best we don't. I'm sure my face is permanently cold-chapped and my hair disheveled, but at least Haeden thinks I'm cute. "Have you had any morning sickness yet?"

She's silent.

I drop next to her on the furs and get in her face. "Tiffany! You did, didn't you! Why didn't you tell me?"

Tiffany rolls her eyes and pulls another stitch through the leather. "Because it's not a big deal? I was a little sick the other morning. Not much, though."

"Are you kidding me? This is exciting!" I cover her hand with mine, stopping her work so she can focus on the exciting topic at hand. "How did you know you were sick? Did you wake up with the barfs or did it come on slowly? How long did it last? Was it a mouth-filling-with-saliva sort of thing or did it hit you by surprise?"

"Do we really have to talk in depth about vomiting?"

"Yes! Because it means you're *pregnant*." Clearly she's not as excited as I am.

"Jo, the fact that Salukh and I resonated and mated means I'm pregnant. Morning sickness is just that. I don't need it to tell me I've got a baby on the way." She smiles and pulls her hands free. "Now, do you mind? I'm trying to fix this cloak for Salukh before he goes out on the trails for a week."

"Okay, well, when I get morning sickness, I'm telling everyone all the details." I sit back on my heels and clasp my hands on my lap as Tiffany takes up her sewing again. I should probably be doing the same, but this is such an exciting time that I can't possibly concentrate on making my stitches even. I'm just so happy for Tiffany . . . and for myself, and I can't stop beaming at her. Best friends, pregnant together.

This is something out of my dreams.

Tiffany laughs, putting her work down and giving me an exasperated look. "I can't do this when you're sitting there just smiling at me!"

I give a little wriggle of happiness. "I'm just excited!"

"Weirdo," she jokes, but her tone holds no venom. She knows how much I've wanted this.

"It just feels like everything's finally falling into place. Haeden, the baby, our lives here . . ." I touch my stomach again. "Everything's perfect."

"Well, since you've got babies on the brain, do you want to work with me on a couple of skins later? I want to make some really soft leather in gender-neutral colors for baby clothes. Like a nice pale green, or a soft yellow."

"Love to!" I beam at her. "But I know mine is going to be a boy."

"Did Rokan say something to you?" She studies her stitches, glancing at me out of the corner of her eye.

"Nope. I just know. That's how it happens in my fantasies," I tell her, flopping onto my back in the furs and watching the fire crackle. "First a boy, and then a girl, and then it alternates back and forth. We'll have at least eight children, too."

"Is that all," Tiffany jokes dryly.

I grin, running a hand over my still-too-flat abdomen. The word "fantasies" has me thinking about last night. How I'd gotten into dirty talk and it had stopped Haeden cold. Hmm. "Hey, Tiff."

"Listening," she says absently, tying off her stitches.

"You ever do something in bed that Salukh isn't into?" I prop up on my side, supporting my head with my hand as I regard her. "Like, have you ever freaked him out?"

"No? But I'm pretty vanilla about that sort of stuff. I don't want adventurous. I'm perfectly happy with what we have."

Hmm. Am I not vanilla? It's not something I've ever thought about. "I don't want to do anything freaky," I clarify. "I'm just worried that Haeden doesn't want to try anything new in bed. It's the same couple positions over and over again. Not that they're not good positions. They are! I just . . . want to try some stuff."

"And he doesn't?"

"I don't know. I hinted at some stuff last night and he kinda froze on me." I chew on my lip, thinking. Normally Haeden is completely enthusiastic about everything in bed. The sex we have is great. So great that I want to try everything now. Like, *everything*.

But I don't want to scare my mate, either. And I don't want him thinking I'm a freak.

"Maybe talk to Nora about it?" Tiffany suggests. "She and Dagesh are a little wilder and he plays along with her games."

I brighten, because that's the perfect suggestion. Everyone's heard Nora and Dagesh having some rough (sounding) sex. It's a small cave and it's that much smaller when someone is squealing for their mate to smack them on the ass. Nora takes all the teasing in stride, though, and she and her mate are happy. If anyone would know how to ease their mate into some exciting games in bed, it'd be Nora. "Great idea. Plus, it gives me a chance to hold her babies."

Tiffany laughs. "You don't need an excuse. I'm sure she'd be happy to foist them off on you for a few hours."

There's a scratch at the cave entrance, even though there's no screen over it. Kemli—one of the elderly sa-khui women and Salukh's mother—smiles at us. She holds a large basket in her hands. "May I join you?"

To my surprise, Tiffany gets a shy look on her face, but she gestures at the fire. "Of course. Come sit. Do you want some tea?"

Kemli shakes her head and ducks into the cave, then sits across from us at the fire. "I was going through my storage and pulled out the clothes from when my kits were young. I thought since you both are carrying that you could see if there was anything you wanted." She pulls an adorable little tunic with decorative zigzag stitching out. "This was Salukh's."

Tiffany makes a completely undignified squeal and takes it from Kemli. "Oh my God. It's so *tiny*!"

"He was a tiny kit," Kemli says, chuckling. "Now Farli, she was the big one." She hands another baby-sized tunic to me, this one a pale white with vivid red flowers embroidered on the shoulders. "She never even wore this one. She was too plump."

I touch it with reverent fingers. "It's so pretty. Oh, Kemli!"

"I would love to see them used again," she tells us. "Have you seen the hats?"

And with those simple words, I forget all about everything but babies once more.

Haeden

"I do not understand it," I tell my friend as I pull a frozen dvisti from a cache. "She said she had been naughty, yet she would not tell me what she had done wrong." I sling the dead meat to the side and eye the rest of the cache's contents. "Two more dvisti and six quill-beasts. We should make sure this is full before the brutal season."

Aehako grunts, his hands on his hips. "I do not like how low the caches are. I suppose it is to be expected with the extra mouths to feed, but I still do not like it. Ah well. More hunting for us!" He rubs his chin. "As for Jo-see, I have not heard anything. You are certain something is wrong?"

"I am not, and that is the problem." I shake my head, tossing the dvisti back into the cache now that we have assessed how much is left. "And she mentioned it at a strange time."

"Strange time?"

"During mating." My face gets hot as I think about it. Jo-see is an incredible mate, and this feels disloyal. I do not want her thinking I find fault with her, because in my eyes, she is perfect. Yet I do not feel knowledgeable when it comes to females. Aehako is much better at this sort of thing. He had a pleasure mate before he resonated to Kira. Surely he will have ideas as to what would cause Jo-see to blurt out strange things when I am deep in her cunt.

"I do not think of Jo-see as the type to break rules. She is not like Leezh." He grins at me. "Jo-see only caused problems when the problems involved you."

I huff with amusement. "Truth." It is no secret that we did not get along well prior to our resonance. I think I was fighting my feelings for her out of fear, and Jo-see was fighting because she thought I hated her. It is easy to look back upon and laugh about now that she is happily in my furs every night and my kit is in her belly. "Jo-see is sweet and kind. I do not understand why she thinks she is naughty."

"Perhaps it is some sort of game in the furs? Like the kind Dagesh and his mate play? Or my brother Zennek? He and Marlenn are very, ah, enthusiastic." Aehako gives a wry shake of his head. "I admire my brother's stamina with that one."

Perhaps it is a mating game of some kind. But why would she wish for me to be angry with her? "Foolishness," I mutter. "Just foolishness."

"You know what my solution is."

"I am not giving her a courting gift." I glare at my friend. "That is not a solution for everything."

He doubles over, laughing and slapping his knee. "Is it not? I do not hear complaints from Salukh! And my mate is well pleased."

I scowl at him. I do not want to get my mate a replica of my cock. It makes me feel strange. Like I am not quite enough for her. I do not like that thought, not at all.

Perhaps I should speak with Dagesh or Zennek, though. Someone that is more confident than I am in how to please a mate. I will be devastated if Jo-see does not find my touches enough. I know in the past, when the tribe was much larger, that some shared their furs with a third to please their mates.

But I do not want anyone but Jo-see . . . and I do not want to share.

I kick more snow over the cache. "Come. Let us get this buried and check the next one. You can tell me all about what Kae is up to."

"I think she will be a huntress," Aehako says with excitement, lifting a hand. "You should see the grip on her."

When I return to the caves later, I bring two fresh hoppers with me—one for my mate's dinner, and one for Dagesh and his female. I hover outside their cave, wondering if I should even speak up. I do not want everyone to think there is a problem between me and Jo-see. She has my entire heart in her hands.

I just do not want to fail her somehow.

So even though I feel like a fool, I clear my throat and scratch at the privacy screen covering the entrance.

Dagesh pulls the screen back and puts a finger to his lips. "They are sleeping."

"The twins?" I whisper, lowering my voice. I try to imagine what I would do if Jo-see carried two kits at once. That might be too much for us to handle. Dagesh and his mate often look exhausted.

"All of them," he whispers back, grabbing me by the arm and pulling me away from the cave. "No-rah, too. What is it?"

It seems a silly thing to ask about now. "I . . . brought meat. So you would not have to hunt." I hold the dead hopper up. "Here."

Dagesh looks surprised at my thoughtfulness. I do not often hunt for him—he has brothers and a father that can assist. "My thanks. Is something troubling you or your mate? Jo-see was here earlier and spoke with No-rah for quite some time."

She did? "I . . . it is nothing." My throat tightens and I cannot make myself say the words. I shove the hopper at him again. "Just take the meat."

"You are sure?" He eyes me. "I am good at keeping secrets."

I scowl, bristling. "It is not a secret. And there is no problem."

"I did not say there was." Dagesh takes the hopper from my tight grip. "My thanks for the hunting. You have saved me a walk out to my traps." The look he gives me is weary but pleased. "Some days are difficult with two young kits at once."

"Do you and No-rah still find time? To mate?" I have to ask. I think of Jo-see and how we cannot get enough of each other. I am eager for kits and a family, but I do not want anything to change from the perfection it is right now. Perhaps that is why I am panicking. I worry I will lose everything because it is too good at this moment, too perfect.

He grins, raking a hand through his mane. "Some days are not good for mating. Some days we just want to crawl into the furs and sleep until dawn. But yes, when No-rah and I can find a moment, we enjoy each other. Is this what you worry over, my friend?"

I pause, considering if I can say it aloud. "Do you . . . have you . . ." Flustered, my tongue glues itself to the roof of my mouth. I do not know how to approach this. "Is your mate a naughty girl?"

Dagesh's eyes widen and he looks shocked at my words. "*What?*"

Immediately, I sense I have made a mistake. I want to fling the other hopper down and storm away, but I want answers. I want to know how to please Jo-see. If I am not giving her something she needs . . . "My mate said a strange thing in the furs," I blurt out. "I think she wishes to play games like No-rah." I sigh heavily. "And I do not know what to do."

"Do you not wish to do them? To pleasure her?"

I have heard Dagesh smacking his mate on her backside and her cries. I am not sure I could do the same to Jo-see. She is so slight and fragile despite her inner strength. "I . . . cannot harm her. Even if she wishes it."

To my surprise, he snorts. "It is not about the harm. It is about pretend."

"Eh?"

"It is about pretending," he says, leaning in. His voice is low and confident. "No-rah does not want me to harm her. Do you think she would be happy if I walked up to her and struck her? She would be furious, and I would never forgive myself. But in the furs, in the moment? It is about pretend." He holds his hand out, cupping his fingers slightly. "I have learned what she wants. I have learned that if I hold my hand so, it makes a loud noise but does not hurt her, and she likes the noise more than the sting. It is the element of danger. Of taking things too far. She trusts you enough to want to play. Has she asked you to pull her mane?"

I stagger backward, shocked. "What?"

"Mmm. No?" He shrugs. "It is something No-rah likes. She likes to be overpowered, but not harmed. She just likes to see that I am strong. That I could take what I want . . . but I do not take. Does that make sense?"

Yanking on my mate's mane . . . overpowering her . . . this all sounds terrible. "I do not know that I can do this."

"Even if it is just a game?" He tilts his head, regarding me.

"It is not a game I understand," I grumble.

"Then you are not listening," Dagesh emphasizes, leaning in. "Your mate is telling you she wishes for something. She trusts you enough to ask this. No-rah trusts me enough that she will let me pull on her mane, knowing that I will not do it outside of the furs, and that I will not do it hard enough to harm her. She likes to give her control to me. It makes her feel good. Safe. Jo-see feels safe with you, so she asks for this. It is a compliment." He reaches out and pats my shoulder. "Trust me. And you can always use your word if things go too far."

What he says makes sense. And yet it is difficult for me to understand. I need to find out if Jo-see truly wishes her mane pulled on or her backside smacked, or if there is another problem. "My . . . word? What word?"

"A safety word," he tells me proudly. "It is a word you establish with your mate to ensure playing does not go too far."

Ah. I like this idea. "I shall think upon this more. My thanks, Dagesh."

"Talk with your mate," he says. "She probably has a good idea of what she wishes but is too shy to ask."

Shy? Jo-see? Bah.

Even so . . . I suppose it cannot hurt to ask. "What sorts of games do you and No-rah play? Can I ask?"

He grins. "Recently we have been pretending she is a huntress."

"A huntress?"

"A very bad one," he agrees, and gestures that I should lean in closer so he can whisper the details.

Puzzled, I lean in. I want to learn everything.

Josie

Even leather baby clothes smell like babies. It's amazing. I sort through the pile that Kemli gave me, just because I can't stop touching them, and I fold each little dress and tunic with admiring fingers. I lift one pale blue leather gown that's so small I doubt it's ever been worn, and I raise it to my nose, inhaling deeply. So sweet. So perfect.

I can't wait for my baby. I can't wait to see Haeden as a father. God, the future is so *exciting*.

"Ho," Haeden calls out, ducking into our cave.

Turning with excitement, I beam at my mate. "Hi! Look at these cute little clothes Kemli gave me! Aren't they precious? I'm picturing Farli in this one." I hold the gown up so he can admire it, and then I smell it again. "They should bottle this scent back home. They'd make a fortune."

He grunts, setting his spear in its regular place, and then pulls the privacy screen over the entrance. Then he turns to me, his hands on his hips, and he gets this imperious look on his face. "You have been a terrible huntress, Jo-see, and I wish to slap you."

I blink, shocked. "W-what?"

My expression must not be what he wants. Immediately, Haeden kneels next to me by the fire, leaning in. "It is a role-play," he whispers, a look of concern on his face. "Am I not doing it right?"

My jaw drops. "We—you—you want to role-play? Right now?"

His eyes narrow and he gets that closed-off, mulish look on his face that tells me he's getting defensive. "I was not told it had to be done at a specific time."

Before he can get to his feet, I grab his hands. "Wait. Haeden. Love. I'm not saying no. I just don't think I want to be slapped?" I've had boyfriends try that shit in the past and I am not down with abuse. "Do you really want to slap me?"

"No." He hangs his head. "The last thing I want is to slap you. I am trying to play games with you. Dagesh says No-rah likes it when he is rough. They play games in the furs, and I thought you were trying to play with me and I did not understand it."

My heart feels as if it's growing three sizes in this moment. I squeeze his hands tightly, so full of love I want to burst. He's trying to figure out how to please me? God, I could kiss him all over. "I love you so much right now," I breathe. "You're the most amazing man ever, you know that?"

The look he gives me is suspicious, but he leaves his hands in mine. "I have not done anything yet."

"But you're trying. That's enough for me." I shift in my seat, my legs crossed, and I face him directly. "Let's talk about this, can we?"

Haeden nods and sits like I am, with his legs crossed. He puts his hands out for mine again and we link hands, and I smile at him, just brimming with affection. How did I ever hate this guy? Seriously? Even when he's scowly and feeling uncomfortable, he's just the most gorgeous male I've ever seen. "Tell me what Dagesh talked to you about."

He rubs his thumb over my skin as he talks, staring at our hands. I know my mate well enough now that I can tell he hates feeling like he doesn't understand something. He hates being made to feel foolish, and it's obvious he feels foolish right now. "Dagesh and No-rah play their games when they mate, yes? You mentioned that you wished to be punished, and I thought you were wanting to play games like her. So I asked him. I do not want you to feel as if your mate is not pleasing you in the furs."

Oh. Oh no. "I don't want you to think that, ever." I hold his hands tightly, as if I can somehow convince him of my earnestness. "You're the only person I've ever really enjoyed sex with. You're the only person that's ever made me come. If I'm asking for more, it's because I'm greedy. I want everything with you. Every position. Every hole. I don't care if it's something I didn't like in the past. Being with you makes me want to try it all again because I know it'll be good this time, because it's with you."

Haeden's gaze is solemn. "You would tell me if there was a problem? You would not try to hide it?"

I shake my head. "Like I said, I'm being greedy with you. Our sex is amazing."

"And you . . . do not want to be struck?" He looks doubtful.

"I do not." I had a boyfriend in the lifestyle once, and he used it as an excuse to get far too handsy and would cite it as "discipline." I know Haeden wouldn't be like that, but I'm fine with our experiments being of a sweeter nature. "When I said that the other day, I was just role-playing. Talking dirty."

"Pretend?"

"Kind of, yeah. Dirty pretend. But if you're not into it, that kinda ruins the fun."

He thinks for a moment. "I am not *not* into it. I just did not understand. Dagesh says we should have a word."

"A safe word? Great." Smart Dagesh. I love that they had this conversation. I love that another sa-khui is making it normal so I don't feel like a freak for asking to play games in bed. "What do you want to use?"

"'Stop.'"

I furrow my brows. "Your safe word is 'stop'?"

I swear, I'm going to start giggling and then Haeden will be annoyed. I press my lips together hard, trying to keep calm. But when he gives me another solemn nod, I lose it. A giggle escapes me, and at his astonished look, I fling myself into his arms. "Oh my God, why are you so cute?"

"'Stop' is not right?" he asks, his arms going around me. "If you ask me to stop, I will."

I crawl into his lap like the shameless thing I am. He settles me against him, adjusting his legs so I can cradle myself in his arms. One of the things I love—well, one of the many—about Haeden is that he's so big and strong. Being with him makes me feel safe and secure, especially when I'm in his arms. "'Stop' is good and all, but what if you're licking my pussy so well that I can't stand it? If I say 'stop,' I don't really want you to stop."

"You . . . do not?" His expression is openly skeptical. "Then why say it?"

"Because you just say shit when you're in the moment. You're trying to get off. You're trying to get your partner off." I reach up and take his long braid in my hand, pulling it over one shoulder. "You'd say anything to come, and sometimes what comes out is 'no, stop' even when you want to keep going. That's why you need a safe word. Because sometimes you're feeling so much that you tell the other person to stop because you can't take it, but you know that if they keep going, they'll make you come. Does that make sense?"

He snorts. "No."

I giggle again, leaning against him. "It's just sex talk. Kinda like when I tell you I've been a bad girl. I want you to play along. I want you to get in the zone with me. Tell me I'm naughty and you're going to punish me. I don't really want you to hurt me, but the thought that you might get a little rougher with me? That you might spank me? It adds a wicked edge to things."

Haeden grunts, digesting this as I play with his braid. He rubs my arm idly, considering. "What other things do people say in the furs? To make their mate excited?"

Oooh. Is he getting into this? I take the tip of his braid and tease it against my lips. "I could call you 'daddy.' That's slang for 'father.'"

The look on his face is pure horror. "No."

Oh God, I'm going to start laughing again. I bite the inside of my cheek and think for a moment. "Teacher and student is a popular one. What if I was a huntress that you were in charge of teaching and I was so very bad?" I wiggle in his lap, leaning in, and I let my voice drop to a husky note. "You'd be oh-so-stern with me, wouldn't you?"

"I am always stern with you. Sometimes you do not like it."

"This is *pretend*."

"So I should pretend you are a terrible huntress and we will all starve in the brutal season?"

Clapping a hand over my mouth, I dissolve into another fit of giggles. I lean against my mate as he caresses my back, and laughter rumbles through his chest, too. Good. I'm glad he's not upset. "That's not how the game goes," I manage, wheezing with laughter. "Haeden, come on."

"It *is* how the game goes," he grumps, but I can hear the smile in his voice. "But yes, if you were a terrible huntress, I would be very upset that you were wasting my time."

Immediately, my laughter dies. "And would you want to discipline me? Maybe a spanking because I'm so naughty?"

"I . . . would consider it."

I press my fingers to my lips, delighted and overwhelmed. Tears threaten again. Not because I'm sad, but because I'm so happy with my wonderful, thoughtful mate. "You're the best, Haeden."

"Because I would strike you?" He looks openly skeptical at my response.

"Because you're willing to play and do things just because I want to try them." I cup his face in my hands and beam up at him, vision blurry with happiness. "I love you so much. I'm so stupidly happy that I feel like it's hard to hold it all in, you know? I feel safe and secure for the first time ever. Like nothing bad is ever going to happen again, and it makes me feel . . ." I pause, trying to figure out the best way to express the intensity of the emotions I feel. "It's like I'm at a buffet. Do you know what that is?"

He shakes his head, even as he leans into my touch.

"Okay, a buffet is a restaurant where they lay out tons of food of all kinds—from salads to soups to meats to sides. Desserts, too. There are always delicious desserts at a buffet. At most restaurants, you pick one food and order it and that's all you get. But at a buffet, you buy a plate, and when you get that plate, it allows you to eat anything you want from the buffet and as much as you want. It's just a crazy amount of food. And when I was a kid, I had a foster family that would go to a buffet, but they would never buy a plate for me. They would just let me have a little extra off of one of their plates. I never got my own plate and I dreamed of being able to pick and choose what I wanted, and as much as I wanted. It never happened, of course. But now with you, it feels like, well . . . sex is the buffet and I finally have a plate. Do you understand now?"

"No," he admits. "I am more confused than ever. But I think you are telling me you want to eat me as much as you can?" He turns his head so he can press a kiss to the palm of my hand. "I am a stringy meal."

I chuckle. "You're my buffet and I want to try everything with you in the furs. I want to lick your cock. I want to lick your horns. I want to lick you between your cheeks—"

His tail thumps behind him, hard.

"—and I want you to lick me between mine. I want to try anal sex. I want to wear silly costumes and pretend like we're strangers and see what it's like. I want all of it, Haeden. I don't know if I'll like all of it, but with you, I want to try *everything*."

He groans, closing his eyes. "My sweet mate. You are a gift. If you wish to try anything, I will gladly do it with you." He opens his eyes again and gives me a hungry look. "I will be your *buff-ay*."

I lean in and kiss his wonderful mouth. "I love you so much. Let's make a word for just the two of us, hmm? Something better than 'stop,' because if I'm pretending, I might demand for you to stop even though I don't want it."

Haeden looks openly skeptical at this declaration, but shrugs. "You pick the word."

I think for a moment, considering what word would be unusual enough to stop both of us in our tracks. "Buffet" seems like a bad idea. There are a dozen human words that spring to mind—bicycle, car, telephone—that mean nothing to Haeden. Then I have it. I give him a wicked grin. "What about the word 'daddy'? You didn't like it, right?"

"If you wish for my cock to wither, it is a good one," he grumbles.

Biting back another giggle, I kiss him again. "Perfect. We only go for that word if we want to stop. Other than that, we play, understand?"

"And what is it you wish to play right now?"

"Naughty huntress, of course." I slip out of his lap and move across the cave, feeling bold. I move toward his spear and pitch my voice low so no one can hear me. "Oh, look—I was supposed to sharpen my spear point and I didn't. Now my fierce, handsome mentor will be *so* mad."

I exaggerate my reaction, putting a hand to my mouth in an "oopsie" expression. Then I bend over, wiggling my butt in the air as I pick up the sharpening tools.

To my surprise, a hand cracks against my backside, spanking me. I squeal in astonishment, nearly losing my balance. Haeden's arm wraps around my waist and then he puts a hand over my mouth, hushing me. "Not so loud."

"Sorry," I whisper, fighting back giggles. "You startled me."

"How? It is what you asked for." He rubs a hand down my flank. "Did I hurt you?"

"No, just startled me with the sound." For all that it sounded as if he cracked me good, it doesn't even sting. "You can go harder next time."

He mock-growls at me. "Do not tell me what to do, huntress."

Oooh. Heat flutters through my belly and I wrestle out of his grip. "Don't be such a bully," I declare, lifting my chin as I face him. "You can't tell me how to hunt. I can do as I please!"

Haeden closes the distance between us, and for a moment, he looks so angry that I feel a hint of panic. He grabs me by the shoulders and turns me around, then smacks my backside again. Once more, the sound is loud, but the actual contact on my backside is nothing at all—probably because of my leathers.

"Stop it!" I hiss at him, and push away.

He pauses, confused, and then his eyes narrow. "That was not the word, was it?"

"It wasn't." I'm breathless and aroused. "And you need to stop spanking me. I don't like it."

"Then do not be such a foolish huntress," Haeden growls back, and tries to turn me around again.

I let out another muffled squeal and try to get away from him, but he grabs me by the waistband and I drop to the furs. A moment later, he rips my pants down, exposing my backside, and delivers another slap to my butt. This time it stings, and I let out another noise of surprise.

His hand remains on my buttock, his fingers hot against my skin. "Jo-see . . . ?"

"Still good," I reassure him. "And I'm still naughty."

He growls again, and this time when he hauls me over his knee and smacks my ass once more, I moan. I never thought I'd be into spanking, but the fact that he's playing with me and being so firm and unyielding like he was when we first met is kinda hot.

Okay, really hot.

"You are a danger to the tribe," Haeden all but snarls at me as he smacks his hand on my ass again. "You need to be *punished*." Again he spanks me, this time harder than before, and I moan again, clinging to his leg. "Do you need to be punished, Jo-see?"

"Yes," I whisper, my pulse throbbing between my legs. "Oh, fuck yes."

He spanks me again, and then his fingers delve between my thighs. I whimper and arch back against his touch as he pushes into my cunt, thrusting into me with a thick finger. "You are wet."

"So wet."

"That does not make you a good huntress," he says, though his voice is thick and distracted. His finger pumps in and out of me quickly, and I rock in time with his touch. "You still need to be punished."

"Punish me," I pant, totally into our game. "Show me who's boss."

Haeden pushes me off of his lap and shoves my pants all the way down to my ankles, and then shucks them off my legs. A moment later, he grabs me by the hips, adjusting me and nudging my thighs apart.

Then, a heavy hand settles on the back of my neck, pushing me into the furs even as my ass is in the air. I moan again as the head of his cock rubs against the entrance to my body . . . and then thrusts into me, hard.

A choked cry escapes me.

"Say if you need your word—"

"No word! No word! So good! Keep going—"

He draws back and then thrusts into me again, and I bite down on my lip, trying to stay quiet. Haeden hammers into me as if I'm a rag doll to be used, and oh God, I absolutely love it. He fucks me hard, his spur stabbing at my backside in a way that feels invasive and exciting at the same time. I love that Haeden pins me down as he snaps his hips against mine, growling. I'm torn between laughing with delight and moaning—and when I come, I'm pretty sure I do both.

My mate hisses between his teeth, and with a few more hard, furious drives into me, he comes, too. I can feel his seed flooding my channel and spilling down my thighs, and I clench my inner walls, wanting to keep him there forever. That elicits another grunt from my mate, and he smacks my backside with a lazy tap that just makes my buttock quiver.

Well, and my belly, too, but it's quivering inside. Deep, deep inside.

"I liked that," I manage as we catch our breath. I feel so at peace in this moment. Just dopey with endorphins and hazy with love for Haeden.

"You are certain?"

"Mmm-hmm." I nod against the furs, and I'm a little disappointed when his hand lifts from the back of my neck.

"Which part was your favorite?" he asks, panting. His hands are skimming all over my bare flanks, touching me everywhere. I don't know if it's because he's trying to make sure I'm not bruised or if he just wants to touch me right now, but I'll take it. "Tell me the things you liked and did not like so I know what to do again."

"I liked all of it. But I think I liked your hand on my neck the most." It's a little surprising to me to admit that. I thought I'd be super into the spanking, but I was more excited about the prospect of Haeden pinning me than anything. "It made me feel trapped but safe, if that makes sense."

My mate grunts and then sprawls on the furs next to me. A moment later, he pulls me against him, flipping me over and arranging me so we can lie on our sides, face-to-face. "None of that made sense, but . . . it was enjoyable anyhow."

I grin at him, leaning in to rub the tip of my nose against his. "You're a good sport."

"And you are a naughty huntress," he grumbles.

"The naughtiest. I can see that I'm going to need *so* much discipline."

Haeden snorts. "Then I suppose it is a good thing I am a tireless hunter. And patient. And understanding—"

"Now who's pretending?" I tease, and break into giggles when he pulls me against him for another kiss.

Haeden always sleeps wrapped around me, with my head tucked under his chin. It melts my heart and makes me feel so special, because it's like he's protecting me even in his sleep. I love it.

Normally I love it, that is.

This morning, I'm a little sore. I've slept on one hip all night and my backside stings on one cheek. I'm feeling smug, though, because we "played games" in bed all night, progressively getting rougher as the night passed. It was so much fun, and Haeden really got into it, which thrills me. So if my butt is a little sore from too much spanking this morning, I'll take it.

It's my belly that feels off. There's a taste of acid in my mouth, and I feel a little queasy. I try to nudge Haeden's heavy arm off of me, only for him to adjust and pull me even closer. Okay, then. I lie quietly against him and try to think of what I ate last night that might have caused my stomach to be upset, and remember that I only ate two bites of dinner, because the stew smelled overcooked.

Thinking of that unpleasant dinner, my mouth suddenly floods with water, and I bolt out of bed, my head cracking against Haeden's chin in my haste. He makes a grunt of pain, and I cradle my head even as I army-crawl over to the basket I've been keeping near the furs for just in case.

And I throw up. A *lot*.

It's horrible. It shakes my entire body and makes me clench with the force of my vomiting. I've been so excited to get morning sickness, but in this moment, all I want is for it to be over. I want my belly to stop trying to fling itself up my throat. I want this taste out of my mouth.

"Shh," Haeden whispers, rubbing my shoulder and stroking my hair back from my face. "Your mate is here. I will take care of you."

"Morning . . . sickness . . ." I pant between heaves. "Baby . . ."

"Do not talk, Jo-see. Relax. Let your stomach settle." He tucks a lock of hair behind my ear and caresses me until the moment passes.

When I'm finally done being sick and there's nothing left in my gut, he hands me a cup of water. I sip it with trembling hands, washing the taste out of my mouth and spitting it into the fire. Now that the worst of it has passed, I'm excited. It's the first real signal I've had that the baby exists. Oh sure, there's resonance, and there's the fact that I've missed my period, but I've missed my period plenty of times before, and resonance still purrs anytime I'm near Haeden.

Morning sickness makes this all feel *real*.

"Rest," my mate instructs as he takes the basket in hand. "I will return with something easy for your stomach." He doesn't look nearly as thrilled as I am at this prospect, but Haeden is a worrier. He'll get used to it.

I finish my water, then lie back down in the furs, my fingers tracing over the still-flat planes of my belly. We haven't thought of names yet, I realize. Well, we've talked a little, but nothing too serious. The baby needs a name that will be the perfect blending of ours. Hae-see? Ugh. Hae-jo? Also ugh. Maybe the Jo part needs to come first. Jo-den?

Hmm, I like that. Joden. It has potential.

Smiling to myself, I drowse in bed, waiting for my mate to return. When he does, it's with a few cold not-potato cakes and a surly look on his face. I'm not surprised at the scowl—Haeden panics anytime something troubles me, which just makes me feel that much more special. "Come sit up and eat," he grumbles, dropping beside the furs and reaching a hand out for me. "Kemli says this should settle your belly."

"Don't be so gloomy," I say, my tone as bright as my mood as he helps me sit up. "It's morning sickness. That means the baby is just settling or something."

He grunts and all but shoves a not-potato cake into my hand. I take it, nibbling on the edges as he gets me another cup of water. "Your belly is protesting because I was too rough with you. We will not do such things again."

What? Is he serious? But a look over at my mate's rigid features tells me yes, he's absolutely serious. I should have guessed that the matter wasn't settled. "Haeden."

"I mean it. I am using my word now. I am daddy."

I snort-giggle, which only makes him scowl harder. "Sorry. Sorry. I'm not laughing at you. I'm thinking we pick a better word for next time."

"There is no next time. We will be gentle in the furs and nothing else." He picks up one of the furs off the bed and tucks it around my shoulders. "You are carrying our kit and I forgot in the heat of the moment."

"Not this conversation again. I'm not fragile, Haeden. I can take care of myself." I'm still smiling, despite my annoyance at his words. I know now that Haeden's intense protectiveness comes from a place of love. That he would cheerfully smother me with affection to keep me safe. I love that. I love all of it. But I'm also not going to let him deprive us of fun because he's a worrywart. "Morning sickness has nothing to do with having frisky sex."

"It was not 'frisky.' I got carried away." He lowers his voice as if ashamed. "I took you *hard*. You say you are strong, but you are also carrying our kit. I must think of both of you." He turns around and frowns at our cave, as if it's bothering him. "I should make a fire."

"No, you should come sit with me." I hold a hand out to him. "And we should talk about things."

Haeden has a mutinous look on his face, and I can tell we're in disagreement. But now that I've got my seat at the buffet, so to speak, I'm not going to let his worries take all of our fun away. I know what I want and I know what my limits are, and we didn't come anywhere close to that. It makes me feel good that my sweet mate is so concerned that he hurt me, but I need him to not panic over every little thing. If all goes according to plan, I'm going to be pregnant a lot, and we should expect morning sickness, along with a lot of other things that come with babies.

But my mate is a good guy, and he sits next to me in the furs and gives me a patient look. I can tell he's trying, even if he's doing his best not to hover too much. Haeden adjusts the fur on my shoulders and tucks it around my legs. "How do you feel right now?"

"I'm better," I promise him. "I think my stomach was too empty and that made things come up. It's fine now."

"Good. Then you can eat another cake." The look he gives me is stern.

"I will . . . after we talk." I turn to face him, sitting cross-legged so my knees can touch his. "Haeden, love, you know that what we did last night has nothing to do with me being queasy this morning." I grip his hand in mine. "You *know* that."

"I do. But seeing you sick worried me, and it reminded me how quickly things can change, and how fragile you are." When I make a sound of protest in my throat, he shakes his head. "I know you will say you are strong and capable. And I know you are. But you are everything to me, and I am allowed to worry. You are carrying my first kit."

But I'm not his first mate. I remember now, and it softens my annoyance. Zalah died from khui-sickness, so of course he's going to panic when I show signs of illness. "I know how it feels for things to be going so well that they scare you," I say. "Trust me, I know. Sometimes I wake up and I worry that this is all a dream and I'm going to be back on that horrible ship."

I reach out and pull his braid over his shoulder, admiring the length of it. My own hair is so fine that I can't grow a nice fat braid like this. I hope our children have his hair. I hope our children have his everything, because he's perfect to me.

"Jo-see." Haeden caresses my cheek with his big hand. "Do you think I am being unfair?"

Maybe a little? But I also understand him so I don't throw this in his face. We're still figuring out how to navigate our relationship, he and I. If this is our biggest problem, I'll count us lucky. "Did you enjoy yourself last night? Because I enjoyed myself."

"I was rough with you—"

I raise a hand. "But did you *enjoy* yourself?"

He narrows his eyes at me.

"I'm going to take that as a yes," I say, smiling to take the edge off my teasing. "And I had an amazing time, too. We don't have to do that sort of thing all the time, but I love trying new things with you. I love experimenting and not having boundaries. Just being with you is enough for me, so if it freaks you out, we'll do things your way. But if you enjoyed what we did, then I don't see why we have to stop. There are things we can do that don't involve being rough with each other. And if it'll make you feel better, I'll go talk to Maylak and make sure that everything is in working order."

Haeden looks mortified. "You would tell her that I struck you?"

Oh boy. I shake my head quickly, and give his braid a little tug. "No, not at all. I'll tell her we got *carried away* last night and I had my first bout of morning sickness this morning, and I just want to make sure everything is great."

He relaxes at that. "I would not mind if the healer checked you over."

"Then that's what we'll do."

Haeden

I know I am being overbearing again.

I know this as Maylak runs her hands over Jo-see's delicate body and my mate gives me encouraging smiles from the healer's furs. The moment we arrived in Maylak's cave, I knew I was being foolish.

I cannot help it. Jo-see is the most precious thing to me. I cannot bear a single scratch on her skin, much less a bruise that I put there myself. The thought of having a mate after so long—and that mate being someone as smart and fierce as my Jo-see—seems like a dream. I will not take her for granted, even if she begs me to smack her backside again.

No matter how much I enjoyed it and everything else we did.

The healer lifts her long, graceful hands from Jo-see's waist and smiles. "You are as healthy as ever, Jo-see. I see no problems."

"And the baby?" my mate prompts. "All is well there?"

"The kit has no khui, so I cannot communicate with it, but your body carries your kit well and everything feels right. I can feel nothing out of the ordinary." Maylak smiles at Jo-see and then turns to me. "Is there something that concerns you both?"

"No," I say quickly.

"Sex is okay right now, right?" Jo-see asks. "It's not going to bother the kit inside me?"

"Why would it bother it?" Maylak seems perplexed.

I rub my ear, which feels hot. My face feels hot, too, and it takes everything I have not to shift on my feet like a small boy.

"What if it's really, *really* vigorous sex?" Jo-see asks.

Maylak tilts her head, a hint of a frown on her face. "Painful?"

"Not painful," Jo-see says, quick to correct her. "Just . . . enthusiastic. Very enthusiastic. And vigorous. And . . . yeah."

The healer chuckles. "It will take more than enthusiastic mating to dislodge a kit. If that were the case, half the tribe would be in danger."

Jo-see gives me a wink and a thumbs-up, a gesture that means all is well. My ears feel hotter than ever.

"As long as your matings are not painful, I see no problem in being vigorous," Maylak continues. "I am always happy to check on the kit if you have concerns, of course."

"Is this a bad time to say 'I told you so'?" my mate asks smugly. "Or should I say 'who's your daddy now'?"

"You should not," I retort.

My mate only gives me a self-satisfied smile and hops to her feet. "Thank you, Maylak. We really appreciate it."

The healer inclines her head at us, and I could swear her face is just as amused as my mate's as Jo-see snags my hand and holds on to me, beaming up at my sour expression. I suspect I am being outmaneuvered by the females, but I do not think it is foolish of me to worry over my mate. Being protective is never a bad thing, as far as I am concerned.

My sweet Jo-see practically struts on her way back to our cave, tugging on my hand and smiling back at me. "Don't you feel better now?"

"No."

She gives me an exasperated look. "Haeden. You're impossible."

I move the privacy screen aside and put a hand to the small of her back, guiding her into our cave. Perhaps we should go and talk with others this morning and see what chores need to be done, but I still have much to say to my mate. "I am not impossible. This is who I am, Jo-see. I will worry about you. Always. You are the most important thing in my life. You are my mate, and you carry my kit. Of course I think of your safety above all else."

She turns as she enters the cave and gives me a soft glance, her hand stealing to her belly. "I know. Like I said, I just have a seat at the buffet now, and I want to gobble you up."

I understand this "gobble." Every time I see Jo-see, I want to grab her and squeeze her to my chest so tightly that I never let her go. I want to wrap my arms around her and protect her from the entire world, from anything that would make a frown come to her face. She deserves nothing but wonderful days from here on out, and I want to give them to her. "We will compromise."

"We will?" She brightens.

I set the privacy screen over the front of our cave once more and then move to her side, rubbing her arm. "Every week, there will be one night where we will try new things. All other nights we will be 'boring' in the furs, as you say."

"Oh, Haeden. Having sex with you is never boring." She reaches up and cups my face in her hands, tilting hers back for a kiss. "I love love love sex with you. I totally want to have sex with you right now because you're being so sexy and overbearing and for some reason that really gets me going." Jo-see chuckles. "It's just having a little fun on the side. It doesn't mean everything else sucks."

Good. Because I, too, love mating with her. I want to touch her constantly. Even now, I want to touch her. I reach for the belt at her tunic and loosen it, tossing it to the floor. "You do not mind touching your sour mate?"

"I *love* my sour mate." She taps my cheek with a fingertip. "Now kiss me."

I do. I lean in and give her a light, teasing kiss full of promise. Jo-see sighs, her eyes fluttering closed, and I rub my nose against hers. Now comes the rest of the compromise. "But even on our adventure night, there are certain things I will not do while you are pregnant."

I expect her to protest. Jo-see likes to fight when she feels I am being unfair, and it is one of the things I love the most about her—and find the most exasperating. But she only nods. "Also fair. Can we discuss what's allowed and what isn't?"

"No striking," I say immediately. "Even if you enjoy it."

She makes a face up at me. "It's not *striking*. It's *spanking*, and it's on my butt, which is very padded." She reaches down and gives her backside a jiggle. "But fine. If it makes you nervous, we won't do it."

I grunt, pleased at her concession.

"What about holding me down? I liked that." Her cheeks flush with color, her eyes bright as she gazes up at me. "Your hand felt very heavy on my neck and that was . . . nice."

Her arousal is going to scent the air soon, I suspect, and my hardening cock twitches in response. "You like it when I take control?"

She shivers with delight. "More than I should."

I bite back a groan at her obvious excitement. Perhaps we can work that into our regular matings as well. "I do not mind pretending, either. I do not see the point of it but I do not mind it."

Jo-see giggles and pulls her tunic over her head, revealing her body. "You don't get the point of it?"

"If you wish to enrage me, you do not have to pretend to be a naughty huntress. You just need to avoid resonance again."

That makes her laugh, and she wraps her arms around my waist, pressing her soft teats to my chest. "But now I know how good it is, so it's harder to pretend. But we can try that." She bites her lip. "What about . . . anal?"

This is not the first time she has brought this up, so it must be something she wishes to try. "You mean . . ."

"The back door, yeah." She wiggles her eyebrows at me. "There's no baby in there."

I am a bit shocked by her suggestion . . . but also intrigued. I am already imagining what it would feel like to push inside her there, and the strangeness of it is as enticing as anything. "It is something you wish to try? It would be pleasant for you?"

"I mean, I did it in the past and it wasn't great, but sex in the past wasn't great in general. Everything's different with you." She smiles up at me. "I already told you—I want to try everything."

Her answer makes desire surge through my body. "My mate is greedy."

"When it comes to you? So damn greedy." Jo-see brushes her lips against my chest. "I want to feast on you for hours. Days. Months. If that's wrong, then I don't want to be right."

"If that is wrong, then we will be wrong together." I slide a hand into her silky mane and grip tightly, testing her reaction.

Her breath catches, and when I glance down, I can see her nipples tighten. "What would you do if I lowered you to the furs right now and mated you?"

"Probably pass out from sheer happiness?"

I grunt. "Never mind, then—"

"Hey!" Jo-see grabs at me, and then laughs when she sees my smirk. "You suck."

I can do that. And when I lower my mate to the furs and pull her leggings off of her, I show her that I can suck, indeed. And lick. And tongue. And nip. Whatever she needs, I will give her.

Josie

ONE WEEK LATER

I clutch the small pot I got from the healer to my chest and try not to giggle to myself. I'm not a child. I can totally get lubricant for my mate and myself in bed. There's no need to snicker over it like I'm naughty.

It's just . . . I know what it's for, and so I'm giggling, but I'm also nervous.

Tonight is our big night. Our big experiment night. To say that we'd both been looking forward to it all week would be an understatement. We've had sex and cuddled in the interim, of course, but knowing that there's something spicy to look forward to at the end of the week has given things a bit of an edge. Now that the day is finally here, I'm jittery and slightly nervous for no reason at all.

And giggly, too. I don't make eye contact with anyone as I slink to our quarters at the very back of the main cave system. What the lube is for feels as if it's written all over my face—JOSIE AND HAEDEN ARE GOING TO HAVE ANAL TONIGHT—and I know

I'll lose what little cool I have if I have to answer a single question.

It's fine, I remind myself. You're fine. You've done anal once before. Except it wasn't with someone that I loved, and the experience was more unpleasant than anything. But with Haeden, everything is new, and that includes this. I wish there was a clock on the wall I could stare at to know when my mate comes home, but until then I'll just have to keep myself busy.

Haeden's out hunting—or rather, he's checking his closest traps. He's been setting a nearby trail, he told me, since the morning that I threw up. He wanted to be close by when I awoke so he could help out if I got sick again. We've been careful with my meals, though, and a little basket of dried, bland slices of not-potato is kept next to the furs so I can chew on one whenever my stomach feels iffy. I have an herbal tea that the elders gave me that I take every morning and it helps keep things settled, too. Soon Haeden will have to go out farther again, even overnight. I'm not looking forward to that, but it's just part of life here.

Until then, I'm going to enjoy having him in my furs every night.

I primp and get ready for my special night with my mate. I wash every part of my body and wet down my hair, tying it into a loose braid. Dinner tonight is going to be leftover dvisti stew. Haeden prefers stew with fish in it, but the smell bothers me, so dvisti it is. I put the leftovers on over the fire to warm, and add a bit of fuel. After washing my hands and changing into my prettiest tunic—one that gathers under my small boobs and makes them look bigger—I sit by the fire and wait, full of anticipation.

And wait.

And wait.

I should probably sew. Or visit Tiffany. She wanted to go gather some herbs but I pushed her off until tomorrow, because I'm antsy. I feigned a headache so I could have an excuse to visit Maylak without getting her suspicions up, and now I'm hiding in my cave like an idiot. Haeden might not be back for hours. He—

There's a rustle at the entrance of the cave, and I turn just in time to see my mate pushing the privacy screen aside. His long braid hangs over his shoulder as he ducks in, and his gaze meets mine.

Heat immediately floods through my system, just like when we first resonated. "Hi, baby."

A hint of a smile curves his mouth and he steps inside, replacing the privacy screen once more. "Have you been waiting for me long?"

"Not too long. Just all day."

He snorts at that, striding toward me. "My thoughts are scattered as well."

Oh no. "Please don't tell me you think this is a bad idea."

"No, I think it is the *best* idea."

I can't help it. I giggle. It's a nervous giggle, but all this pent-up energy needs to go somewhere and I'm so antsy it's hard to sit still. "Oh, thank goodness. Because if you walked this back on me after I went and got lube from Maylak, I was going to get annoyed."

"You got 'lube'?"

"Lubricant," I explain, and pick up the little pot that's been occupying my thoughts. I pull off the tightly stretched leather lid. "We can use this to slick things up. It'll make it easier for you to get inside me, and for me to take you back there, because you're pretty big."

Haeden grunts, and my face fills with heat. I swear, I'm acting like a shy virgin. This is ridiculous, but this moment just feels . . . momentous. Which is also ridiculous, because if we both hate anal sex, then we won't do it again.

It's more that we're pushing the boundaries in our relationship. We're going to be vulnerable together, as vulnerable as when we first resonated, and that excites me.

We stare at each other for a moment, me brimming with nerves. Finally, Haeden rubs his bare chest and sighs. "I should go bathe."

Oh. I don't want him to leave. Not when the cave feels charged with energy and anticipation. "I'll wash you," I blurt out. "I'd love to wash you."

"You would?"

I nod, my pulse fluttering.

"I am sweaty."

"I like you sweaty." I hop to my feet and fill the bowl I keep for bathing, then drop a scrap of material and a few soapberries into the water. I watch with excitement as my mate strips off his loincloth, leggings, and boots, and I'm not surprised to see that his cock is already hard and erect. Not surprising, because I'm probably wet as hell right now. The anticipation of this moment has been building all week, and I suspect the second he touches me, I'll pop off like a rocket.

Which, in the scheme of things, is not necessarily a bad thing.

Haeden stands near the fire, his tail still as I dip the towel into the water and then begin to wash him. The moment I touch him, the tip of his tail flicks, as if he's desperately trying to hold still and cannot. It makes me smile, and I take great care washing my mate's chest, outlining each pectoral and making sure that every ridge is clean.

When his front is satisfactory, I move to his back, sliding his braid over his shoulder and then washing down his spine. He shudders as I touch him, and I kneel lower, washing his buttocks because, gosh, I just love his body. I love how muscular he is. I love how he's a taut, velvety blue all over. I love his tight buns and that tail he's desperately trying to control. I love his long braid and his big arms and . . .

"Jo-see," Haeden rasps.

"Mmm?"

"You just moaned."

My eyes widen. "I did?"

Haeden turns to look at me over his shoulder, his eyes slitted in that way that means he's barely in control of himself. It makes me clench with anticipation. "Undress for me."

As if he has to ask me twice. I all but jump to my feet, ripping off my tunic and leggings. I get stuck on my boots, because I always do, but when I finally kick them off, Haeden reaches for my braid and winds it around his hand, drawing me in. I move closer, until his hard cock presses against my belly, dripping precum against my overheated skin. He gazes down at me, his expression intense. "Can we still kiss?"

What? "Of course we can kiss—"

With a hungry sound, my mate leans down, capturing my mouth with his. His kiss is utterly voracious, and he steals my breath away. I link my arms around his shoulders, moaning as his tongue slicks into my mouth. Haeden drags me onto the furs with him, my body under his as his weight pins me down, and we kiss. And kiss.

I could kiss Haeden endlessly, I think. I love the way his mouth fits against mine, the perfect amount of intensity between us. I even love the way he tongues me, not too wet, and just teasing enough that it makes me want more. He lifts his head, nipping at my lower lip in a way that makes me quiver, and then looks me in the eye. "How do we do this?"

Do this? Oh. "Any way you want," I say, breathless. "We can put something under my hips and face each other, or we can do it doggy style . . ."

"And my spur?" His nose brushes against mine in a way that makes my pussy clench and my heart melt.

"Oh, right. Maybe we should try face-to-face, then," I murmur dreamily, dazed by his kisses. If we're face-to-face, his spur will go inside my pussy instead of jabbing against my tailbone, and the thought sends a prickle of excitement through me.

He kisses me again. "Your cream?"

"I'll get it." I reach over him to the spot by the fire, and as I do, he teases my nipples with his hand, as if he can't bear to stop touching me. He mouths one as I slide back in place, whimpering as he continues to suck on my nipples. "They're really sensitive right now."

"Because of our kit?" He presses a tender kiss to one tip. "I love that."

I do, too. "They should get bigger, too, which will be nice."

"I like you just the way you are."

"Of course you're saying that," I tease. "You're about to get laid."

"It is the truth." He kisses the tip of my breast again and looks up at me. "Do we grease your back-cunt as well as my cock?"

Oh lord, is that what we're calling it? I suppose it's better than "butthole" but not by much. "Do both, yes."

His tongue flicks over my nipple one last time and he sits up. "Will you touch me, then?"

"I'd like nothing more." I sit upright, curling my legs under me, and scoop a generous portion of the lotion onto my hands. Rubbing them together to warm it, I slide my slick fingers over his length, making sure to lubricate each and every ridge. The head of his cock is flushed and dripping, and I can't help but give him a teasing squeeze as I work over him. "How's that, love?"

His tail thumps the furs, hard, and a fresh bead of wetness appears on the head of his cock. "This grease . . . changes things."

"It's fun, huh? I like it." I kinda want to give him a hand job just to test out the lube, but I also get distracted easily. We should probably focus on the task at hand. "I'll get more from Maylak next time I see her. I wanted to make sure it'd be something that wouldn't make us break out in a rash when we put it in sensitive areas."

Haeden nods, and then gives me a heated look. "Lie back on the furs, Jo-see. It is your turn."

Oh shit, I nearly come just at that. Pussy practically quivering with anticipation, I wipe my slippery hands on my braid, then grab a pillow and shove it under my hips as I lie on my back. "Ready."

I hear a slick squelch as Haeden puts his fingers in the pot, and I part my thighs. The angle makes it hard to see what he's doing, so when a slick finger brushes up the crease of my backside, I wriggle, ticklish, and bite back a squeal.

He pauses. "You remember your word?"

I nod, breathless. "I'm not going to use it, though. You just startled me. I'm better now."

My mate says nothing, but his fingers skate up and down my backside, and then one slick one pushes into the right spot. I suck in a breath, because it feels tight and strange. Not bad strange, just different strange. Before I can comment on this, he pushes in deeper, and his thumb strokes into my cunt.

I cry out, arousal flooding through me. "Oh, fuck, Haeden, that's good."

"Pretty," is all he says, and that teasing finger pushes in and out of the pucker of my backside, his thumb moving in and out of my cunt at the same time. I writhe on the pillow, panting and desperate. Did I think this was a good idea? It's a fucking *great* idea, and I'm so incredibly turned on I feel as if I'm about to lose my mind.

Haeden withdraws his fingers, and I make a sound of protest.

"More cream," he tells me. "I want to make sure you are ready for my cock. It is much larger than your body."

"Use two fingers this time," I pant, trying to hold still as he rubs at the entrance to my backside again. "Stretch me a bit if you can."

He does, and this time it feels tighter, burning slightly at first. I grab fistfuls of the furs and clutch them to my shoulders, desperately trying to hold on to something as he works them in and out of me. His thumb slipping in and out of my cunt is the perfect tease—enough to make me crazed with lust, but not enough to make me come.

I'm reduced to shamelessly begging. "Please, Haeden. Please come inside me now. I need you so badly."

Haeden takes my legs and pushes them against my chest. I clutch the backs of my thighs to help out, and watch his face as he lines up his cock to the entrance of my body. He's disheveled, strands of hair escaping his tight braid, and there's a faint sheen of sweat on his handsome face. His expression is intense with concentration, and he presses against the pucker of my backside, and then frowns. "I do not know if this will work—"

"It will," I encourage. "Push into me. I promise you can't hurt me. Just go slow."

He makes a frustrated sound in the back of his throat, but a moment later, I feel him push harder, the head of his cock pressing against the entrance to my body. I try to relax, because I know if I tense, I'm just going to make things worse, but it's hard not to clench up in response. The press of him is intense, and for a moment I think things won't work after all—

—and then my body gives, and the head of his cock lodges inside me.

I suck in a breath at the same time he groans. Oh. Okay, that feels like a *lot*. I quiver, my pussy aching and empty feeling, and the other parts of me feeling far too full. But I'm the one that wanted to try this, and I don't want to stop now. Not when Haeden's eyes flutter closed and his tight expression is something close to ecstasy.

"Slow," I whisper. "Go slow until you're all the way in."

He leans forward, pressing on my thighs with his arm, and I'm folded in half like a human taco, my feet dangerously near my ears. "Tell me if I hurt you," he breathes, and I can hear the strain in his voice. "We will stop the moment you are in pain."

"I'm fine." I breathe in and out slowly as he presses into me. It's a jarring sensation, and one I don't know if I like or not. There are parts that are good, but it also feels strange and invasive. "How does it feel?"

Haeden groans, the sound ragged. "Tight. So tight, Jo-see."

Oh, that sounds good. His response makes me clench with arousal, and when I do, he gasps. Oops. "Sorry. Sorry."

"Very tight," he says again, his face full of concentration. He leans heavily on me, and even though my muscles strain a little, I like it. I love being pressed into the furs by him. I love all of it, honestly. Even the strange fullness that comes with back-door sex.

Something pushes into my core and I gasp as sensation floods through me. At first I think it's a finger, but when Haeden groans and stops moving, I realize it's his spur. It's dragging against the bottom of my channel, just enough to provide sensation. *Oh.* This, I like. I run a hand up Haeden's arm. "How do you feel?"

His response is another ragged groan, his eyes closing.

"I'm going to assume that's good. Are you in all the way?"

He nods. "Should I . . . move?"

"You should fuck me."

Haeden makes another intense sound, his eyes opening a slit. That raw look on his face hardens and his hips twitch, and he presses into me. I gasp, because just that small bit of sensation changes everything.

"Move," I whisper. "It feels good."

He draws back, his movements slow, and watches my expression the entire time as he rocks back into me again. I bite my lip, teasing one of my nipples as he languidly pumps into me once more. These are different kinds of sensation, I realize, no less intense than regular cock-in-pussy sex. My skin prickles with the power of all of it, goose bumps rising. And when he sinks in again, I moan.

"My mate. My sweet, wild Jo-see. You are so beautiful like this."

I love every breathless word, and I don't even care that he's telling me I'm sexy with a dick in my ass and my ankles at my ears. I love this moment. I love that we're exploring our boundaries together. I love that despite the weirdness of anal sex, this feels good because it's with him, and he's careful with me. He wants me to enjoy this, too. It's not just about him and his needs.

Haeden speeds up over time, his pumping thrusts going from slow, steady movements to quicker, stronger snaps of his hips as we both descend into the moment. I pinch my nipples, hard, whimpering his name as he pounds into me, the lubricant making everything slick and gliding and wonderful. "I'm going to come," I tell him when I'm close. "Make me come, Haeden. Make me come—"

He draws back and, before I can plead again, reaches between our tangled bodies and pinches the top of my pussy, my clit squeezed by the outer folds of my cunt. This time when he drives into me, I go over the edge, clenching up around him and crying out his name. At some dazed spot in the back of my mind, I realize the orgasm feels a little different, too, but it's still good.

So good. Because Haeden makes everything good.

Breathless, I dig my nails into his shoulders and murmur wicked things as he thrusts into me. I tell him how big and strong he is, and how naughty I am and how he's using me, and I babble on, my intention to make him come. His teeth grit, his lips curled back, and then he makes a delicious choked sound as he sinks into me, his body shaking with his release.

I hold him against my folded body, so full of love that I want to shout with how happy I am.

Cleaning up after back-door sex involves more washing, and some giggling as we get the slippery lubricant everywhere. After everything is cleaned and the furs exchanged for fresh ones, we curl up together, my backside pressed against his now-softening cock. I'm a little tender there, I realize, and I'll probably feel an ache in the back of my legs tomorrow, but that was awesome.

"I love you," I tell Haeden, wrapping his arms around me. "Did you enjoy that?"

"Eh," he says.

With a gasp, I turn in his arms. "What—"

Haeden smirks down at me, that self-satisfied, superior look on his face that always drives me insane. "I liked it. But I like everything with you. If you are asking if I wish to do that again, the answer is yes, of course. I like being in your cunt, and I like taking you there, too." He drags me down by my braid so he can kiss me. "Are you satisfied?"

"For now," I tell him, mollified. I tuck myself against his chest once more and breathe in his scent, of sweat and velvet skin and the faint tang of Maylak's lubricant. "We'll just have to think of something even more exciting for next week, though."

Haeden huffs with amusement. "Give me a moment to catch my breath."

"You have an entire week." I can't stop grinning. I love this. I love him. Everything is so perfect.

"I will need it."

"Oh?"

Haeden nods. "Aehako gave me the idea. What do you think of a courting gift? A week should give me time to carve one."

A . . . courting gift? Does he mean an enormous dildo like the one Aehako gave Kira as a prank? He'd give me one for real? To play with in bed? "Um, I think that sounds amazing."

He chuckles and kisses the top of my head, and I feel so, so loved. "I thought you would."

AUTHOR'S NOTE

Hello there!

I can't believe I'm writing the author's note for Josie and Haeden's special edition. Huge thanks to Berkley and Penguin Random House for making these happen. I love seeing the special editions come to life, and a huge thank-you to the artist, Kelly Wagner; the art director, Rita Frangie Batour; and my editor, Cindy Hwang. Your vision together is *chef's kiss.*

Once upon a time when I wrote the first book in the Ice Planet Barbarians series, my initial goal was to get to Kira's book. Then, when I realized people were still into the series after Kira's story was done, my next "end game" was Josie and Haeden. I thought surely, *surely* everyone would be done with blue barbarians after six books.

Ha. Ha ha.

But then I had so much fun working on Josie and Haeden's book and people were so enthusiastic that I started to realize that maybe, *maybe* I needed to think longer-term. Josie finding the crashed ship (the one Kira crashed in book 3) made sense.

The fact that it had a few more kidnapped humans made sense. It just all came together beautifully and allowed me the opportunity to continue the series without it feeling forced or stale. Even though I've expanded the series many times now, I've tried to be thoughtful about it and stay true to the rules of my universe. At the same time, I gauge the reactions of my audience. If people seem tired of the stories, I'll know it's time to wrap them up.

(I'm writing this in December 2022, and I'm about to start the third spin-off series of Ice Planet Barbarians, entitled Ice Planet Clones, so it's safe to say that no, no one is tired of blue barbarians just yet!)

Speaking of Josie and Haeden (I mean, since it's their book and all), this is the couple that I get asked about the most, other than Liz and Raahosh. Everyone is invested in their happy ever after, and I get so many happy emails about their relationship. It's classic grumpy/sunshine, and who doesn't love that, right? When I initially plotted out the tribe, I knew Haeden had a sad past and had lost a mate, and that I wanted him to resonate again. In keeping with the world-building I had established, he couldn't resonate a second time without a second khui, so he lost his (and his mate) during the khui-sickness that plagued the tribe fifteen years prior to the humans landing.

(Another funny note: At some point I had a plan to have the khui-sickness return and kill off some of the elders and a few of the humans, especially Ariana. Sorry, Ariana! Turns out no one liked that idea, not even me, and it was scrapped. I get too attached to everyone.)

Josie is one of my favorite characters. She's just easy to love. On paper, she's arguably had more trauma than anyone else in the tribe, but she's constantly looking to the future and to happiness. Her history was modeled after that of my father, who grew up in a state home and for whom family is everything. Dad, I love you and I sincerely hope you read none of this book. Mom, read this part aloud to him and nothing else. *Nothing. Else.*

Also during this book, I started seeding future plots. Some eagle-eyed readers noticed a very casual mention of a possible green island in the sea itself. I wanted to gently steer readers toward the fact that this is a big world and our tribe only knows their small part of it. There's so much more to explore! I like to seed in things that intrigue me and leave myself threads to pull for the future. It's a bit like Chekhov's gun—or in romance writing, Chekhov's anal. If someone mentions the gun over the mantel, it has to show up in the story. If someone mentions interest in anal sex, it has to happen in the story or readers feel cheated out of a scene.

And speaking of scenes . . . let's talk about the bonus novella. You would think the Ice Planet Honeymoon stories would be easy to write because I'm just revisiting old characters. I learned quickly that this isn't the case. Not only do I need to fact-check myself against future story lines, but I'm weirdly protective of my characters and their happy ever afters. I've nixed most plot concepts because they would make the characters unhappy, and I want to preserve that feeling of contentment you get at the end of the book, when everything is awesome. I don't want to turn around and rip you through the wringer again. So this honeymoon, like the others, is very slice-of-life. It's Josie and Haeden, figuring each other out and settling into being mates.

Oh, and it has anal. Because Chekhov said so.

RUBY

THE PEOPLE OF
BARBARIAN'S MATE

The Main Cave

THE CHIEF AND HIS FAMILY

VEKTAL (Vehk-tall)—Chief of the sa-khui tribe. Son of Hektar, the prior chief, who died of khui-sickness. He is a dedicated hunter and leader, and carries a sword and a bola for weapons. He is the one who finds Georgie, and resonance between them is so strong that he resonates prior to her receiving her khui.

GEORGIE—Unofficial leader of the human women. Originally from Orlando, Florida, she has long golden-brown curls and a determined attitude.

TALIE—Their infant daughter.

FAMILIES

RAAHOSH (Rah-hosh)—A quiet but surly hunter. One of his horns is broken off and his face scarred. Older son of Vaashan and Daya (both deceased). Vektal's close friend. Impatient and rash, he steals Liz the moment she receives her khui. They resonate, and he is exiled for stealing her. Brother to Rukh.

LIZ—A loudmouth huntress from Oklahoma who loves Star Wars and giving her opinion. Raahosh kidnaps her the moment she receives her lifesaving khui. She was a champion archer as a teenager. Resonates to Raahosh and voluntarily chooses exile with him.

RAASHEL—Their infant daughter.

HARLOW—One of the women kept in the stasis tubes. She has red hair and freckles, and is mechanically minded and excellent at problem-solving. Stolen by Rukh when she resonated to him. Now mother to their child, Rukhar.

RUKH—The long-lost son of Vaashan and Daya; brother to Raahosh. His full name is Maarukh. He grew up alone and wild, convinced by his father that the tribe was full of "bad ones," and has been brought back by Harlow.

RUKHAR—Their infant son.

ARIANA—One of the women kept in the stasis tubes. Hails from New Jersey and was an anthropology student. She tended to cry a lot when first rescued. Has a delicate frame and dark brown hair. Resonates to Zolaya. Still cries a lot.

ZOLAYA (Zoh-lay-uh)—A skilled hunter. Steady and patient, he resonates to Ariana and seems to be the only one not bothered by her weepiness.

ANALAY—Their infant son.

MARLENE (Mar-lenn)—One of the women kept in the stasis tubes. French speaking. Quiet and confident, and exudes sexuality. Resonates to Zennek.

ZENNEK (Zehn-eck)—A quiet and shy hunter. Brother to Pashov, Salukh, and Farli. He is the son of Borran and Kemli. Resonates to Marlene.

ZALENE—Their infant daughter.

NORA—One of the women kept in the stasis tubes. A nurturing sort who was rather angry she was dumped on an ice planet. Quickly resonates to Dagesh. No longer quite so angry.

DAGESH (Dah-zzhesh; the g sound is swallowed)—A calm, hard-working, and responsible hunter. Resonates to Nora.

ANNA & ELSA—Their infant twins.

STACY—One of the women kept in the stasis tubes. She was weepy when she first awakened. Loves to cook and worked in a bakery prior to abduction. Resonates to Pashov and seems quite happy.

PASHOV (Pah-showv)—The son of Kemli and Borran; brother to Farli, Salukh, and Zennek. A hunter described as "quiet." Resonates to Stacy.

PACY—Their infant son.

MAYLAK (May-lack)—One of the few female sa-khui. She is the tribe healer and Vektal's former pleasure mate. She resonated to Kashrem, ending her relationship with Vektal. Sister to Bek.

KASHREM (Cash-rehm)—A gentle tribal tanner. Mated to Maylak.

ESHA (Esh-uh)—Their young female kit.

SEVVAH (Sev-uh)—A tribe elder and one of the few sa-khui females. She is mother to Aehako, Rokan, and Sessah, and acts like a mom to the others in the cave. Her entire family was spared when khui-sickness hit fifteen years ago.

OSHEN (Aw-shen)—A tribe elder and Sevvah's mate. Brewer.

SESSAH (Ses-uh)—Their youngest child, a juvenile male.

MEGAN—Megan was early in a pregnancy when she was captured, but the aliens terminated it. She tends toward a sunny disposition when not abducted by aliens. Resonates to Cashol. Pregnant.

CASHOL (Cash-awl)—A distractible and slightly goofy-natured hunter. Cousin to Vektal. Resonates to Megan.

CLAIRE—A quiet, slender woman who arrived on the planet with a blonde pixie cut and now has shoulder-length brown hair. She had a failed pleasure-mating with Bek and resonated to Ereven. Her story is told in the novella "Ice Planet Holiday."

EREVEN (Air-uh-ven)—A quiet, easygoing hunter who won Claire over with his understanding, protective nature. Resonates to Claire.

AEHAKO (Eye-ha-koh)—A laughing, flirty hunter. The son of Sevvah and Oshen; brother to Rokan and young Sessah. He seems to be in a permanent good mood. Close friends with Haeden. Resonates to Kira and was acting leader of the South Cave.

KIRA—The first of the human women to be kidnapped, Kira had a large metallic translator attached to her ear by the aliens. She is quiet and serious, with somber eyes. Her translator has been removed, and she gave birth to Kae.

KAE (rhymes with "fly")—Their infant daughter.

KEMLI (Kemm-lee)—An elder female, mother to Salukh, Pashov, Zennek, and Farli. The tribe's expert on plants.

BORRAN (Bore-awn)—Kemli's much younger mate and an elder.

FARLI (Far-lee)—A preteen female sa-khui. Her brothers are Salukh, Pashov, and Zennek. New pet parent to the dvisti colt Chompy.

ASHA (Ah-shuh)—A mated female sa-khui. She is mated to Hemalo but has not been seen in his furs for some time. Their kit died shortly after birth.

HEMALO (Hee-mah-lo)—A tanner and a quiet sort. He is mated (unhappily) to Asha.

TIFFANY—A "farm girl" back on Earth, she suffered greatly while waiting for Georgie to return. She has been traumatized by her alien abduction. She is a perfectionist and a hard worker, and the running joke amongst the human women is that Tiffany is great at everything. Resonates to Salukh.

SALUKH (Sah-luke)—The brawny son of Kemli and Borran; brother to Farli, Pashov, and Zennek. Strong and intense. Very patient and helps Tiffany work through her trauma.

JOSIE—One of the original kidnapped women, she broke her leg in the ship crash. Short and adorable, Josie is an excessive talker, a gossip, and a bit of a dreamer. Likes to sing. Family is everything to her, and she wants nothing more than one of her own. Resonates to Haeden.

HAEDEN (Hi-den)—A grim and unsmiling hunter with "dead" eyes, Haeden formerly resonated but his female died of khui-sickness before they could mate. His current khui is a replacement, and he resonates to Josie. He is very private and unthaws only around his new mate.

THE UNMATED HUNTERS

BEK (Behk)—A hunter generally thought of as short-tempered and unpleasant. Brother to Maylak.

HARREC (Hair-ek)—A hunter who has no family and finds his place in the tribe by constantly joking and teasing. A bit accident-prone.

HASSEN (Hass-en)—A passionate and brave hunter, Hassen is impulsive and tends to act before he thinks.

ROKAN (Row-can)—The son of Sevvah and Oshen; brother to Aehako and young Sessah. A hunter known for his strange predictions that come true all too often.

TAUSHEN (Tow—rhymes with "cow"—shen)—A teenage hunter, newly into adulthood. Eager to prove himself.

WARREK (War-eck)—The son of Elder Eklan. He is a very quiet and mild hunter, with long, sleek black hair. Warrek teaches the young kits how to hunt.

ELDERS

ELDER DRAYAN—A smiling elder who uses a cane to help him walk.

ELDER DRENOL—A grumpy, antisocial elder.

ELDER EKLAN—A calm, kind elder. Father to Warrek, he also helped raise Harrec.

ELDER VADREN (Vaw-dren)—An elder.

ELDER VAZA (Vaw-zhuh)—A lonely widower and hunter. He tries to be as helpful as possible. He is very interested in the new females.

THE DEAD

DOMINIQUE—A redheaded human female. Her mind was broken when she was abused by the aliens on the ship. When she arrived on Not-Hoth, she ran out into the snow and deliberately froze.

KRISSY—A human female, dead in the crash.

PEG—A human female, dead in the crash.

ABOUT THE AUTHOR

RUBY DIXON is an author of all things science fiction romance. She is a Sagittarius and a Reylo shipper, and loves farming sims (but not actual housework). She lives in the South with her husband and a couple of geriatric cats, and can't think of anything else to put in her biography. Truly, she is boring.

CONNECT ONLINE

RubyDixon.com
RubyDixonBooks
Author.Ruby.Dixon